THE DENALI DECEPTION
A SEAN WYAT THRILLER

ERNEST DEMPSEY

ISBN-13:
978-1-944647-16-2

GET FREE BOOKS

Get Ernest Dempsey's Best Selling Novel and two introductory novellas FREE.

Become a VIP reader and get the free ebooks at http://ernestdempsey.net/vip-swag-page/ or check out more details at the end of the book.

Prologue

Washington, DC
April, 1865

Mary wandered over to the window and pulled back the curtain to steal a peek outside. The streetlights flickered along the sidewalks, illuminating the road for the few carriages that were still out at this hour. Her eyes panned from one end of the street to the other, making sure there was no one loitering where they shouldn't.

Over the last few months, her guests had come to meet at the boarding house in secret. They'd taken precaution on top of precaution to ensure no one would know what they were up to or who was involved.

Even with all the safety measures in place, Mary couldn't keep her paranoia at bay. To say what they were doing was risky would have been the understatement of the nineteenth century.

Satisfied nothing out of the ordinary was going on outside, she turned away from the window and looked over at the men around the warm embrace of the fireplace.

She returned to the little meeting and sat down in her rocking chair a few feet away from the discussion.

"All clear," she said to the man to her left.

His name was John. He had thick black hair and a tight matching mustache. His clothes were fashionable for the time, and he carried himself with an air of distinction, even in the way he sat around the table with the other men. Mary figured it was from his acting background, but she had no way of knowing. He was the only actor she'd met as far as she knew.

The other three were rougher around the edges, though handsome in their own right.

"You're certain of this?" John asked one of the others.

Lewis, a young man with hair brushed to one side, nodded. "I've never been more sure of anything in my whole life." His accent was firmly rooted in the Deep South. A native of Alabama, he'd been a supporter of the Confederacy since the beginning of the war. The others at the table were likewise backers of the rebellion.

The war was all but over, though, and the South had lost.

Robert E. Lee had surrendered at Appomattox just days before. With military engagements officially ending, all hope had been lost...except in the eyes of those sitting in Mary Surratt's boarding house.

To them, the The War of Northern Aggression wasn't over until they'd taken one last desperate measure.

Originally, they'd plotted to kidnap the Union

president, Abraham Lincoln. Six of the conspirators had planned the abduction in intricate detail. Lincoln was supposed to arrive at a specific location where the kidnappers waited in the shadows. Hours went by before the group had come to the conclusion that Lincoln wasn't coming.

None of them were sure why the president didn't show up that day, although they figured he might have been tipped off to their plan. By whom, none of them were certain.

They were going to take the president to Richmond, the current capital of the Confederacy. Now that Union forces were crawling all over Virginia, the plan would have to be modified.

John Wilkes Booth stared down at the sheet of paper Lewis Powell had put on the table. "If you're right about this, Lewis, we may have just found a way to tip the scales in our favor."

"Even though we already surrendered?" George asked. His accent had a strong hint of German upbringing.

"Countries surrender and strike again later on," John said. "Look at the Brits. They were defeated in the Revolution and then came back to invade this very city a few decades later."

"I'd rather not wait decades for it to happen," said the man closest to the fire. His name was David Herold. His hair was combed to one side atop a rustic, chiseled face.

He was the sixth of eleven children born to his parents and the only one who survived to adulthood. Being so close to so much death created a hardened demeanor in him. David was known for keeping his feelings to himself, except when it came to his sympathy for the rebellion. He'd made it known early on that he believed the president handled the situation with the south poorly. Upon meeting other like-minded individuals such as Booth, David found what he believed to be his true calling. With his family all gone, there was even less cause for worry. If he failed and was executed, no one would miss him. He was quite literally a man with nothing to lose.

"If what he's saying is true, we won't have to wait that long."

"It's real, all right," Lewis said. "My sources tell me that the secretary has been sending men all through this region to map it and find out all they can. Word is, he's planning on buying the entire territory."

George guffawed. "Pfft. Why would they do that? It's nothing but an icebox up there."

"That's what everyone else thinks, too. They believe the Alaska Territory is nothing but a bunch of snow and ice and wild animals. But this letter"—he tapped his finger on a piece of paper—"and this map prove what Seward and Lincoln are really up to. They found something in that frozen wilderness. And I'm willing to bet the Russians have no idea it's there."

John listened to his comrades, considering every element of the scheme.

A younger man stood in the corner of the kitchen, doing his best to appear as though he wasn't paying attention. His name was also John, named after his late father, John Surratt, who'd died from a stroke some years before.

John Jr. had been doing his part for the Confederacy for several months, working as an undercover courier delivering medical supplies, ammunition, and other important equipment to various drop spots all over the border between North and South.

He'd become so active that at one point the Union placed three hundred troops around the Surratt farm to keep an eye on their activities.

John Jr. shut things down for a short time to throw off the heat, but now he listened closely as the men in his mother's boarding house discussed their elaborate plan.

"It's hard for me to believe Seward's explorers found something so big in such a remote area," George said. "What if we're wrong? What if there's nothing there? That map doesn't even have a specific location marked on it."

"Yes," Lewis added. "George makes a good point. It's a vast wilderness. You could search for years and not find anything."

The look in Booth's eyes intensified. "If we're wrong, the worst we'll do is rid the world of a tyrant and his toadies. I'm not wrong about this, though. Three years ago, President Davis was getting ready to send a group of men west to

Alaska. Rumor had it there was something big underground near the Denali Mountains. Locals and natives talked about it. Most of what came out was nothing but rumors and legends. A few bits of information, however, were legitimate enough that our president wanted to investigate."

"I guess he didn't find anything," George said. He took a sip of whiskey and set the little glass back on the table. "Nothing valuable anyway."

Booth shook his head. "Actually, his men never left. A group of Lincoln's spies infiltrated the operation's headquarters in Atlanta. The entire unit was killed in their sleep. Then the spies tried to escape by stealing a train and heading north."

"Wait a minute," Lewis interrupted. "You're not talking about the locomotive chase, are you?"

Booth nodded. "Indeed, I am. Their leader was a civilian scout, a volunteer for Lincoln's little secret mission. After they stole the information about the Alaskan objective and executed the men set to carry it out, they boarded the *General* and took off toward Chattanooga, Tennessee. From there, they planned on stealing another locomotive to carry them west where they could arrange passage to the Alaskan Territory.

"Their mission was twofold. General Mitchel— the one who put the entire operation together— would move his forces in and take Chattanooga. Andrews and his men would disable the railway and telegraph wires between Atlanta and Chattanooga so their military lines couldn't be reinforced. I have to admit the whole thing was pretty brilliant. Most people just thought it was a raid to destroy the Confederate railroads, but that was only one piece of the puzzle. The other motive behind the sabotage was to cover up whatever is in the Alaska Territory." He paused for a short breath. "And so they could take it for themselves."

"They were stopped before they could reach Chattanooga," Lewis said. "Several of the men, including Andrews, were caught and executed. Most escaped. Union sympathizers were all over the place. Couldn't trust anyone. Still can't." He spat the last words out.

"Right," Booth agreed. "But now the war is coming to an end. Lee has already surrendered. If we don't act now, our cause will be lost for good. Our only hope is to take out Lincoln, Seward, and Johnson. When we do, the Union government will be thrown into disarray. While they're trying to settle the chaos, we'll find whatever is hiding in the Denali Mountains."

"And just how are we going to find that? You're talking about going all the way out to Alaska. That map isn't even complete. Where's the other half of it?" Herold asked. "What do those letters at the bottom mean?"

"Not to mention the fact that you're talking about murdering the president of the United States," George said with an eyebrow raised.

Booth's eyes narrowed as he stared down everyone in the room, making sure they understood the gravity of the situation.

"This is only half of the puzzle," Booth said, tapping on the map. "When Andrews and his men ran out of fuel, they fled the locomotive and ran for their lives. They'd devised a plan to split the information in case they were caught. Once Lincoln and his allies are dead, we'll find the other half. Then everything will become clear."

"Just how do you figure on finding the other half? Those Yanks could have hidden it anywhere."

Booth looked from one pair of eyes to the other until he'd made contact with everyone. "It's in North Georgia."

"How do you know that?" George asked.

"One of the men from the locomotive chase had a penchant for drink. Let's just say when he's drunk, he gets real mouthy. I overheard him in a bar, talking about something that would make the Union invincible. So I followed him out of the tavern, and when the moment presented itself, I pulled him into an alley and coaxed the information out of him."

"So, once this is done, with the president and his allies, we go to Georgia, find the other half of this, and then off to Alaska?" David said. "Seems like an enormous task."

"It is. Great victories come with great sacrifice and incredible risks. This will turn the tide in our favor," Booth said. "Lincoln will be the hardest target. I have a plan for him, and I'll see to it personally. Seward and Johnson will be easier, especially Seward. He's in his home in Auburn, New York, recovering from an accident. He'll be in bed and an easy target with few guards around."

Booth could see the hesitation in some of the eyes looking back at him. Lewis was the only one who appeared to be comfortable with the idea.

"So, what do you say, gentlemen? Are you ready to make history?" Booth asked.

The others glanced at each other as if confirming their resolve, then nodded.

"Good. Soon, the tyrant will be dead, and the South will rise again."

1. Upstate New York

Sean Wyatt was dead.

His heart still thumped in his chest, his lungs inhaled and exhaled air, but he was dead. And he knew it.

He watched the snowy countryside of western Upstate New York pass by outside the heavily tinted window. The darkness of the glass was an irony in itself since civilians weren't allowed to tint their car windows that dark. It made seeing inside nearly impossible. Looking out during times of low light must have been difficult as well, or at least Sean figured as much.

He wasn't concerned about the government-issue tinted windows, though. It was merely a passing thought in his mind.

His concern was where he was being taken and why.

The answer to the first part of that question wouldn't be known until they arrived, but he knew exactly why. The guns in the laps of the men surrounding him, the utter silence of the SUV's cabin, the matching black outfits the men wore—all told Sean everything he needed to know about why.

These men worked for the government. And they were going to execute him.

He'd seen assets like the ones around him before. They wore the typical tactical gear; each had a small earpiece planted in the right ear. Back in Sean's day—when he worked for Axis—there would have been a wire attached to the tiny device. Now everything worked on Bluetooth.

The only man in the group who appeared to be over thirty was the driver—his age given away by the sparse strands of gray in his beard. All the others had naked faces, like they'd never had to shave in their lives.

Sean knew that didn't change the fact that these men were well trained and would execute their mission without batting an eye. He'd seen it before, though he never expected to be on the receiving end—at least not from his fellow Americans.

He averted his gaze to the road ahead. Snow was piled up along both sides of the asphalt. Winter had hit the area hard of late, dumping a few feet of powder on the countryside.

Were he not heading to his death, Sean would have enjoyed the drive in the serene beauty of a winter landscape.

They hadn't seen a car in twenty minutes. It wouldn't be long now.

Sean knew better than to ask questions. These guys wouldn't say anything. Their hardened expressions told him everything he needed to know. Well, not everything. He would like to know who they worked for, why they were going to kill him, but those questions wouldn't be answered.

Not by these men.

Sean's only hope was clutched in the palm of his hand. It was in the shape of a small, black disk: a gift from a friend at DARPA.

When the hit squad nabbed Sean in Auburn, New York, he'd seen them coming. Sensing trouble before the men made their move, Sean grabbed one of the disks from a little pouch on his belt and kept it in his hand. There was no point in trying to fight the men off—not yet anyway. When he saw them approaching with their weapons drawn, he'd surrendered without a fight. Sean's pistol had been left in the car. He figured there was no reason to make the museum curator uncomfortable if there was no need.

Very few crazy things happened in the quiet little western New York town.

Sean should have known better.

It was always when one least expected something bad to happen when things started to go south.

He'd been all over New England from Massachusetts and Connecticut to Vermont, New Hampshire, and even southern Maine. In the end, his search brought him back to where he began this particular quest—at the home of Abraham Lincoln's Secretary of State, William Seward.

The initial reason Sean went to Auburn was at the request of his friend, President Dawkins. Sean and Tommy had been instrumental in helping the president with issues on more than one occasion.

In fact, the leader of the free world had called so often over the last few years that Sean wondered if Dawkins had memorized his phone number.

In this case, Dawkins had come across a peculiar letter from former Secretary of State William Seward. It was written to Lincoln in 1864.

Sean asked the president how he'd come by the letter. Dawkins was happy to explain that he'd been looking through an old book in the White House when the letter fell out from amid the other pages. It was only later that Dawkins realized that the book was a first edition from the early nineteenth century and had been in the White House for over 160 years.

"Keep this between you and me," Dawkins said when he handed Sean the letter. "I don't know exactly what this means, but if anyone can figure it out, it's you and Tommy."

"I'll do my best, sir," Sean said.

Now, months later, he'd been unable to find anything.

The cryptic letter was pretty vague, a fact Sean had made known to the president. Dawkins had insisted that Sean at least give a look around the Seward estate. And when the president of the United States insisted that someone do something, they usually did it.

Tommy was busy back in Atlanta, showing his parents the entire operation at the International Archaeological Agency. For nearly two decades, Sean's best friend, Tommy Schultz, had believed his parents to be dead. He'd used his inheritance to establish the IAA in their honor to continue the search for lost artifacts in hopes of exposing new and genuine history to the world. His parents certainly had a lot of catching up to do. For nearly 20 years they'd been imprisoned by North Korea's Chairman, otherwise known as the Dear Leader. When he died and his son took over, one of the head generals continued to keep Tommy's parents hostage, demanding they unravel a mystery that would lead to what the general believed was an ancient power that would make his military unstoppable.

Now they were safe, back home in Atlanta with their son.

That gave Sean plenty of time to take a look into the matter with the president's letter. He'd read it so many times, Sean nearly had the whole thing memorized.

"Dear Mr. President,

I write this correspondence to you with the utmost urgency.

I recently received word from my men in the Denali region. The anomaly they reported discovering before is, apparently, extremely dangerous. Our head geologist recommends we bury the anomaly so that no one else will be hurt by it. One of our men tried to touch the strange device and was instantly struck dead. None of the physicians or researchers on the team know what happened to him, only that there was a bright blueish light that sparked over his head before he died.

As your Secretary of State, I recommend the following actions be taken, both for national security and to continue in the steps of Manifest Destiny as set forth by our forefathers.

One, we must close off the mountain where the anomaly was found.

Two, I recommend we make an offer to the Czar to purchase the territory west of Yukon.

This land will provide numerous resources for our nation, and by owning the land, we can monitor it to make sure no one strays into the mountain and finds what I can only assume was meant to never be discovered by mere mortals.

I believe the Russians will accept a sum of around seven million, but we may try for less. I know that the war has taken a great toll on our finances; however, I deeply believe this is necessary.

Sincerely,
William Seward
Secretary of State
United States of America

What had Seward's men discovered in Alaska that caused him to be so afraid? According to the letter, one of the men died in what sounded like some kind of electrocution accident.

There was no way to know without seeing the anomaly in person.

The driver turned off the main road, and Sean

snapped back to the present. His wandering thoughts about the last few months hadn't been productive. In fact, all the time he'd spent on the project had produced almost no results, except for one.

He discovered a note that appeared to be written in Seward's handwriting, albeit somewhat rushed. The note was short with no formal heading or footer denoting who it was from or who might be the recipient.

It had said, *"The KGC are aware of the oddity and are preparing an expedition. Proceed with Operation Iron Horse."*

Sean had no idea what Operation Iron Horse was, but he knew exactly what the KGC was. It was an acronym for the Knights of the Golden Circle, a "secret society" of Confederate supporters who often worked behind the scenes—and sometimes in full view—to help the efforts of the rebellion.

Rumors about the KGC being involved with the assassination of Abraham Lincoln had been floating around since the late 1800s. Most of the information was hearsay or hypothesis. There was rarely anything substantial, as was usually the case when it came to secret societies. They were called secret for a reason, and Sean knew it wasn't because they took their rules and guidelines lightly.

The KGC stepped deeper back into the shadows in the years following the American Civil War. Maybe they ceased operations. Or perhaps they just took on a new position from which to manipulate events.

Sean shook the thoughts from his mind. The SUV was slowing down as they approached a clearing. Another SUV was already parked off to the side of snow-covered side road. It appeared to be nothing more than a trail with two ruts, most likely used by people with four-wheel-drive who liked to get out on the weekends and do a little off-roading.

As he looked through the windshield, Sean could see two men standing by a pile of dirt. Shovels were lying atop the mound.

"At least you took the courtesy of not making me dig my own grave. I appreciate that," Sean said.

No one in the vehicle said anything to his smart-aleck comment.

The driver turned the wheel to the right, maneuvering the SUV off to the opposite side of the other. Snow crunched under the tires as it plowed into fresh unpacked drifts. He stopped the vehicle and got out. The men in the back with Sean didn't need to be told what to do. They immediately opened the doors and motioned for the prisoner to exit.

Sean obeyed, knowing there was no point in delaying things further. No cavalry was on the way to help him. If he was going to get out of this situation, he'd need a miracle. That or a little improvisation.

He noted the H&K submachine guns dangling from the shoulders of the men by the grave. The guys who'd been in the back of the SUV with Sean had similar weapons. The man in charge—or so Sean figured—was carrying a SIG 9mm he'd tucked in a holster.

Sean stepped down into the snow and squinted. The sun peeked through the clouds above, shining brightly off the white blanket of this time of year. His guards winced as well, but their sunglasses kept away most of the glare. Sean kept his fist clenched tight to make sure none of the men saw what was in his hand.

The smell of fresh snow and evergreen trees filled the air. Snowflakes fluttered from the clouds above, adding to the serenity of the moment. It was a calm Sean knew would either end in a bullet to the head or a chaotic escape. He was hoping for the latter.

One of the guards put his hand on Sean's shoulder and ushered him forward, toward the grave.

The snow crunched with every step. Sean's shoes sank deep into the white powder. He was thankful to be wearing a winter coat. The SUV had been too warm. Stepping out into the fresh air was a welcome change, except for the fact he was about to be executed.

He stopped by the big hole in the ground, and the driver motioned with a nod to one of the guys behind Sean. Immediately, the guard pressed Sean down to his knees. Sean looked around at the partially covered faces. The men didn't need to hide their identities. After all, a dead witness was a silent one.

Sean felt the cold of a muzzle press against the back of his skull. It was something he'd felt before. It made him squeamish every time, though no one could tell from looking at him.

The man in charge stood right in front of Sean with hands folded across his belt line.

"So, Sean, this is where I ask you why you were snooping around the Seward estate. Then you tell me where I can shove my questions, and then I tell you it's your last chance before you die. Of course, you won't tell me what I want to know, which will result in me having my associate behind you put a bullet through your knee. That may or may not get you to talk, so we'll continue torturing you until you either pass out—at which point we shoot you in the head—or you tell us what we need to know, which will also result in a bullet to the head."

The man stared down at Sean with a look colder than the icicles on the trees around them.

"So, should I have him go ahead and begin, or do you want to skip all that pain and just tell me what you were doing looking around the museum?"

Sean drew a long, icy breath through his nose. He returned the stoic glare to the man in charge. "Drew Porter, is it?" he asked. Before the man could answer, Sean went on. "I thought that was you. CIA if I recall correctly. You were a good agent. Showed a lot of promise, from what I remember. Emily considered you for Axis at one point. Said your psychological didn't check out. That's a bummer. What was it? Oh, that's right. I remember now. The shrink said you had a problem with authority, that you would probably break the rules."

"Don't believe everything you hear from a shrink," Drew said.

"Hey, I don't judge it. I've been known to break a few rules myself. Shame it didn't work out with Axis. I can tell you're a real swell guy. Most people would have made me dig the grave myself. Not you, though." Sean looked over at the guys by the dirt mound. "Thanks to you two, by the way. I imagine digging that must have taken a while, what with the dirt being frozen and all. Hope you didn't blister your fingers."

Sean's comment was received with a hard backhand across his cheek. The frigid air made it sting more than normal, and he cringed for a second until the pain subsided.

"Answer the question, Sean, or I have him take out your kneecap."

Sean shook his head slowly. He was out of time. These guys wouldn't give him the chance to stall. The only reason they hadn't killed him yet was because they wanted information. How they were CIA and didn't already know the answers puzzled him.

There were more questions, too. What were they trying to cover up at the Seward estate? Why was the CIA involved? He didn't have to wonder how they knew he was snooping around. The CIA was good at keeping watch of important things. He'd probably been under surveillance for some time, though he wondered why they hadn't apprehended him sooner.

His mind raced with the possibilities. What had he learned in the last few days that would have triggered this kind of response from the CIA? And were these men rogue or acting on orders from their official chain of command?

He wouldn't get the answers right now, but he would eventually. That is, if he managed to escape.

Sean decided to play the ultimate trump card and see what would happen. It might give him at least a few of the answers he needed.

"The president sent me here," he said. The blunt response did little to change the demeanor of Porter and his men.

"And why did the president send you here?"

Sean shrugged. "I don't know. He wanted me to take a look at some historical stuff at Seward's mansion. You know I work for an archaeological agency, right? I mean, we do this sort of thing all the time."

"So, the president knows about Denali," Porter said. "Very well. I suppose he will have to die, too."

Sean's eyebrows cinched together. What did that guy just say? Kill the president? Not what Sean expected.

"Whoa, take it easy there, Drew. Dawkins has nothing to do with this. And I don't know what you're talking about with Denali."

"Oh, but you just said he sent you here to investigate something. Now, what was it he wanted you to look into?"

"He didn't say. All he told me was that he wanted me to talk to the museum curator and ask to see the archives. I've been on this project for a few months now and haven't found anything useful." He hoped they bought the lie.

"You mean, in regards to the letter?" Porter held up the letter the president had given Sean.

Well, it was worth a try, Sean thought, considering his effort at misdirection.

Porter and his men must have seized it from Sean's room. He'd hidden it away in a tattered folder. Apparently, he hadn't done a good enough job of concealing the secret document.

Sean raised an eyebrow. "Yes, that's the one." He made the faux confession with a broad, exaggerated grin. "I guess I forgot...That letter mentions Denali, doesn't it? My mistake."

"Not a problem," Porter said. "You won't be around long enough to meddle anymore. And neither will your friend in the White House."

Porter looked up at the man holding Sean at gunpoint and gave a nod. Sean saw Porter take a step back and knew the man was moving out of the splash radius.

Sean squeezed the little black disk in his palm and let it dangle from his fingers.

"If you're going to kill me," he said, "the least

you can do is look me in the eyes, Drew."

Porter stopped and crossed his arms. "Oh, I intend to."

The patch of clear sky above gave way to another front of dark gray clouds, an ominous sign from the heavens.

Sean didn't have a moment to lose. He dropped the device into the snow behind his feet and closed his eyes tight. He felt the gun press harder into his skull for a second and then pull away as the gunman was about to fire.

A loud pop came from behind Sean's back.

2. Upstate New York

Sean felt a surge of heat rush past his legs and up his back as his eyelids brightened for a second from the flash of light the device gave off.

The gunman behind him screamed. Porter yelled something unintelligible. Sean fell to his side just as the gunman blindly squeezed the trigger. The weapon fired, sending a round plunging into the snow beyond where Sean's head had been a second before.

Sean rolled onto his knees, wrapped his hands around the weapon, and twisted while jamming his elbow into the man's forearm. The gunman yelped, bending down on one knee as Sean continued to wrench the appendage until he heard the bone break. Then the screaming grew louder.

As the gunman craned his neck back, Sean rose from his knees and chopped the bridge of his hand into the man's throat. The yelling stopped instantly, and the guy fell face-first into the snow, clutching his neck as he desperately gasped for air that would not come.

Sean raised the weapon to aim it at Porter, but the head man had managed to stumble over to the SUV and take cover behind the hood. Sean spun around and whipped his leg out to sweep the other guard's ankles. The top of his foot struck the man on the lower calf. Combined with the temporary blindness, the sudden blow knocked him off balance.

The guard fell hard onto his back and scrambled to get up. Sean spun to his feet and pounced, driving his knee into the guard's temple. The man collapsed to the snow, unconscious...possibly dead. Sean didn't have time to check.

The two men near the shovels were the first to recover from the flash bang. Being several yards away kept them at a safe enough distance that the sudden bright light only blinded them for a few seconds.

Sean grabbed the dead gunman from the snow and propped him up as a human shield as he fired over the man's shoulder. The first two rounds missed, exploding in the snow around the two shooters' feet. The third caught one guy in the thigh and dropped him to the ground.

The other opened fire, peppering Sean's human shield with a dozen rounds before he had to reload.

Sean dropped the body back into the snow and stood up, raising his weapon to eye level. He took a menacing step forward and fired a single shot. The bullet thumped into the shooter's chest. He wavered for a second, still holding his new magazine, and then toppled backward.

Another gunshot rang out from the SUV.

Porter and his last henchmen were tucked behind the truck's open doors. Sean whipped around and took aim. His first two shots plunked into white car paint. The shooters kept firing. Sean was out in the open, an easy target for expert marksmen, even from forty feet away.

Sean took a step back as he aimed for Porter's feet that were exposed under the door. As he was about to squeeze the trigger, a bullet caught him in the upper right part of his chest. His weapon fired as he staggered backward, losing his balance.

He hit the bottom of the grave with a jarring thud. The impact increased the burning pain in his chest for a second. He winced and clutched one of the wounds. His body reacted by forcing a cough.

This is it, he thought. His mind wandered to Adriana, the woman he loved. She was back in Madrid, visiting relatives. He didn't think that when she left for the airport it would be the last time he saw her. Then his thoughts drifted to Tommy, his lifelong friend. Tommy wouldn't know what happened either. Sean's body would be covered up and left for time to forget.

Suddenly, another weapon fired from somewhere behind the grave.

It was a hunting rifle based on the sound. Sean struggled to breathe; the pain in his chest felt like two knives were jammed into his lungs.

The new weapon fired again.

Then he heard the SUV's engine rev to life. The sounds of the vehicle speeding away through the snow echoed down into the shallow hole.

Sean's vision started to blur, and a chill began creeping into his bones. He felt the cold metal of the pistol in his hand, and he held it up to defend himself from whoever was still on the ground above.

"Hello?" a gruff voice shouted. "You in the grave. You still alive?"

Sean tried to answer, but all he could muster was a faint squeak. He could feel warmth spreading across his chest as blood leaked from his body.

Just before he lost consciousness, he saw a silhouette of a man in a long black coat standing over him. Then everything went dark.

* * *

Sean's eyes cracked open. He didn't feel cold anymore. Instead, his body was embraced by a strange warmth. He coughed and closed his eyes again. The pain in his chest wasn't as bad as before. He tried to turn his head, but the movement caused his vision to spin for as second.

"Where...where am I?" he whispered through cracked lips.

His nostrils filled with the smell of smoke. A dim orange light flickered from the corner of his eye, and he realized wherever he was had a fireplace. He tried to open his eyes wider, but the lids felt caked together. He raised his right hand and rubbed his eyes for a moment until his sight cleared.

Sean surveyed the room, taking in his surroundings. He was in an old log cabin, lying on a sofa. The fire crackled in the hearth on the opposite side of the living room—about twelve feet away. He could see the kitchen off to the right. There was a doorway nearby, just behind his head, though he couldn't maneuver enough to see what else was there. He looked down and noticed the IV in his wrist. A stand with a bag of clear liquid hanging from it was propped up next to the couch.

"Whose cabin is this?" he asked himself. "Doctor Quinn?"

"Not hardly," a man's voice answered from the shadows.

Startled, Sean attempted to sit up, but vertigo took hold once more and forced him to keep his head on the pillow.

"Who are you? Where am I? What do you want with me?"

The gravelly voice chuckled. "You sure do ask a lot of questions for a dead guy."

Sean knew he wasn't dead. That didn't change the fact he had zero ideas as to where he was.

Before he could say anything, his host spoke up again.

"You're lucky I came around. Those guys were bent on killing you." The voice had a Southern draw to it—definitely out of place in this part of the country. "So how's about you answer my questions first. That is, if you're feeling up to it."

Sean's body still felt heavy. He was too weak to move or protest.

"What do you want to know?"

"That's more like it. The name's Jack. Jack Scoggins. What's your name?"

Sean sighed. "Wyatt. Sean Wyatt. I work for—"

"Now hold your horses, Son. I didn't ask who you worked for. Truth is I don't rightly care. What I do care about is why those men wanted you dead. You a criminal? Was this some kind of Mafia hit?"

A chuckle escaped Sean's lips. The brief spat of laughter sent a fresh jolt of pain through his chest and turned to coughing.

"No," he said finally. "I'm not a criminal. Like I was saying, I work for the International Archaeological Agency in Atlanta."

"Okay. Pardon me for being a bit skeptical, but why on earth would a group of men armed like those fellas want to execute an archaeologist? Did you have some sort of treasure they wanted?"

Sean struggled to keep from laughing again. "No. Nothing like that. And I'm not technically an archaeologist. I just enjoy history. My job is research and security. I find lost relics and bring them in for further study, stuff like that."

Jack didn't respond for a moment. Sean figured he was assessing the explanation.

"What brings you to this part of the country? Kind of remote out here. I can't imagine there's much in the way of archaeology going on around these parts."

"Looking...for a clue," Sean said, struggling to get the words out. He was so weak, even the act of talking took a concerted effort.

"Clue?"

"Yeah. I'm on a mission from the president. He

found a letter in the White House that had to do with William Seward. I thought I'd poke around the Seward museum and estate to see what I could find."

"Looks like what you found was trouble," Jack said.

"So it would seem."

Sean heard the wooden floor creak under slow, heavy footsteps. A man with a thick gray beard appeared in the light of the fireplace, standing five feet from the couch. His eyes were lively and green, seemingly out of place in the older man's face.

"Nice to meet you," Sean said. He glanced down at the IV in his wrist. "I guess you have some kind of medical training. This is a clean line."

"You could say that," Jack said. "Before I came out here, I was a doctor."

Sean's eyebrows shot up. "A doctor? What kind of doctor?"

"Surgeon. That was a long time ago." There was a twinge of sadness in his voice.

"So, you retired and came up here to get away from everything?"

"Something like that. Let's just say I didn't have anything else keeping me in that line of work."

Sean immediately figured the man was a widower. That or he went through some other major tragedy. People didn't usually just pick up and move out to the frozen wilderness unless they wanted a big life change. That desire was typically driven by sadness in one form or another.

Jack pointed at Sean's chest. Two white bandages were taped to his skin, stained a brownish red. "You lost a lot of blood. Wasn't sure you were going to make it. Been giving you some pain meds and saline for the last two days. For a minute, I thought I was going to have to take you back to that grave those guys dug for you."

"Wait. Two days? I've been here for two days?"

"Yeah. And you're lucky it's not a permanent stay. Whatever you did to those men, they wanted to make sure you didn't do it again."

Sean tried to push himself up from the couch. His arms gave out, and he collapsed.

"Just take it easy, Son. You're safe here. My cabin is a half mile from where they tried to kill you."

"They'll be back. I have to get out of here. You won't be safe until I'm gone."

Jack stepped forward and put his finger to Sean's forehead, pushing him back to the pillow.

"I said you need to take it easy. I tell you what, back when I was a surgeon, I had the same problem with patients. No one ever wants to listen to the doc. You're going to be here a few more days, Sean. High time you get used to that idea. And if you think those men will be back looking for you, I doubt it."

"What...what makes you say that?" Sean said in a feeble tone.

"Because I've been keeping an eye out for them. If they haven't come back in the last forty-eight hours, I doubt they will now. My guess is they think you're dead. You're very fortunate those bullets didn't do any permanent damage. If I were you, I'd take the good doctor's advice and get some rest. When you're feeling a bit stronger, you can get up and move around."

Sean gave a weak nod. "Okay, Doc. I'll do what you say."

"That's better. Now, here's some water. I'm sure you're thirsty even though that thing is pumping fluids in you."

He set a cup with a straw next to Sean on a little end table. Sean picked it up and took a sip. The water was cold and had a slight taste of iron to it, but he didn't care. He *was* thirsty.

"Thanks for saving my life," Sean said as he set the cup back down on the table. "I'd be dead if not for you."

"Yep. You probably would." The curt answer almost caused Sean to start laughing again, but he fought it off. "And you're more than welcome. I took the bullets out. Saved them in a bowl in the kitchen in case you wanted to keep them. One was pretty close to your heart. You're lucky. I guess it wasn't your time yet."

Sean wriggled into the sheets and stared at the ceiling. Too many things were running through his head. Questions about who had attacked him and why were some of the more pervasive. He also realized he'd need to get in contact with his people. "Jack, I need you to do me a favor."

"Name it."

"I'm going to give you a phone number. I need you to call it and ask for a woman named Emily Starks. Tell her it's from Sean and it's urgent. They'll ask for a security code. It's three, seven, four, eight, six."

"Ain't got no phones here, but there's a diner a few miles away on the main road. If you need to make a call, you can do it from there when you feel better or I can go into town tomorrow morning and do it for you."

No phones? Not even a cell phone? Apparently, this guy was living all the way off the grid. Sean had a cabin that wasn't connected to the world, but he could always get online via satellite if he needed to and he always had a cell phone with him. His phone had been taken away by the CIA guys who'd abducted him. Now he was on a snowy island in the middle of nowhere with no connection to anyone or anything except a former doctor turned hermit.

"Okay," Sean said, resigned to the fact that he wasn't going to be strong enough to get up anytime soon. "If you're going to make a call for me when you go into town, let's go ahead and make it three calls."

"Got people who will be worried about you?" Jack asked.

"You could say that."

3. Washington

Secretary of State Kent Foster waited patiently for the door to open. He'd been sitting in the Oval Office for just over twenty minutes. It wasn't unusual for the president to keep him waiting. For a man who was on such a tight schedule, it seemed Dawkins was perpetually running behind.

Secretary Foster looked down at his phone and tapped one of the app icons. He made a quick note of something he didn't want to forget later in the day before putting the phone back in his pocket. He did so just as the door to his left opened.

He stood up as the president, two Secret Service men, and one of Dawkins's advisers walked in.

"Mr. President," Foster said in a polite tone.

"Good morning, Kent. Please, have a seat."

The secretary did as instructed and returned to his seat. The president's adviser left a note on the Resolute Desk before disappearing out the door again. It closed behind him leaving the room in momentary silence.

"So, tell me what's so urgent that you had to meet with me this morning." Dawkins eased into his seat and folded his hands on the desk's surface. His brown, wavy hair was combed to one side as best as could be done, though it seemed to often have a mind of its own.

"We have an issue, sir."

"Obviously, Kent. What kind of issue?"

"Actually, sir, there are two," Foster said. "The first is the Russians. We have reason to believe they are pushing closer and closer to Alaska. I've been briefed by the council. Things are starting to get tense. They've gone so far as to begin installing oil rigs just off the Aleutian shores. I've heard that they've even been so brazen as to send geological experts to a few locations to investigate potential drilling sites. This is a direct encroachment. We're going to need to take a stand."

"I've been told the same thing by the members of the council," Dawkins said. "Which is why we are meeting with them in two hours."

"Yes, sir. I'm aware of the meeting."

"This couldn't wait until then?"

Foster tilted his head toward the floor for a second, slightly embarrassed by the question. "I'm sorry for the inconvenience, sir. It's just that...the Russians get more emboldened every day. Their president has claimed rightful ownership of Alaska and wants the United States to return it to them."

"Again, I've heard this stuff before, Kent. How in the blue blazes that guy thinks he can just push us out of that territory is beyond me. He's just blowing smoke. He wouldn't dare try an invasion, not this day and age."

Foster cleared his throat. "While it is certainly a possibility that this is just a case of the Russian leader trying to show a little bravado, we still have to take this threat seriously, sir."

Dawkins leaned back in his chair and crossed one leg over the other, resting his ankle on the other knee. It wasn't the first time he'd had to deal with the Russian president. A few years before, the man had been brazen enough to invade a section of Ukraine, claiming it had always been Russian land and Russian citizens still lived there. Remarkably, the international community did little more than blast the move on social media, which was basically like throwing snowballs at a tank.

President Dawkins had watched everything unfold from afar, waiting to see what would happen before issuing any executive orders. He'd adopted a strong policy of neutrality when it came to most international conflicts. Dawkins firmly believed in a strong defense but without trying to police the world. The rest of the planet had made it abundantly clear that they didn't want the United States poking its nose in everyone's business. And so, President John Dawkins all but refused to openly jump into conflict.

Of course, what the public didn't know was that he'd secretly ordered elite units to take care of certain situations abroad.

A warlord in Sudan had been wreaking havoc on the country and its people. Women were being victimized in horrible, unthinkable ways. Children were brutally murdered. People were starving and exposed to the elements with no shelter.

His predecessor had stayed away from such

situations, probably because there was no money in swooping into a central African nation to help people in need. His predecessor had focused more on oil countries.

Not Dawkins.

He had ordered a tactical strike on the Sudanese warlord that took out the man and most of his followers in one swoop. Next, Dawkins had sent tens of millions in aid to help feed the people and get them back on their feet.

The attacks on the warlord were never publicized, never shown in the media, because that's how covert ops were supposed to work. Dawkins wasn't a fan of bragging. He didn't put his triumphs out there for everyone to see so his approval ratings would go up a fraction of a point. He just got the job done, and the people loved him for it.

He'd handled several situations in much the same way, helping people who couldn't help themselves.

The Ukraine situation, however, was different.

The Russians had been stewing for a long time. Their national resources were vast, but severely restricted and less cost effective than getting them somewhere else. That, or implement new laws and regulations that would enable the country to get back on its feet with more renewable resources and better management of nonrenewable ones.

While Dawkins couldn't fly in and bomb the Russians back across their border with the Ukraine affair, he had every right to defend Alaska. A full-on military assault wasn't his first choice, especially when the people infringing on U.S. borders were mostly civilians.

"I realize we must take this threat seriously, Kent. Believe me, I have no intention of letting Nikolai Zhirkov think he can make idle threats without me noticing. Don't worry. I'll handle it, just like I've handled every other threat in the past."

Foster appeared to accept the answer, so the president continued. "What was the other thing you wanted to talk to me about?"

"Well," Foster said with an uneasy voice, "it's about Axis, sir."

"Axis?" Dawkins sat up a little straighter. Only he and a few other select people knew anything about the elite secret agency. They operated quietly, sticking to the shadows most of the time. Their missions were the ones no one else could handle, or they simply didn't want to. It was much like MI6 in the UK, only smaller.

"Yes, sir. I don't know how to say this. I know that you are personal friends with Director Starks as well as Sean Wyatt."

"Wyatt? He's no longer with Axis, Kent. You should do your homework."

Foster nodded. "I'm aware that former agent Sean Wyatt is no longer working for Axis, sir. However, this does involve him."

"Wyatt? How so?"

"Sir, I don't know how to tell you this, but we think that Sean Wyatt might be working with the Russians."

It was all Dawkins could do to keep from bursting with laughter. After a minute, the laughter died as he realized Foster was serious.

"You're kidding, right?" Dawkins asked, his face turning grave.

Foster folded his hands in his lap atop a file he'd been holding. "Unfortunately, sir, I'm not. I just received word from the CIA that he's gone rogue. He took out three operatives. Another is recovering from a blow to the head."

"Three operatives? Why on Earth would you send CIA assets after Sean Wyatt in the first place? You do realize he's like a badger. Corner him, and he is more dangerous than pretty much anyone you know."

"We are aware of his skill set, sir."

"You are aware?" the president said in a mocking tone. "Obviously, you didn't think before you put people in play with him. And that brings me back to the first question. Why were you sending men after him?"

Foster took the file from his lap and laid it on the desk. He pushed it closer to the president with one finger.

Dawkins read the cover. It was like a million other files he'd seen come across his desk in the years he'd been president.

Classified.

He opened it and noted the pictures of Sean taken by—most likely—a CIA surveillance operative.

"Those images were taken a few days ago by one of our assets. You can see there, Agent Wyatt is on the premises of the William Seward estate."

"So? I told you before, he's been working on a special assignment from me. And he's doing it as a favor."

"That may be, Mr. President, but take a look at the next image."

Dawkins glared at Foster under his eyebrows before returning his gaze to the pictures in the folder. The next one showed Sean sitting at a cafe table on a street. There was a cup of coffee in front of him.

"Okay, what am I looking at now? A picture of Sean drinking a cup of coffee? Looks like he's texting someone."

"You would be correct in that assessment, sir. He is texting someone. The NSA intercepted the text message and forwarded that to our team. The number he was sending that message to is based in Moscow."

The president's face remained stoic, but inside he was fighting off a stern frown.

"You'll find the messages and the number behind those images, sir."

Dawkins scratched the side of his head and moved the picture. He looked over the numbers on the list and then noted the messages.

There was reference to Alaska, Denali, and a device, though the verbiage was vague.

"You do realize Sean has contacts all over the world. And while we should probably be wary of whatever the Russians are doing right now, I'd hardly say these texts are reason to go after one of my trusted friends."

"We agree, Mr. President. The CIA team simply wanted to ask Sean some questions. He got hostile and killed three Americans. That is something we cannot ignore, sir."

Dawkins knew the secretary was right. He couldn't ignore it. Something wasn't right, though. He couldn't put his finger on it, but John Dawkins was no fool. If Sean Wyatt killed members of the CIA, he wouldn't have done it without good reason. He decided to keep that thought to himself for the moment.

"What do you propose we do, Kent? Bring him in?"

"That is what the CIA team was attempting to do. They merely wanted to ask him some questions."

"You mean interrogate him."

"Call it what you will, sir. Wyatt is a threat. And if you look at the next page, you'll see what I'm talking about."

Dawkins scanned the next piece of paper until he came across a line that struck him as odd. *I will personally make sure Big D is down.*

He shook his head. "Big D? What does that

mean? You trying to tell me Wyatt is going to attack Dallas?"

Secretary Foster shook his head. "No, sir. YOU are big D."

Dawkins swallowed hard at the implication. Sean had been a friend for several years. It was unfathomable to think he'd be involved with a plot to kill him. Based on the intel in front of him, it seemed that was exactly what was going on. He drew in a deep breath and then exhaled slowly before speaking again.

"What do you suggest we do, Kent?"

"I've already taken the necessary measures. Wyatt will resurface sooner or later. And when he does, we'll be ready."

4. Upstate New York

Sean sat up on the couch and looked at the Band-Aid on his wrist. Jack had taken the IV out a few days before, and ever since Sean had been drinking fluids normally and switched to pills for the pain in his chest.

He'd recovered faster than expected and was even getting up to move around a bit. There wasn't much to do in the cabin except for reading old books Jack kept on a shelf near the fireplace. Sean thumbed through a few of the pages once, but the story didn't hold his attention.

On the third day after Sean had awoken in the cabin, Jack went into town to get some supplies his unexpected guest requested. The host had planned on doing it the previous day, but blustery conditions brought in another round of snow that kept the old doctor at home for another day.

When the weather subsided, he ventured out in his old truck and disappeared down the trail.

Sean watched until the tail lights disappeared before he got to work testing out his muscle strength. He knew Jack wouldn't approve and would likely tell him to take it easy for the next few weeks, but Sean didn't have that kind of time. Someone had tried to kill him, which meant he was onto something. What it was, he didn't know for sure, but he intended to find out.

He eased himself down to the floor and propped his weight up on his hands and knees. He tried to lower his chest to do a push-up, but the pain on the right side of his chest was too much, and he crumpled to the wooden floorboards in a heap.

His lungs rose and fell as he gasped for air. He'd only been in the cabin for four or five days—according to Jack—but he'd weakened significantly.

"Maybe I'll start with the legs and work up to the arms and chest," he said to himself.

He pushed his weight off the floor and stood next to the smoldering fireplace. He put his arms out in front of him and bent his knees until they were hovering over the tops of his feet. Then he stood up, completing one squat rep. He let out a sigh and repeated the process until he'd done ten reps.

A bead of sweat rolled down the side of his head. The cabin was surprisingly warm seeing that the world outside was covered in snow and ice.

He wiped his forehead and noticed the logs stacked by the fireplace. Outside, a larger stack of uncut wood was piled by the back door. A shiny axe leaned up against the logs.

Sean raised an eyebrow.

Two minutes later, he was standing in a foot of snow next to the cabin, chopping wood in Jack's pajamas and his shoes. The swinging motion didn't hurt much. It was more of an irritation than a hindering pain. He split a log in half, then set one piece back up on its end and cut it in half, repeating the process several times until he'd worked up a sweat. His heart pounded in his chest from the exertion.

"That wasn't so bad," he said.

He heard a car coming down the trail.

He hurriedly put the axe back where he got it and rushed back inside, careful to stamp the snow off his shoes and clean himself off before getting back into his makeshift bed on the couch.

Jack's truck rumbled to a stop, and the engine cut off a moment later. Sean heard the door slam shut, the footsteps coming up to the door, and then Jack appeared in the doorway. He closed the door behind him and set a few bags of groceries on the little round table in the corner of the kitchen.

"Looks like someone's been up and about," Jack said, staring at his patient with a condemning glare.

Sean did his best to look innocent, but the older man wasn't fooled.

"I was getting antsy," Sean said. "And besides, I'm feeling much better."

"Yeah, I've heard that from patients before. Know what we call that in the medical field?"

"Noncompliance?"

"Oh, seems we have a know-it-all in our midst," Jack said with a shake of the head. "No one wants to listen to the doctor. Everyone knows better than me."

"I didn't do much," Sean said. "Just a little exercise to build up my strength."

Jack made his way into the kitchen carrying a carton of milk and a container of butter. "I don't care what you do, son. I took the bullets out of you. If you want to go hurting yourself or putting more bullets in, that's your business. Can't say I'll be there next time, though."

"Hopefully, I won't need it."

Jack closed the refrigerator door and took his coat off. He hung it on the chair and lumbered over to the small pile of wood next to the fireplace. He placed another log on the fire and stoked it with the iron leaning against the wall.

"I see you split some wood out back. Hardly what I'd call easy exercise."

Sean said nothing. He didn't have to defend himself to this guy, even though the man had saved his life. The sooner Sean could get back to civilization and figure out what was going on, the better.

"No need to thank me for the chopped wood," he said.

Jack kept his eyes on the fire. "Good, because I wasn't going to."

Sean grinned at the response. He liked the old guy. Part of him wanted to know the full story about why Jack was out here on his own, but a little voice in Sean's head told him to let sleeping dogs lie.

"I made your phone call," Jack said, standing up

straight again. He turned and faced Sean, who sat up a little straighter on the sofa.

"And?"

"And...the people at Axis said they'd never heard of you. They claimed they'd never heard the name Sean Wyatt before. And that security clearance number you gave me didn't check out either. Did you give me a wrong number or something?"

Sean's heart rate jumped. Had he heard Jack correctly? No one at Axis knew his name? That couldn't be right.

"I'm sorry; you said they don't know me?"

"Yeah. They said they'd never heard of you."

"And you spoke to Emily Starks?"

Jack nodded and eased into his recliner near the fireplace. "Yep. Seemed like a nice gal. Kind of direct, to the point, but not rude. Claimed she had no idea who I was talking about."

Sean shimmied to the edge of the seat cushion. *This is worse than I thought. Axis has been compromised.*

"What about the other number? Did you call Tommy Schultz?"

"Yeah, but all I got was his voice mail. Left a message that he had a friend who needed to let him know he was okay. Thought it might be better if I didn't give specifics in case someone else was listening to the call."

Sean's eyes narrowed. "Why would you think that?"

Jack took a pocket knife out of his jeans and

picked up a piece of wood he'd left on the chair's arm. He whittled away at the wood for a second before answering.

"Son, I've seen a lot of crazy things in my life. I once had a man come into the ER with a kitchen knife sticking out of his forehead. Darned thing split right down the middle of his brain. He was fully conscious, too. One of the strangest things I've ever seen. We ended up getting the knife out. He survived and went on to live a normal life. I've seen it all. So when I see someone who has pissed in a hornet's nest, I know it."

Sean ignored the metaphor, although he thought it a good one. His host was insinuating something Sean hadn't considered. Were he at both full strength and 100 percent mental faculties, he likely would have thought of it as well.

The men he fought in the clearing, the ones who were going to execute him, obviously worked for the government. That meant they'd be watching all Sean's friends, monitoring any contacts that were made. No doubt, if they were watching Tommy's phones and email, they would have noted a call coming in from the remote region of New York— the same region where Sean had been abducted.

His mind raced. If the government was watching Tommy's communications, his friend could be in danger. He had to get to Atlanta, and fast.

He stood up and wavered for a second, dizzy from the sudden movement. "Where are my clothes?" he asked.

"Over there, on the table. I went ahead and washed them for you. Although your shirt and coat are ruined. I took the liberty of getting you a new jacket, and you can have one of my T-shirts."

Sean stalked over to the kitchen table and picked up his pants.

Jack acted like he wasn't paying any attention to his guest, but he could see Sean out of the corner of his eye.

"What's got you in a tizzy?" Jack asked.

"I...I have to get back to Atlanta. My friends could be in danger. If what you're telling me is true, the men that came after me might go for them next."

"Of course what I'm telling you is true." Jack turned to face Sean. "Look, Son, I know you want to get back home and help out your friends, but whoever wants you dead is a real power player. Who was it that you said sent you here in the first place?"

Sean swallowed back the lump that rose in his throat. "The president."

"Right. And do you trust him?"

"He and I have been friends for a long time, Jack. John Dawkins may be a politician, but I trust him."

"Fine. You trust your president. That doesn't change the fact that you need to lay low for a while and recover. It will be a while before you will be back to normal physical condition, whatever that is for you."

More thoughts flooded Sean's brain as he slipped out of the pajamas and back into his jeans.

If Emily had disavowed knowledge of Sean's existence, that could mean whoever was behind all this had gotten to her.

He shook off the notion. He and Emily went back a long time. They'd worked together as partners when he first joined Axis. She'd begged him to stay on when she got promoted to director. If there was anyone Sean could trust in the government, it was Emily Starks.

If she was acting oddly, that could mean only one thing.

"Jack, do you have any money sitting around that I could borrow? I'll only need enough to get me back to Atlanta."

Jack nodded. "Sure. There's a cigar box on the counter. That's where I keep my cash. Should be a few hundred dollars in there. Take whatever you need."

"Are you sure? I don't want to put you out."

"Son, you strike me as a man who is going to do what he wants to do. There's nothing I can do to stop it, so I may as well help expedite your journey. I just hope the final stop isn't a grave like the one I pulled you out of the other day."

Sean stepped over to the cigar box on the counter and pried it open. As Jack said, there were folded twenty-dollar bills stacked inside. He took a hundred and closed the lid. "This should get me back," he said. "I'll return the money to you when I get all this worked out."

"It's no big deal. I have plenty of money. Just do what you have to do. A fella like you shouldn't have any problem getting a new debit card and cash from your bank."

"Yeah, that's just what I'm worried about," Sean said in a distant tone. "I think I've been burned."

5. Atlanta, Georgia

Tommy stared at the check for a moment and then looked up at the waiter.

"I'm sorry, sir," the waiter said. "This card was declined, too. Do you have another one you'd like to try?"

"No...I...those are the only ones I have."

June looked across the table at him with sympathetic eyes. "It's okay," she said, fishing a gold credit card out of her black leather clutch. "I got this one." She handed the waiter the card and the check. "Run it on this one."

Tommy ran his fingers through his hair. "I am so sorry. There must be some kind of mistake."

"Sweetie, it's okay," she said. "I don't mind paying. I have money, too, you know."

"I know, but it's embarrassing."

"It's fine. Like you said, the bank must have just made a mistake."

Three banks, he thought. It wasn't the first time something like that had happened with one of his cards. It *was* the first time, however, it had happened with multiple cards. That fact set off an alarm in his head.

"I appreciate you picking up the tab," he said, pushing the growing panic to the back of his mind. "I can pay you back."

"Honey, really, it's okay. You know I make decent money, right?"

Tommy knew.

June was a research scientist in Germany. During her time in the field, she'd worked for a pharmaceutical company for several years before switching employment to the university. They didn't pay as well as the previous job, but she'd made enough in pharmaceuticals to support her lifestyle for a long time. Plus, the university job paid pretty well, too.

"Thank you," he said.

"It's fine. Seriously, don't worry about it." She glanced at her watch, and her eyes widened. "Shoot, I have to go. Early flight back tomorrow. Need to get some rest."

Tommy sighed. He was glad to have been able to spend the last two weeks with her. He'd never met anyone quite like June. She was smart, successful, respected by her peers, and she was beautiful. On top of all that, she was secretly tough, trained in self-defense and able to hold her own in a fight.

She was the perfect woman for Tommy, which only served to ravage his anxiety with the constant barrage of *Don't screw it up; don't screw it up* on repeat in his mind.

He'd hired a personal trainer to help him get in better shape in spite of June telling him she loved him just the way he was. The results had been astounding and helped his self-confidence. He was stronger and fitter than ever before. Still, decades of insecurity caused him to worry about losing the woman of his dreams.

He pushed those thoughts aside and smiled at her. He reached across the table and took her soft hand in his. "I wish you didn't have to go. These last few weeks have been so good."

She returned the smile and tilted her head to the side. A strand of blonde hair broke loose from the tight ponytail and hung down by her ear. "I know. I wish I didn't have to leave, too. But we'll see each other again next month. You're still planning on coming over, right?"

His head rocked up and down. "Yeah. Already got my ticket."

"See? It won't be that bad. Time will fly by, and before you know it we'll be sitting on the Italian coast sipping espresso and eating pizza."

"That sounds amazing. Just the two of us, relaxing at a cafe overlooking the Mediterranean...that might be as close to heaven as I can get in this life."

The two stared at each other for another long moment before they got up and left the table. Outside, a winter rain shower had come through downtown, soaking the streets and sidewalks. By the time Tommy and June were outside, the rain was gone and a cold wind was blowing through the city.

"Rain followed by freezing wind," Tommy said. "Welcome to winter in the South."

"Yeah," she said, looking around at the

downtown buildings. "It's a shame there's no snow. I bet the city is beautiful under a blanket of white powder."

"When we get it, it's rarely powder. More like slush. Although, we do get a good snow every now and then."

The two walked down the sidewalk and made a right. They went two more blocks until they arrived at June's hotel. At the door, they stopped and faced each other again.

"So..." Tommy said.

"So..." June echoed.

"I guess this is goodbye for now."

"I guess so."

He wanted to walk her to her room, to ask to stay the night, but he didn't. Tommy had remained a gentleman during their relationship. He wasn't going to change course now.

"Call me when you get back to Germany, okay?" he said.

"Of course."

He leaned closer and wrapped his hand around her lower back, embracing her tight as their lips locked.

"Be careful."

Her face scrunched into a smile. "Careful? You're the one who runs all around the world getting shot at. I just sit in a lab."

He bit his lower lip. "Point taken."

"I'll see you in a few weeks," she said and walked through the automatic sliding glass doors.

He watched until she disappeared around the corner inside before turning to walk away. His car was just across the street, and he looked both ways to make sure there was no traffic before trotting over to his parking space.

June had spent the last few weeks in a guest room at Tommy's place in the Virginia Highlands area of Atlanta, but with her early flight the next day, she'd wanted to stay in a hotel on her last night so she could be a little closer to the airport.

He looked back at the hotel as he opened his car door, lingering for a moment to savor the feel of her lips, the smell of her perfume.

The sound of footsteps from nearby brought him back to the moment. He turned and saw a man walking alone in a black trench coat, typing something on his phone as he made his way down the sidewalk. He seemed oblivious to Tommy's presence.

Tommy swung his car door open farther and was about to get in when a voice stopped him.

"Mr. Schultz?"

Tommy spun around and saw a man in a dark green tactical jacket with black cargo pants.

"Yes. And you are?"

The man held up his wallet, displaying his government identification to Tommy.

"Kyle Sherman. I work for the federal government. We'd like to ask you some questions about your friend, Sean Wyatt."

Tommy's eyebrows cinched as he frowned.

"Sean? What about him?"

Tommy sensed another man approaching from behind him and another one from his left. He was being hemmed in.

"Am I under arrest or something?"

"No," the man said, pushing out his bottom lip for a second. "We'd just like to ask you a few questions. That's all. You are free to go whenever you like."

Tommy's pulse quickened. He glanced to his left at a guy who'd stopped next to his car. He didn't have to turn around to know the other person had positioned himself a few feet behind him.

"What's this about?"

Kyle put his wallet back into one of his pockets and crossed his arms. "Mr. Schultz, we have reason to believe that your friend is engaging in treason. We think he might be working with the Russians on something big. We were hoping you could help us put together a better profile on him so we know what we're dealing with."

Tommy chuckled. "The Russians? I thought the Cold War ended a long time ago."

"As I'm sure you're aware, tensions have been growing between them and us lately. Now it seems that your friend is working with them."

"Sean? Russians? No way. Seriously, zero chance that's what's going on."

Kyle reached into his jacket and pulled out a photo. He held it out so Tommy could see it.

"This is Wyatt at a rendezvous point with his

Russian contact. They met last week at a coffee shop in Portland, Maine. We also have text records and phone calls to and from a number connected to Moscow. We need to know what he's working on and any relevant information you can give us."

Tommy stared at the photo. It was definitely Sean in the picture, but it was difficult to tell who was sitting across the table from him. Or even if the other person in the picture had actually been there. Photoshop made things far too easy to manipulate.

"Look, Kyle, is it? I appreciate what you're trying to do, but Sean isn't working with the Russians. I can tell you that with 100 percent certainty. Last I heard from him, he was working on a special project for the president. I don't know what it is, exactly. From what he told me, he doesn't know what it is either. Why don't you reach out to him? I can give you his number if you like."

Kyle fired a sidelong glance at his man on the sidewalk. The guy shifted a little, exposing the weapon bulging out of his jacket.

"We've tried. He's not answering."

Tommy sensed the man moving closer behind him. Something about this interrogation was off, and it was getting worse by the moment. Either these guys weren't who they said they were, or they were up to no good.

"Well, maybe he's just busy. Or maybe he doesn't answer calls from numbers he doesn't recognize. I know I don't. If I get a call from a number I don't know, I let it go to voice mail."

"You know," Kyle said ignoring Tommy's explanation, "your friendship with Sean goes way back. Doesn't it?"

Tommy shrugged. "Sure. I've known him most of my life."

"It would be a shame if we found out you were covering for him."

"Whoa. Covering for him? Covering what, exactly?"

"That's what we intend to find out."

Tommy heard a footstep close behind him. He was still holding his car door open. He had less than two seconds to make a decision. These guys were going to try to take him. He didn't know why, but he knew enough to know that wherever they were going wasn't going to be good, at least not for him.

"Maybe you should come with us. We'll get out of the cold and into someplace warm where we can talk more about it," Kyle said.

Tommy clutched the edge of the door and eased it forward a few inches. "Yeah, sure. Whatever I can do to help."

He felt the man less than a foot away behind him. Suddenly, Tommy jerked the door back. It slammed into the approaching man's knee with a loud thud. The guy instinctively bent down to grab the throbbing joint. As he did, his nose met Tommy's knee on the way up. Tommy drove his leg hard, pounding the man's face with his kneecap.

The blow knocked the guy onto his back on the wet street, blood instantly pouring from his face.

Kyle stepped toward Tommy, but Tommy anticipated the move. He stepped to the side, into the open street where he could maneuver better.

"You shouldn't have done that," Kyle said, reaching into his jacket.

Tommy lunged at the man before he could draw his weapon and plowed his shoulder into Kyle's midsection. Caught off guard, Kyle was helpless to keep the stronger man off. Tommy's legs pumped hard as he drove the agent into the side of his car, jarring his hand from the jacket. A gun fell out of the bottom of the coat and clacked on the ground.

The sudden impact with the car threw Kyle off for a second, but he immediately recovered and swung his elbow into Tommy's jaw.

Tommy staggered back a step. Kyle used the moment to go on the attack. He charged, firing punch after punch at Tommy's face.

For most of his life, Tommy had been a brawler, getting through fights with brute strength and size. Now he was leaner, faster, and stronger than before. And he'd been learning a few things on the side.

His hands moved fast, blocking one punch, then another, and another, repeating the moves he'd learned from his trainer.

Kyle tried a close-quarters kick, but Tommy twisted to the side and blocked it easily with his leg.

Frustrated, Kyle lunged a little too far with his
right hand. Tommy snatched the man's wrist and
yanked him forward. He raised his knee and
plunged it into Kyle's abdomen. As the agent
doubled over, Tommy chopped down with his
elbow, driving it into Kyle's lower back with such
force it dropped the man to his knees.

The guy on the other side of the car drew his
weapon, but Tommy was a step ahead. He grabbed
Kyle by the collar and lifted him up, holding him
between the gunman and himself.

"Drop the weapon," Tommy said.

The other agent had an intense look in his eyes.
A mixture of fear and anger—a bad combination
for someone holding a gun.

"You don't want to kill your boss, do you? So
drop the weapon, and nobody gets hurt. You can go
back to wherever it is you're from, and no one will
be the wiser."

The guy shook his head. "Doesn't work that
way."

Not what Tommy wanted to hear. He recognized
a sense of finality in the man's voice. Also not what
he wanted to hear. He instantly realized that—for
these guys—failure was not an option. Their job
was to bring in the mark, no matter the cost.

"Then I guess we have ourselves a stalemate,
huh?"

The man said nothing as he continued to stare
down his opponent, waiting for a slipup—a tiny
mistake that would give him the clear shot.

Tommy was careful to keep any part of his head and body out of the gunman's sights. Highly trained operatives could be deadly from short range, even with a narrow target margin.

"Seriously, man. Put the gun down. We're both Americans. We're on the same team here. We keep standing here like this for too long, a cop or someone is going to drive by and see this whole standoff."

On cue, a red luxury sedan approached just down the block. It was followed by a line of other vehicles.

"See?" Tommy said, motioning to the oncoming traffic without revealing too much of his head. "If you think all of them are going to ignore this little scene, you underestimate the meddling public. One of them will call the cops. Then what will you do?"

"Let them. We own the police. Just like we own you."

The gunman suddenly dropped out of sight as if yanked down by a ghost. Tommy craned his neck to get a better look, still wary that the gunman could be trying to sneak around the car to get a better angle.

"Hello?" he said. "Threatening gunman? You still there?"

"Sorry," a familiar voice said from the other side of the car. "He's going to be out of commission for a while."

Tommy subconsciously let go of the man in his arms, letting him drop awkwardly to the ground.

"Sean?"

"Yeah, it's me." Sean popped up from behind the car. He looked down the street in both directions as the cars began passing by in the two lanes. "What do you say we get out of here? Having a couple of bodies lying around is bound to get some attention."

"Good idea." Tommy started to get in his car when he had an epiphany. "Wait. We can't just leave June here at the hotel. If these guys can track me here, they can find her, too."

Sean bit his lower lip and nodded. "You're right. Hurry. I'll take care of these bozos."

Tommy's head twitched to the side, curious as to how his friend was going to handle the matter of three unconscious, full-grown men on the asphalt. He decided not to ask and waited for the last of the cars to drive by before sprinting across the street and into the hotel.

Sean worked fast. The guy he'd taken out was mostly out of view from the street, resting quietly on the sidewalk behind the right side of the car. The other two...were significantly more conspicuous. He ran around the car's back end and grabbed the guy Tommy'd been holding. With another look down both streets, Sean took the guy by the ankles and dragged him up and over the curb. He left the body next to the other one and rushed back to get the third.

The man was starting to roll his head around, eyes cracking open as he regained consciousness.

"Shh," Sean said. "Go back to sleep."

He lifted the man's head and dropped it to the pavement with a sickening thud. The guy instantly stopped moving again.

Sean stole another look around before hooking the guy under the armpits and dragging him around the front of the car. This time, he kept moving, tugging the body into a dark alley. When he reached a couple of garbage cans, Sean let go of the man and let him slump into a heap out of view from the street.

He took a couple of deep breaths as he hurried back to the sidewalk to grab the next guy. His legs burned as he pulled another agent into the hiding place, the man's weight starting to strain Sean's muscles.

"Two down," he said, wiping his forehead. Despite the frigid winter temperatures, hauling so much weight had the tendency to get one's heart rate going.

Sean trotted back out to the street and saw more cars approaching from both directions. Fortunately, the last hit man was hidden behind Tommy's car, but not from the pedestrians walking down the sidewalk. It was a young couple, laughing and strolling hand in hand, probably enjoying the end of a lovely date. Any second now, their laughter would turn to screaming and chaos the moment they noticed the body on the concrete.

Sean had to think fast. Remembering something he'd had to do in college for more than a few friends, he scooped up the last guy in his arms and wrapped one arm underneath the opposite armpit, holding the guy up like he'd sprained his ankle. As casually as possible, Sean took a step back and leaned against the car, pretending to rest with what he hoped appeared to be a drunk friend.

The couple slowed down as they approached the two men. Their laughter dissipated, and they tried not to make eye contact as they passed.

Sean smiled awkwardly at them as they passed. "He had way too much to drink," he said. "Can't believe he was actually going to try to drive home."

The couple kept walking, only acknowledging Sean's statement with a few uncomfortable nods before they sped up and walked away.

He looked back over the top of the car at the entrance to the hotel. "Hurry up, Tommy," he said quietly.

6. Atlanta

By the time Tommy and June appeared on the sidewalk, Sean had already dragged the last of the hit squad into the alley and dumped him with the others.

"Took you long enough," Sean said as Tommy and June neared the car.

June was carrying her clutch while Tommy pulled a rolling suitcase behind him.

"I was crawling into bed," June explained. "My flight is pretty early tomorrow morning, you know."

"Nice to see you again, June," Sean said. "Sorry for the change of plans. Seems your boyfriend ran into a little trouble."

Tommy's eyes darted around. "Speaking of trouble, what did you do with them?"

Sean jerked a thumb toward the dark alley. "I dumped them in there."

"You...you just hid dead bodies in there?" June asked, more appalled than frightened.

"They're not dead," Sean said. "At least I don't think they are. Can we talk about this in the car? I'd rather not be around when they wake up. And we need to get you to a safer place."

"Good points," Tommy agreed. He turned to June. "Just get in. We'll figure it out on the way."

They stuffed June's sparse luggage into the back seat and sped away, hanging a right at the next intersection, squealing tires on the wet asphalt.

"You mind telling me what is going on?" Tommy said, steering the car down another side street.

"I wish I knew," Sean said. He noted the direction they were heading. "Go north."

"North?" Tommy asked.

"Yeah. Head to Helen and Mac's place. June can crash there for the night. They'll be able to take you to the airport in the morning," Sean said, turning his attention to June in the front passenger seat.

"Their place is like an hour from the airport?" Tommy said.

"Would you guys mind telling me what in the world is going on?" June interrupted. "I know it's probably something to do with international villains and ancient mysteries, but what have you two done this time?"

Tommy glanced in the rearview mirror at his friend in the back. "Sean?"

Sean sighed. "I'm not entirely sure yet. I was working on the Seward project. Then several days ago, a group of guys approached me in Auburn, New York. They put me in the back of their SUV and drove me out to the middle of nowhere."

"Jeez. Seriously?"

"Unfortunately, yeah. They were government. One of them is, or was, definitely CIA. I met him a long time ago. Name is Drew Porter. Cocky young buck. First impression I got from him was ego and ambition. Looks like I wasn't too far off. I guess someone with money and secrets took him under their wing. He wanted to know why I was looking around the Seward estate."

A momentary silence filled the car before June broke it. "Why would the CIA care about your research?"

Sean rolled his shoulders. "No idea. But if there's one thing I do know, it's that they come after you when you've found something you weren't supposed to."

"Why didn't you just tell them you were doing a project at the request of the president? That should have gotten their attention."

Sean snorted. "You know, I thought the same thing. Turns out mentioning President Dawkins's involvement might have been a bad thing."

"Why do you say that?"

"They must not have known he was the one who made the request. As soon as I said so, they said something about eliminating him."

"What?" June gasped.

"Yeah. They said they're going to take out Dawkins. Which means we need to warn him."

"Warn him?" Tommy asked.

"Right. Only problem is, there's no way I can even get close to the president now. I've been burned."

"Burned?" June asked. "What do you mean?"

"It means that whoever is behind all this has wiped out my bank accounts, credit cards, everything. If I so much as set foot anywhere close to the president, I'll probably be arrested on sight."

"Are you sure?" Tommy asked, looking back in the mirror again.

"Yeah. I'm sure. And to make things worse, I can't get through to Emily either, which means they've infiltrated Axis, too. Whoever is pulling the strings behind all this is a major player."

The car went silent again as Tommy guided it onto the interstate heading north. Atlanta's skyline passed by outside. New high-rise condos and apartments lined the road across from Georgia Tech. The taller buildings in Midtown climbed into the darkness, casting a dull glow on the low cloud ceiling above.

"I wonder..." Tommy said, letting his voice trail off.

"Wonder what?"

"Earlier this evening I tried to pay for dinner, but my cards were declined. You don't think—"

"They burned both of us," Sean finished the thought.

A lump dropped from his throat into his stomach. He hadn't considered that possibility. Now he cursed himself for bringing Tommy and June into this mess, although it wasn't his fault. He had started the project thinking it was innocent enough. There was no way to know it would turn into something like this.

"Oh no," Tommy said.

"What?" Sean asked and then realized the issue

before his friend could respond. He saw the blue lights flashing behind them. "Were you speeding?"

Tommy shook his head. "Are you kidding? Downtown? No way. Those guys are always lurking down here. They have speed traps set up all the time."

"That's what I was afraid of."

"What should I do?"

"Just be cool. If he pulls us over, just relax."

"Easy for you to say."

The squad car sped toward them, closing the gap rapidly.

"He sure is in a hurry," June said, glancing in the right-side mirror.

Tommy eased off the accelerator and flipped the blinker on, merging into the far right lane. He prepared to pull off into the emergency lane as soon as the cop was right behind them.

Suddenly, the car with the flashing blue lights surged by them in the next lane over and zipped by. He kept going, chasing down a black Ferrari about a tenth of a mile ahead.

The luxury sports car slowed down and pulled off on the side of the road with the cop right behind him.

Sean, Tommy, and June breathed a collective sigh of relief as they passed the routine traffic stop and kept going. Once they rounded the curve where I-75 and I-85 split, the blue lights disappeared from view.

"That was close," Tommy said, his voice still

trembling.

"The sooner we get to Mac's, the better," Sean said.

"How do you know they haven't gotten to them, too?" June asked.

"I don't, but it's our only play right now. We need to get out of the city. Once we're at their place, we can figure out our next move."

"Which will be what, exactly?" Tommy said. "You said yourself, no way you or I can get close enough to the president."

"We won't have to. I've got someone else who can."

"Adriana?" Tommy asked.

"Yeah. She's on her way back from Madrid as we speak. I reached out to her father and asked him to relay the message. She's going to meet us at Mac's. Adriana is the only one that can reach Dawkins. He knows her and trusts her. If she tells him something is going on, he'll know what to do."

"What about us? What do we do? Lie low until he can clear up this mess?"

"No. If we hang around too long, eventually these guys will check all our connections. You need to get in touch with your parents. Make sure they're safe. Then we'll need to keep moving."

"Mom and Dad are in Aruba."

That was information Sean hadn't heard yet.

"Aruba? What are they doing there? I thought they were getting acquainted with IAA, you know, learning about what their son has been up to for the last twenty years or so?"

"They did all that. Said they needed some time to decompress, preferably in a warm place with beaches. So I sent them to Aruba."

Sean raised his eyebrows. "Okay then. Good. Check that off the list. That still doesn't take care of us, though. Those guys back there, the ones who came after me, they'll find us again. It's only a matter of time."

"I guess that only leaves one thing for us to do," Tommy said, reading Sean's mind.

"Yep. We have to figure out what these guys are hiding. The letter from Seward was pretty cryptic."

"The one Dawkins gave you? I don't understand."

"The very same. In the letter, Seward suggested to Lincoln that they buy Alaska, both to expand our borders and to secure the area around Denali. Dawkins felt like there must have been something important for Seward to want to make such a purchase during a time of economic struggle. Heck, buying Alaska must have been a big contributor to the recession that plagued Johnson's presidency."

"It was, though no one talks much about it."

"So, all this has to do with a letter to Abraham Lincoln?" June asked, cutting in again.

"Seems that way," Sean said.

"Well, there's more to the story," Tommy said as he swerved around a semi. "Those guys back there, the ones who were trying to arrest me or whatever they were doing, they said something about you working with the Russians."

"Russians?"

"That's what I said. Where you suppose they came up with that?"

Sean thought hard for a minute. The men who'd tried to kill him in New York were definitely not Russian, at least not that he knew. Porter was American, and while the other men in his outfit hadn't said much—if anything—Sean didn't get the impression they were from the former Soviet Union.

"Looks like we may have gotten ourselves in deeper than usual."

"We always get ourselves in deeper than usual."

"Sure seems that way, doesn't it? So, we get to Mac's, meet with Adriana, tell her to warn the president, and then what?"

Sean looked out the back window. He'd been doing it intermittently since they got in the vehicle. If they were being followed, he wanted to know it. So far, he didn't notice anything out of the ordinary.

"We have to get to the bottom of this letter. And I think I know where to start."

"Where's that?"

"I was hoping you could help with that," Sean said with a devilish grin. "I didn't mention it to the men who tried to kill me, and I haven't told anyone about it until now. While I was at the Seward estate, I found an odd note. Couldn't tell who it was for or who wrote it, though it may have been Seward himself. It said something about proceeding with Operation Iron Horse. Got any idea what that might be?"

The car cabin fell silent once more. Tommy kept his eyes on the road, navigating the late night Atlanta traffic as they neared Marietta. He narrowed his eyes, thinking about his friend's question.

"Operation Iron Horse?" he asked, making sure he'd heard correctly.

"That's what the note said. It was faded, almost unreadable. Probably because the thing is over a hundred years old."

"If it was from Seward, more than 120 years old."

"Right. So, any idea what that could mean?"

Tommy thought for another minute, searching the archives in his mind for anything that came close. He'd absorbed history since he was young, as had Sean. Between the two of them, they had several dozen textbooks worth of information about the past memorized. The note had vexed Sean, however, and he couldn't think of anything concerning the mysterious Operation Iron Horse.

"Wait a sec," Tommy blurted. "I think I've got it."

The other two occupants stared at him, waiting with breathless anticipation.

"What if—and this is just a theory—but what about Andrews' Raiders?"

The idea punched Sean right in the gut.

"You really think that might be a possibility?"

"Would be crazy, right? I mean, all these years to have that right under our noses."

June was doing her best to follow along, but Tommy and Sean had clearly ventured into an area where inside information was required to continue.

"What are you guys talking about? What's Andrews' Raiders?" she asked.

"You wanna field this one, or should I?" Tommy said.

"Be my guest," Sean said.

Tommy cast a sidelong glance at June out of the corner of his eye. "We grew up in Chattanooga. Just across the Tennessee/Georgia border in the little town of Ringgold, there's a monument next to an old country road. The monument commemorates what was called the Great Locomotive Chase. There was a movie made about it in the 1950s."

He could tell she was trying to piece things together, so he went on. "During the Civil War, a civilian named James Andrews took a unit of undercover Union agents deep into the South. Their objective was to steal a train in Atlanta and make their way north, burning bridges and sabotaging the railroad as they went. The unit ended up being called Andrews' Raiders."

Sean took over the tale. "History books tell us that the objective of the operation was purely to undermine Confederate efforts to resupply the lines in Chattanooga while Union forces pushed farther into the South. Chattanooga was a critical railroad center. It was effectively the gateway to the entire Southeast, and even to the western parts of the Confederacy. The North knew that if they could cut off supplies from Atlanta and the rest of the South, they could establish a stronghold in Chattanooga from which they could begin to slowly strangle the rebellion."

June reflected on the story. "Okay. So, you think maybe this Andrews' Raiders group has something to do with all this trouble?"

"Maybe," Tommy said. "Andrews and his men ran out of fuel just outside Ringgold. All the time it took for them to stop, burn bridges, and sabotage rails cost them. Eventually, their pursuers caught up. They would have been caught sooner, but Andrews and his men cut telegraph lines from Atlanta so there was no way to get word north to cut them off. When their train slowed to a halt, they had no choice but to make a run for it. Some of them made it into the forests around White Oak Mountain. Others split up and tried to get through the valley. Almost all of them were caught. Some were tried and hanged, including Andrews. Knowing their companions' fate, many of the captured men escaped and made their way back to Northern lines. Nearly all of the soldiers were awarded the Medal of Honor. Andrews wasn't because he was a civilian. Several of them were buried in the Chattanooga National Cemetery.

There's a monument by the graves commemorating their mission."

"What Tommy is saying, June, is that we don't know if it has anything to do with what's going on with us or not, but right now it's the only lead we have."

"It's possible," Tommy said, "that the sabotage story was a cover-up to the real purpose. Seems like an awfully desperate move from a military that was already winning the war. The South was on the run. The North was closing in, and it would only be a matter of time until the war ended."

"Unless they found something that could turn the tide," Sean said.

"Right. Like a massive fortune. The Confederacy was strapped for cash, and they didn't have the manufacturing the Union had. There was no way they could keep their men supplied with weapons and ammo at the same rate as the North. But if they had money, they could buy supplies from an old enemy of the United States."

"The British?" June said.

Tommy nodded. "Possibly. There were others, too. But the British certainly had a vested interest in the war's outcome."

"Or maybe they found something more powerful than money," Sean said in an absent tone.

The two in the front looked back at him.

"Like what?" Tommy asked.

Sean looked out the window again, keeping his eyes on the lanes behind them. "I don't know, but maybe we need to make a little trip back home."

7. Atlanta

Yuri rubbed his eyes. He hadn't slept in almost twenty-four hours. His eyelids felt like ten-pound weights were hooked to them as he struggled to stay awake on the road. He couldn't stop to sleep, though.

His mark hadn't. So he wouldn't either.

He'd been following Sean Wyatt around New England, and now all the way into the Southeastern United States. The American's ability to go without rest was impressive. Yuri knew why, of course.

Over the last month, he'd studied Wyatt, learned everything about the man...or what he could learn, at least.

Wyatt wasn't exactly secretive for someone who'd once-upon-a-time been an exemplary special agent. With that kind of experience, Yuri imagined, sooner or later someone would come looking for payback. Although, according to Wyatt's dossier, the way he operated didn't leave many opponents alive, which might be why the American was so comfortable being in the open.

Yuri started dozing off again and almost veered into the oncoming lane. He smacked his cheek for what must have been the fifth time in the last twenty minutes. The fresh sting on his skin snapped him back to reality.

His assignment had been simple enough, or so it seemed on the surface. He was to follow Wyatt until he found something.

Simple and also vague.

Yuri asked his superior what Wyatt was looking for or what was meant by the term "found something."

"What will he find?" Yuri said.

"We...don't know. Just stay with him. This mission is of the highest importance."

They didn't know what Wyatt would find? That fact had struck Yuri as beyond strange. As a good soldier, though, he wouldn't question orders.

He'd always done what he was told. Being raised in a strict home had yielded that mindset.

Yuri's parents were hard-working middle class people. His father worked in a steel factory, his mother as a custodian in a hospital. He'd yearned for something more as a child, wishing to travel the world and see magnificent sights.

His father, however, spent more money on vodka than taking family vacations. As Yuri went through school, he soon realized that if he were going to ever get a chance to leave home, it would be in the service of Mother Russia.

He'd been in the military since he was of age. Four years in, his superiors recommended him to a special branch of their Spetsnaz (special forces). It didn't take long before Yuri's commanding officers saw his potential. They contacted the main intelligence directorate—GRU—and requested he be trained as a spy.

Most of Yuri's work had taken place in Chechnya, Ukraine, and Georgia, but he'd been to more countries than he could remember.

Sure, he had to kill people now and then, but he was living his dream of seeing the world. It wasn't a typical life, that much he knew. Yuri also didn't care.

He watched the line of cars in front of him, making sure the one carrying Wyatt didn't leave his field of view. He couldn't see the American's car, but he knew it was there. One of the things he'd learned early on was how to trail a mark without being detected. An expert like Wyatt would most likely be on the lookout for trouble. Yuri knew he would be if the roles were reversed. So far, he'd managed to follow Wyatt from New England to Atlanta without being noticed. He couldn't screw up now.

His mind drifted to the events in upstate New York. He'd watched as a group of men abducted Wyatt. Following those men had been much more of a challenge, requiring mere guessing on several occasions as to the direction their SUV had gone. Yuri was lucky, and had managed to keep up with the mysterious men until they pulled off onto a side road, far out in the country.

Hiding his car a half kilometer away, he trudged back to the side road on foot before ducking into the forest and making his way to the meadow.

From the safety of the trees, he watched as the men—Americans from what he could tell—threatened to execute Wyatt. They had a grave dug for him before they arrived, fully intent on disposing of the man permanently.

Yuri wasn't sure what to do. Should he protect Wyatt and take out the men but risk exposing himself? If he did, Wyatt would know someone was following him. If he didn't save the American, the odd trail Yuri had been on would come to an abrupt end.

Fortunately, he hadn't been forced to make that call.

Wyatt had managed to free himself of his captors, killing a few of them in the process. A stranger also appeared with a hunting rifle and scared Wyatt's captors enough that they fled the scene. Two bullets in Wyatt's chest, no communications, and being stuck out in the middle of nowhere were a recipe for certain death.

At least it would have been had the stranger not shown up and pulled Wyatt out of the grave.

Yuri watched as the older man hauled Wyatt back to a cabin in the woods. There, over the course of days, the stranger nursed Wyatt to health.

Not knowing how long he'd have to sit and wait near the cabin, Yuri found a town not far from there and bought some supplies. He lined his crossover with blankets at night to keep the interior as warm as possible. Sleeping in the cold had been something he learned as a child when there wasn't always enough heat in their rickety Moscow apartment building.

During his first night near the cabin, he set up a laser tripwire on the driveway in case anyone left. For several days and nights, the only person who went anywhere was the old man. At one point—when the cabin's owner drove into town—Yuri risked venturing to the cabin and taking a quick look inside to make sure Wyatt was still there. It would have been Yuri's luck for the American to make a sneaky escape in the back of the old guy's truck.

Wyatt, though, was still there, recovering from his wounds.

When the American did finally leave, Yuri followed, all the way to Atlanta.

After several days of sleeping in his car, his exhaustion was near the point of driving him insane.

He kept his wits, though, and continued his pursuit of Wyatt. Yuri had a mission to complete.

"Where are you going now?" he said quietly. He found talking to himself helped keep him awake better than just thinking.

A few dozen miles north of Kennesaw, Yuri saw the sedan suddenly move over to the right lane. He checked the green sign noting the name and number of the exit. From the looks of it, his mark was heading to Cartersville.

"Cartersville? What is it you're looking for here?"

he said.

His phone rang in the passenger seat. He glanced at the number, picked up the device, and answered it.

He answered the phone with a simple "yes" in Russian.

"What's your status?" the man's voice said through the earpiece.

"Still observing."

"Anything yet?"

"Nothing worth reporting," Yuri said. His superior didn't bug him often, but it was enough to be irritating. If there had been something he needed to relay to the boss, he would have already done it. He decided to risk a proposition.

"You know, sir, it could be that there is nothing to find. I've been over here for several weeks, and there have been no developments. Is it possible we have made a mistake?"

"No. There is no mistake. Just stay on it."

"Perpetually?" It was a legitimate question. Yuri didn't mind doing his duty, but at some point, his superiors needed to call a wild goose chase what it was.

"We will give it forty-eight more hours, Agent Stolov. If the American doesn't find anything by then, abort the mission."

"Yes, sir." He paused for a moment before speaking again. "I almost forgot; there is one thing you need to be aware of."

"I'm listening."

"When we were in New York, Wyatt was abducted by a group of armed men. They looked like Americans."

"Abducted?" The voice sounded angry. "Why didn't you tell me this to begin with?"

Yuri sighed. It was the reaction he'd expected. "I apologize, sir. I've been without sleep for over a day. Also, Wyatt got away. He managed to escape, killing a few of his captors in the process. My question for you is, who are those men, and what do they want with Wyatt?"

A long silence seeped into the phone. Had Yuri not heard the other man breathing on the other end, he would have wondered if they'd lost the connection.

"We'll have to get back to you on that. Were you spotted?"

"No, sir."

"Are you certain? At any point in time did these men or Wyatt see you?"

"I'm certain. I've not been seen or heard. If I was, I wouldn't be speaking to you right now."

The man seemed to accept the answer. "See to it things stay that way. If Wyatt doesn't find anything in the next two days, return home."

"Yes, sir."

The call ended, and Yuri placed the device back in the passenger seat. He shook his head, half to keep awake and half out of irritation.

Why were the higher-ups so interested in this Wyatt guy? They'd been incredibly sparse with the details.

Yuri understood it wasn't his place to question authority. He was also glad he only had to stay on this mission for two more days. His thought was if Wyatt was going to find something, he'd have already found it.

"Two more days, Yuri. You can do anything for two days."

8. Fairfax, Virginia

Drew Porter sat in his SUV, flipping through the news feed on his phone. Tensions were growing between the United States and the Russian Federation. The Russian president, a man named Nikolai Zhirkov, had invaded land on the Black Sea that once belonged to Ukraine. Like getting beat up by a bully in the school yard, there wasn't much the Ukrainians could do to stop the attack.

Some retreated farther into their country. Others stayed put, accepting the way things were with their new overlords.

Porter didn't buy into the stories the media wove for the public. He knew better. He should. After all, he was on the inside making the real news happen, pulling strings from behind shadowy curtains.

He raised his wrist and glanced at the time. The man he was meeting would be arriving any minute. Porter had chosen the place, an old cemetery outside of Washington, just across the border in Virginia. He'd have preferred to meet at night rather than the morning, but as long as he got paid, Porter didn't care.

"I'm glad you didn't keep me waiting," a voice said through the open passenger side window.

Porter wasn't startled. He noticed the older man approaching in the side mirror a second before he spoke.

"I don't like being late," Porter said. "It doesn't reflect well on one's character."

"I agree," the other man said, keeping his face pointing forward.

He was wearing sunglasses and a black trench coat. His ears were pink from the biting winter air. Breaths came out in big clouds before dissipating.

"What happened in New York?" the man asked, never facing Porter directly.

"Wyatt didn't have anything, so we took him out. Just as ordered."

Trench Coat nodded. "Yes, I read the report. But that isn't the whole story, is it?"

Porter clenched his teeth. He hated bureaucrats. They drove him nuts with all their questions. He doubted this particular one had ever spent any time in the field. He knew the man had never served in the military, so that was one strike against his credibility right off the bat.

"Are you referring to the men I lost during the mission?"

"No," the older man shook his head. "In case I need to remind you, I said I read the report."

"Yes, you did say that, sir. So, what else do you want to know?"

The man drew in a long breath and released it through tight lips. The air almost made a whistling sound as it passed through the little hole. "Oh, I don't know. How about the fact that the man you were supposed to kill, and reported as dead, is actually still alive?" He turned to face Porter for the first time.

Though the man's eyes were hidden behind his sunglasses, Porter knew they were narrowed with irritation. What he didn't know was what the guy was talking about.

"Alive? That's impossible. You must have gotten some bad information, sir."

Porter hadn't confirmed Wyatt was dead. In the sudden chaos to get away, there wasn't time. He knew Wyatt took two to the chest. It was highly unlikely he could have survived.

"You know," Trench Coat said, "I thought you might say something like that, which is why I brought you this."

He tossed a black-and-white photo into the passenger seat, close enough for Porter to clearly see the image. He tilted his head to make sure he was seeing correctly before returning his gaze to the older guy.

"Where did you get this?" Porter asked.

"Atlanta. Traffic camera. It was taken last night—in case you were going to ask when, too."

"Last night?"

"That is correct. You mind telling me how in the world Sean Wyatt was shot twice in the chest and managed to show up in Atlanta, healthy as can be, almost a week later? He wasn't wearing a vest, was he?"

Porter shook his head. "No. He definitely was not." He stared in disbelief at the photo.

"So, what are you going to do about it?"

"I'll take care of it," Porter said, trying not to show his frustration. He hated being wrong about something. This was a bad time for him to be wrong. The people he was working for didn't accept failure.

"Oh?" Trench Coat raised both eyebrows. "You'll take care of it, huh? Because you've done such a bang-up job of that so far? Sorry, but I'm going to need a little better than 'I'll take care of it.' Come on, Porter. You don't even know where he is."

"You just said he's in Atlanta."

"So? He could be anywhere by now. What if he left the country? Then what are you going to do?"

Porter sighed. His employer had a tendency to panic, overreact, and just be plain impatient. It was understandable. He had a lot riding on this mission. If Wyatt was able to find anything on the Denali Project, there would be big trouble.

"He didn't leave the country, sir. We took precautions."

"Precautions? What kind of precautions?"

"Wyatt is on a national watch list. If he so much as tries to take a leak across the river in Canada or look at a churro in Mexico, we'll know, and we'll grab him. Every airport will be on the lookout for him, too. All of his credit cards, his bank accounts, even his mortgages have been frozen. So, sir, he couldn't have gone far. Odds are he's still in the Atlanta area. I'll have my team check all his contacts in and around the city. More than likely, he is lying low at a friend's or colleague's place. That's what I mean by I'll take care of it."

"You burned Wyatt?" Trench Coat asked, sounding mildly impressed.

"This is why you pay me, sir. I get things done. So, if Wyatt did survive and he is in Atlanta, he won't be around for long. I can promise you that."

Trench Coat turned his head, facing toward the street beyond the cemetery fence. "I hope I don't need to remind you the price of failure, Porter. I realize you're a tough guy with lots of resources and know-how. But if you screw this up—"

"Yes, sir. I understand. Don't worry. I said I'll take care of it, and that's exactly what I intend to do."

Trench Coat seemed to accept the response and gave a curt nod. "Good. See to it you do."

He turned and started walking back down the winding sidewalk.

Porter watched him disappear around the bend on the path before he rolled up the window and looked ahead.

One more reason to hate bureaucrats, he thought.

They thought they knew everything.

He flushed his anger deep down inside and thought about the problem at hand. His team had been decimated in New York. He still had two men he knew he could count on. Luckily, they were in Washington awaiting further instructions. So, they would be easy enough to pick up.

Porter would also need someone he could trust in Atlanta. And he'd need it immediately. Getting to Atlanta would take time. Time wasn't something he had in spades at the moment.

Fortunately, he knew a guy. Porter just hoped he was available.

Like the man in the trench coat said, he and the men he worked with didn't take failure lightly. It wasn't an option, and Porter knew it. He'd seen what those men were capable of. It made what he'd done to Sean Wyatt look like child's play.

Porter hadn't mentioned his plan for the president to the guy in the trench coat. He thought it better that way. The less his employer knew, the better. He'd be thanked later on, of course, once the president was out of the way. The vice president would be a puppet, easy to manipulate.

He pulled up his phone contacts and found the first name he needed. It was time to put the presidential plan into action. As soon as he issued the order to take down Dawkins, Porter would take care of the situation in Atlanta.

Sean Wyatt might be alive, but not for long. And soon, he'd have every person in the country with a badge looking for him.

9. Cartersville, Georgia

Sean didn't sleep much during the night. When he finally drifted off after an hour of tossing and turning, it was into a fragile, troubled sleep.

He, Tommy, and June arrived at Joe and Helen McElroy's place late into the night. Sean lost his phone in New York and had been forced to pick up a burner phone. At his request, Tommy and June both shut off their devices and removed the batteries—further insurance against being tracked.

He knew the hour was late, but Sean also knew that Joe and Helen wouldn't mind them showing up at a moment's notice. They'd been friends for a long time, and eventually Tommy ended up hiring them to work for the IAA. That fact turned out to be a problem when the three arrived at the McElroy cabin in the woods just outside Cartersville.

Joe and Helen were gone on a trip, taking a little vacation time to tour around the county and do some camping with their dog.

Luckily, Sean and Tommy both knew where the spare key was and helped themselves into the home. The alarm started beeping, but as soon as everyone was inside, Sean reset the alarm.

They were all too tired to discuss things further and went to bed.

Sean woke early, after scraping together a tight five hours of rest. The sun still hadn't come up over the mountains to the east. There wasn't even the residual rim of light yet.

The utter exhaustion had been no match for his overactive brain. Hundreds of ideas and hypotheses about James Andrews and his Raiders blitzed his mind. Some were wild, fanciful notions that had absolutely no plausibility. A few, however, were certainly worth checking into.

He looked out the window from his seat at the computer desk, staring into the darkness for several minutes until the caffeine from his coffee kicked in. His fingers wrapped around the computer mouse, and he moved it around on the desk, bringing the monitor to life. The most promising theory revolved around an old story he'd heard from his dad when he was a child. He'd heard it several other times throughout his life, due to the fact that his father told and retold tales without knowing who'd heard them and who hadn't.

According to the story, during the Confederate retreat from Chattanooga, the army had to take the Old Federal Road and pass through a gap between White Oak Mountain and Taylor's Ridge, where Interstate 75 South cut through in the present day.

The legend went on to say that some of the men in the retreating army had loot they'd taken earlier in the war. Knowing that time was of the essence and they'd need to move fast, some of the soldiers broke ranks and made their way up the side of Boy's Mountain, two miles to the southeast. A Confederate hospital wasn't far away, located by Cherokee Springs. Knowing the group would rendezvous at the hospital before heading south toward Atlanta, they ran up Boy's Mountain to a cave.

During their occupation of the area, Confederate forces had built trenches on the side of the mountain from which they could fire upon the enemy from a high vantage point. The cave was just below the trenches, having been seen by almost everyone who was assigned to that area, so hiding anything in there before then wouldn't have made much sense.

The story suggested that these men hid gold, money, and other valuables inside the cave. Another detail that made the tale less credible was that it suggested the fleeing men stuffed their treasures inside the barrel of a cannon.

The legend certainly had some blurry spots to the tale. Things got twisted, added, and lost through the passage of time.

There had been other stories about hidden Confederate gold somewhere along the Old Federal Road. They seemed far less credible than the one about the fleeing soldiers, however, and it wasn't the treasure in a cannon that had Sean's interest. It was a story about the men from Andrews' Raiders.

Sean heard the story from his grandfather, which told him early on in life exactly where his dad got the habit of spinning long yarns.

According to Sean's grandfather—and history—the Raiders ditched the locomotive in the valley near White Oak Mountain. The few men who ran toward Chattanooga ended up safely behind Union lines. Some ran toward the mountain, hoping they could get the high ground and have a defensive advantage or perhaps find better hiding places to wait out the pursuit.

Most of those men made the mistake of running straight into the Confederate forces on the other side of the ridge. One who evaded the pursuers for two days was eventually captured in the hills outside Ringgold. The story suggests he tried to make a deal with one of the soldiers and even told him he'd be handsomely rewarded if he'd been let go.

The Confederate guard refused the bribe. The prisoner was tried and hanged in Atlanta shortly after. Whatever secrets he may have been keeping died with him. Unless he'd left something somewhere in a place few people would look or think to look.

Sean had been down inside the cave on one occasion. Neither time did he think it was possible or practical to get a cannon in there.

He'd been in high school the last time he ventured down into the darkness of the cave. He didn't remember seeing anything unusual, but he also hadn't explored as deeply as he would have liked.

With the strange events of the last few months, Sean couldn't help but wonder if there was something in the cave, something that would help shed some light on the Seward mystery.

It was a long shot, and Sean knew it. Unfortunately, he and Tommy didn't have a ton of good leads, so they needed to give it a try. If they found nothing helpful in Ringgold, they'd keep digging until another lead presented itself. That's how it went in their line of work. Sometimes you hit a home run, and sometimes you swing and miss.

Sean moved the arrow on the computer screen and clicked on a link. The computer lagged for a second before zipping him to a web page with a black-and-white map at the top. A red line was drawn from Atlanta to an area just east of Ringgold. He took a sip of the coffee as June and Tommy entered the room, dragging their feet and rubbing their eyes.

"Good morning," he said. "Coffee's ready if you want some. There's milk and creamer in the fridge. I left the sugar on the counter."

"Thank you," the other two said in tandem.

Outside, the sun still hadn't peeked over the horizon, leaving the cabin bathed in darkness. The thick forests surrounding the place made it seem even darker.

"How long you been up?" Tommy asked from behind the kitchen counter as he fumbled through a collection of coffee mugs.

"A while," Sean said as he took a sip from his steaming cup.

"I figured."

"Did you sleep okay?" June asked.

"Okay enough for me," Sean answered. "I don't usually sleep much anyway. Too many thoughts running through my head to get any rest. Especially right now."

"Any of those thoughts useful to our current predicament?" Tommy asked. He finally chose a mug and started pouring.

"Maybe," he said, pointing at the screen. "We don't have a lot to go on in terms of Operation Iron Horse."

"Yeah, I was thinking about that. What's that?" Tommy motioned at the computer.

"A map of North Georgia. The line represents the starting and ending point of the Great Locomotive Chase."

"So, that's where we're headed, huh?"

"The first thing we need to do is get June out of here." He shifted his gaze to the blonde, who was taking a sip from her cup.

She swallowed and shook her head. "Hey, I'll be fine. I can handle myself."

"I know you can," Sean said. "But these guys are dangerous."

"As opposed to the ones we dealt with before? Pretty sure it doesn't get much more dangerous than that."

"That may be, but if we can avoid it by getting

you back home, I'd prefer that."

"He's right," Tommy agreed. "I'd feel much better knowing you were back across the pond. Whoever these people are, they probably don't know about you and me. I'd rather keep it that way for now."

She tilted her head forward, and her eyebrows pinched together. "Sounds like you're trying to get rid of me."

Tommy shook his head vigorously. "No, that's not it."

"I'm messing with you," she said. "Really, it's okay. I have to get back to work anyway. I have to say, though, I don't like the fact that you might be in danger."

She pulled close to him and wrapped her arm around his back.

"Okay," Sean said, interrupting the intimate moment. "As I was about to say, I have an idea about where we should go after we take her to the airport."

"Oh yeah?"

Sean nodded. "Yeah. There's an old legend about a cave in Ringgold. I think we should start there."

"Cave, huh?"

"I know. Another cave. But it's the only thing I can think of. It's less than three miles from the place where the *General* ran out of fuel, and it butts against White Oak Mountain, where several of the Raiders tried to escape. It's worth a shot."

The other two listened for a moment,

considering the idea.

"You said it's a legend," June spoke up. "Do you two normally chase after any random myth that comes along?"

Tommy was in the middle of taking another sip of coffee and froze in place. He looked over the rim of the mug at his friend.

Sean chuckled. "Sometimes. But only if we don't have any other options. This is one of those times."

She shrugged and raised the coffee mug to her lips. "Just asking," she said with a playful smirk.

Sean turned his attention back to Tommy. "After you take her to the airport, get yourself a burner phone. We can't make it easy for these guys to follow us."

Tommy nodded. "Gotcha. Wait..."

"What is it?"

"The kids. You think they'll be okay?"

"They'll need to hunker down for a few days, but they should be fine. I'm sure the men coming after us will be watching the building. As long as they stay put, they'll be okay. I doubt anyone will try to go in."

"I hope you're right," Tommy said, dubious.

"Tell you what," Sean said. "You take June to the airport, and I'll make sure the kids are okay."

Tommy wasn't sure he liked the second part of Sean's idea. Going back into the city could be dangerous. The new IAA building would be under surveillance, and if either one of them so much as showed their face within a block of there, they'd have trouble.

"So, you're going to go back into the hornet's nest?" Tommy asked.

"You got a better idea?"

The long pause after the question told the tale.

"I'll do it," June said suddenly.

The two friends jerked their gaze to her.

"No," Tommy said. "You need to get out of the country. And besides, you said you have to get back to work."

"I have some extra paid time off. There will be a fee to change my flight this late, but I can handle it. I can go into your headquarters and let the kids know what's going on."

The kids, Tara Watson and Alex Simms, pretty much lived at IAA headquarters. Constantly embedded in research with new artifacts or historical oddities, they each kept a bed and several days' worth of supplies on hand in case they ever needed to stay put. This situation fit that description perfectly.

The two men exchanged uncertain looks.

"Come on," she pushed. "You need someone to let them know what's going on. And who knows, maybe I can help out in case you guys need something. In fact, my phone is probably the only one that isn't being traced right now. If you have a question, you can call me, and I'll relay the information to Tara and Alex."

Her offer made a lot of sense, so much so that Sean and Tommy were having a hard time coming up with a reason not to let her do it.

"Fine," Tommy said after a long moment of thought. "I suppose we do need someone on the inside to keep the kids safe."

"Thanks for the vote of confidence," she said with a caked-on layer of sarcasm.

"I just don't want you to get hurt."

She stepped closer to him and put her hand on his chest. "I appreciate that. But I'm a grown woman. Like I said, I can take care of myself."

He ignored her comment, focused on the task at hand. "You'll need to lock up the building."

"The kids and I will be fine," she said with a warm smile. "You boys run along and figure out this mystery."

10. Washington

Adriana waited patiently inside the Oval Office. She stared through the window, beyond the shrubs and out onto the White House Rose Garden. Not everyone could get into the fabled office of the president of the United States. One either had to be a part of his operation or be highly trusted.

Fortunately for Adriana, she was the latter.

The side door opened, and John Dawkins walked in, taking the usual long stride that had become as much a part of the man as the navy suit and red tie he often wore in public.

She stood up as he entered, but he held out a dismissive hand. "You don't have to do that. Please. You're a friend, not some ambassador from insert random country's name here."

Adriana's lips creased at the comment. Dawkins had a good sense of humor. It was an endearing quality she'd come to appreciate over the years.

"Thank you for seeing me on such short notice, sir."

He shook his head. "Enough with the formalities, Adriana. You don't have to call me sir. Now, what's going on? From what I heard, you have something urgent you needed to tell me." He paused for a second, cocked his head to the side, and then spoke again. "You look tired. Can I get you a coffee or something?"

"Actually, coffee would be great, sir...I mean...yes, please. I've been up a long time."

"Yes, I know. You were in Madrid yesterday, and now you're here, in my office." He leaned back in the big chair and put his hands in his lap. "Must be pretty important for you to fly halfway across the world just to meet with me."

She looked around, uncertain if anyone was listening. The Secret Service man at the door stared straight ahead like he was studying the wallpaper on the other side of the room.

"Is...is this room secure?" she asked.

The president raised his eyebrows, curious about her line of questioning. "Of course. It's one of the most secure rooms in the world."

Her head twisted back and forth rapidly. "That's not what I meant. I mean, is someone recording what we say?"

Dawkins swallowed, still displaying a puzzled expression on his face. "No, Adriana. Nothing like that. Why?"

She drew in a deep breath and exhaled. "Sean is in trouble. Someone abducted him outside of Auburn, New York. He said he was working on a project for you. Whoever took him tried to kill him, but he managed to escape. Now he's on the run."

The president's head drooped. He put his right hand over his eye, massaging his forehead as he listened.

"That's not all," she went on. "Whoever is behind

this completely wiped out his bank accounts, credit cards, savings, everything. His phone was taken, so he got a burner phone. That's how he called me."

The concerned look on the president's face deepened. "Sean was burned?" he asked.

"That's what it sounds like. Whoever he ticked off must have some pretty strong connections." She waited to steel her nerves for a second before continuing. "There's something else. The men who tried to kill Sean are coming after you. That's why I'm here, Mr. President. Sean asked me to warn you. Someone is going to try to kill you, and it's probably going to happen soon."

The president's expression couldn't have been graver. He blinked rapidly for a couple of seconds before he leaned back and crossed his arms.

"I'm sorry. I got here as soon as I could to tell you. Sean would have done it himself, but he's on more watch lists than most known terrorists right now."

Always unselfish and perpetually caring about those close to him, Dawkins addressed the matter with Sean first. "Is Sean okay?"

"He's fine, lying low for the time being. He went to Atlanta to warn Tommy. I think his plan is to figure out what these people are hiding. He said that's the only way to make sure you and everyone else are safe."

"Well, that's Sean, isn't it? Always taking care of his friends."

Adriana agreed with a slight nod.

"I'll be sure to alert my security detail to the threat. They'll take care of the rest. The Secret Service is the best in the world when it comes to things like this. I'll be fine."

"I heard you're giving a speech today," she said.

"Yes, that's true. And in light of the information you just gave me, I'll have to pass that along to my guys."

"Will they have enough time to recheck everything?"

"They should be able to handle it," he said with a wink. "They are extremely thorough when it comes to that sort of thing. No building within a mile will go unchecked." An idea struck him as he was talking. "Adriana, would you like to come along? The speech will be boring. Please don't tell my writer, Gerald, I said that. It's not his fault. The topic just isn't exciting."

"Who's it for?"

He sighed. "It's a big luncheon for an environmentalist group."

"You've done a lot of good things for the environment during your presidency. I thought it was something you cared about."

"Oh, it is. I will always be a proponent of taking care of the planet. It's not that. This event, though, is just a bunch of patting people on the back. There's no real point to it. I guess it will raise awareness. At any rate, I have to be there in an hour, so if you want to tag along we'll need to get ready to leave soon."

Adriana considered the offer for all of three seconds before she agreed. "Sure," she said. "I'd love to."

She didn't tell the president the real reason for agreeing to go with him. Sean had told her the guys behind his abduction were CIA. That meant they would have connections in the government, potentially to security details surrounding presidential appearances.

The president probably didn't realize it at the time, but he'd just picked up a little added security.

"Shall we?" he said, standing up and motioning to the door.

"Absolutely." She stood as well and made her way across the room. "By the way. I was wondering if you could put me in touch with Emily."

He stopped and turned to face her. "My goodness. They blocked him from Axis, didn't they?"

Adriana wasn't sure how he knew. She attributed it to the president's ability to sense things better than most people. Perhaps it was his gift.

"Yes. He said when he called they claimed to have no knowledge of a Sean Wyatt and that the security clearance he gave them was invalid."

Dawkins scratched his chin. "He's been disavowed."

Her eyes widened. "You mean...they erased him from their systems?"

"Sort of. With elite groups—like Axis—the agents operate under a very strict policy that if they are ever captured or killed in the line of duty, the agency will disavow any knowledge of their existence. It's like they never walked the earth."

Adriana had heard of that kind of thing, but she didn't think too much of it. She figured it was only in movies. Still, it was hard to fathom Emily would do such a thing to a longtime friend.

"But Emily—"

"She will do whatever is necessary to protect the agency. And she will do whatever she must to keep Sean safe as well. If what you say is true, I doubt Emily would turn her back on him. At the same time, she has a duty to keep the rest of the agency safe and running smoothly. Once we are done with this speech, I'll set my dogs on the case and see what's going on. Maybe they can find something."

He reached out and opened the door leading into the next room full of desks, computers, phones, and several dozen people busily doing whatever office tasks the White House required.

Two more Secret Service men were waiting outside on either side of the door.

Adriana noticed the guards as they passed through the doorway. The men immediately fell in line behind her and the president.

"I hope you don't mind riding with me," Dawkins said. "Will be quicker that way."

"No," Adriana said. "I don't mind at all."

One of the president's assistants approached as he and Adriana made their way down the corridor. The young assistant looked like she was in her mid-twenties. Her dark green dress fluttered in the air as she strode toward the commander in chief.

"Mr. President, here is your itinerary for the event." She passed him a sheet of paper.

He took a glance at it and then thanked her. "I appreciate it, Grace. Keep things running smoothly 'til I get back."

She grinned, appreciating his sense of humor. "I'll do my best, sir."

Outside, the motorcade waited with several police cars in front and back. More Secret Service men stood around the black limousine, waiting and watching. They almost looked like robots, standing perfectly still and twisting their heads back and forth as they scanned the area for any potential threats.

One of the guards opened the rear door to the limo. The president and Adriana got in and slid into the back seat. A young man with black-rimmed glasses and curly brown hair sat across from them in the seat facing backward.

"Morning, Gerald," Dawkins said. "I trust you remember Adriana?"

"Yes, sir. We've met before," Gerald said with a smile.

"Good to see you again," she said. "Did you write his speech for today?"

Gerald bit his lower lip. "Yeah, although this one won't be exciting. Pretty standard stuff."

Adriana sensed the president's smile, recalling their previous conversation.

The convoy started moving, wrapping around the long driveway and out onto Pennsylvania Avenue.

Riding in the president's limo presented a whole new world to Adriana. Every time she'd been in Washington, the traffic had been a nightmare. The stoplights only seemed to last for a few seconds before changing, and with so many people in one place—many of them tourists—the streets were constantly clogged.

For the first time, Adriana experienced an almost nonstop ride through the city. The motorcade passed historic buildings and monuments, the National Archives, the Smithsonian, and dozens of other impressive buildings as it wound its way through the district.

Adriana had always been impressed by the nation's capital. It stood as a symbol of power and balance in a world often dominated by chaos.

After 10 minutes, the motorcade rolled to the entrance of one of the older hotels in Washington. A green-and-red-striped awning stretched out over a red carpet leading to a pair of glass doors. A doorman in a uniform and white gloves stood waiting by the door with a pleasant smile. Adriana imagined the man had been thoroughly searched before allowing him to go about his business.

Secret Service flooded the area under the awning. Six men took up positions on both sides of the red carpet as the doorman opened the entrance. Two more men in black suits and sunglasses went through the door and waited inside.

"Shouldn't you go in through a back door or something like that?" Adriana said as the president flattened his suit jacket and prepared to exit the limo.

"You'd think so," he said. "But awnings help give a little extra security in case of snipers. It limits a potential shooter's field of view."

"Ah." She hadn't thought about that before and would probably always think of it whenever she saw an awning.

One of the Secret Service guys ducked his head into the limo. "Ready, sir?"

Dawkins nodded and followed the man out of the car with Adriana and Gerald tucked close behind.

The president shook the doorman's hand as they passed through the entrance and into the hotel lobby.

Marble tile stretched out from one end of the grand room to the other. An opulent chandelier hung from the ceiling. The fixture featured hundreds, maybe thousands, of crystals shimmering around dozens of electric candle lights.

The lobby was clear of people except for the concierges working behind the desks. Police officers stood in every corner, keeping their eyes open for potential danger.

The president and his entourage walked quickly

through the lobby, passing marble pillars, giant ferns in ornate vases, and a row of hotel staff standing at attention against the right-hand wall.

The procession went down a short series of steps into a lower level and then turned right into the first pair of open doors where another pair of men in black suits stood guard.

Dawkins gave them a curt nod as he passed through the doorway into a grand ballroom to the sound of "Ladies and gentlemen, the president of the United States."

"Hail to the Chief" started playing through a public address system, and everyone in the room stood up and started clapping.

Adriana suddenly felt overwhelmed. Hundreds of people in tuxedos and fancy dresses stared in her direction as she followed the president and his security detail through the path winding around the tables.

She leaned over toward Gerald as they made their way to the front of the room. "I feel very underdressed," she said, referring to her black pants, white polo, and the black overcoat she donned.

"Don't worry about it," Gerald whispered. "They're all looking at him anyway. No one ever notices us."

When the procession reached the front of the room, the president ascended three steps onto a stage. Gerald gently tugged on Adriana's arm, pulling her to the side of the stage where they would stand during the speech.

Adriana was relieved to be out of everyone's line of sight and relaxed a little, looking around the room at all the people.

The music came to a stop, and the applause died down.

Dawkins began his speech by thanking everyone for coming. Then he went straight into the meat what he had to say.

"What is this thing anyway?" Adriana whispered to Gerald.

"Founders brunch," Gerald said. "Most of the people in this room are entrepreneurs. They're business people from Washington, Virginia, Delaware, and Maryland."

"Delmarva?"

Gerald raised an eyebrow. "I've never liked that term," he said with a quiet chuckle.

The two hushed as the president continued talking about contributions to the local economy, keeping taxes low for businesses, and everything that had come about as a result of the efforts of everyone in the room.

Adriana's eyes panned the large chamber. Some of the faces were young, easily in their early twenties. Some were much older, covered in wrinkles and gray hair. No one looked like a threat, and every person in the place sat almost perfectly still as they listened to the president's speech.

Maybe Sean was wrong about the threat to kill Dawkins. It was rare, she had to admit, but now and then Sean was incorrect about things. Usually, that was a bad thing. In this instance, however, she was hoping that was the case.

Her head slowly moved from left to right as she continued searching the room. Secret Service men were stationed in several places along each wall, separated by police officers. All of them were doing the same thing as Adriana: watching for trouble.

She noticed a subtle movement in the back of the room. It came from high up on the wall where one of the spotlights shone brightly, casting its yellowish-white beam on the podium where the president stood.

Was Adriana's mind playing tricks on her? It had to be. She thought she saw a long, black silhouette just behind the spotlight. Her eyes narrowed as she tried to focus.

The spotlight was set in a square opening fifteen feet up from the floor. Access to the control room and the spotlight must have been through a side door outside the ballroom.

She returned her gaze to the opening and peered into it. Her eyes widened suddenly. There it was again. A long, black tube moved to the left with fluid, robotic motion.

"Oh no," she said.

Adriana looked at the president. He was still talking about the benefits of entrepreneurship and how it made the economy go, providing jobs and building a strong foundation for the country.

He had no idea what was going on.

The nearest Secret Service man to her was twenty feet away.

She thought fast. Only one idea came to her mind, and she didn't like it. The black tube stopped moving, and she knew there were no other options.

Adriana pumped her legs as fast as she could, leaping onto the stage and sprinting at the president.

"Shooter!" she yelled as she ducked her head and drove her shoulder into the president's midsection. The form tackle would have made any football defensive coach proud.

Adriana and Dawkins hit the deck a half second before gunfire erupted.

The chain gun whined loudly amid a constant series of pops, sending dozens of rounds at the stage per second. The podium was torn apart almost instantly as bullets shredded the wood.

The two nearest Secret Service men charged the stage to cover the president while four others zeroed in on the source of the gunfire and drew their weapons.

Panic flooded the ballroom. Men and women ducked under their tables. Several women screamed. Two or three people closest to the exit ran for the doors.

Adriana held the president down until one of the Secret Service agents arrived.

The gunfire from the spotlight window had stopped and been replaced by loud pops from the other guards' weapons. Sparks flashed off the spotlight. The bright bulb suddenly exploded as one of the rounds struck it in the center, turning the big tube dark.

Police rushed out of the room toward the access door outside to make sure the shooter couldn't escape.

One of the guards pulled Adriana off the president and pinned her to the stage. He drew his weapon and pressed it to the back of her head.

"Don't move," he barked.

Dawkins was lying facedown with his head turned toward her. One of his guards was lying on top of him to protect the president.

"Put that gun away," Dawkins ordered. "This woman just saved my life."

"Yes, sir," the guard said and stepped away from Adriana.

The gunfire had ceased, but the chaos had only just begun.

"Get him out of here!" she said in a commanding voice to the guard atop the president. "Now!"

The two Secret Service men glanced at each other and then nodded. They knew what to do. Two more joined them as they ushered the president off the stage to the right and out through a side door.

Adriana stood up and scanned the room. Everyone was in a panic. Or were they?

One man in the far right corner in the back was walking calmly toward an exit door. Adriana frowned. The guy was way too collected for a civilian.

She glanced back at the spotlight window. Through the opening, she saw security forces rushing through the room.

No one had noticed the man leaving in the corner.

Adriana took a deep breath and leaped off the stage.

11. Ringgold, Georgia

Sean stared out at the grand view from atop the hill. Tommy stood next to him, also admiring the landscape that rolled out before them. He tightened the gear bag strapped to his back, making sure it was snug enough to stay in place for some light spelunking.

They stood atop Boy's Mountain just a couple of miles outside the little town of Ringgold. It was— for Sean—a very real homecoming. His parents had owned the property for nearly thirty years, moving here from Chattanooga when he was in high school.

The rise was more of a large hill than an actual mountain. White Oak Mountain—just a few thousand yards away—was taller and longer, stretching far into Tennessee and deep into Georgia, nearly reaching all the way to Summerville. Still, the little mountain provided incredible vistas, especially on a clear, cold day.

"I can see why your folks never sold this place," Tommy said. "You can see all the way to the Blue Ridge Mountains from here."

"Yep," Sean nodded. "I don't miss living here, but every time I come back it gets harder and harder to leave."

After taking in the scenery for another minute or

two, Tommy turned to his friend and asked if he'd made arrangements for them to search the property next door.

"Yeah, I spoke to the lady who owns the place. She said it's cool for us to walk around down there. With it being winter, snakes won't be a problem."

Tommy tightened the zipper on his coat. "No kidding. A reptile would be frozen solid in this weather."

The two trudged beyond Sean's father's shed and began the short descent toward the cave. After only two minutes, they arrived at one of the Confederate trenches. Even a casual observer would have realized the earthworks were a military trench. The position was perfectly placed to take out an enemy as they rounded the bend on the Old Federal Road several hundred feet below. Soldiers could have poured musket fire and cannon balls into the bottleneck, obliterating anyone who crossed their path. Due to the trench's position, anyone going through the pass wouldn't realize what was happening until it was too late.

"You ever bring a metal detector up here and look around?" Tommy asked.

"Oddly enough, I never have."

"Really?"

Sean chuckled. "We've been friends for about thirty years. If I'd done something like that, I would have invited you to join me."

"That's true." He pointed to a strange opening in the earth another hundred feet away. "Is that the cave over there?"

"Yep," Sean said as he marched forward, through the shallow trench and down the hill.

Tommy followed close behind, kicking dead leaves with the tips of his shoes along the way.

"How long did you say it's been since you went down there?"

"I don't know. Twenty years?" Sean said. "Last time I went in, we had to use a rope to climb out. The hill leading down into the cave is kind of steep."

"Do we need a rope?"

"Not sure. We'll know in a second."

The two traversed the face of the mountain until they reached a broad opening in the earth. The cave mouth was about twenty feet in diameter. To get to the actual entrance, they had to lower themselves down a steep incline, fifteen feet to the bottom where the ground leveled off. It wasn't a straight drop to the entrance, but having something to hold on to as they made their way down was definitely a plus. Lucky for Sean and Tommy, someone had left a fifty-foot extension cord tied to a pine tree.

Sean tested the makeshift rope by pulling on it and then leaning back, putting all his weight on the cord.

"Looks like this will hold," he said, giving it one last tug.

Tommy wasn't as convinced. "Maybe we should go check out your dad's shed and see if there's a rope or something else in there."

"Shed's locked, and my parents aren't around. Don't worry. This will hold."

Sean started lowering himself down the steep slope one hand over the other. It took him less than half a minute to reach the bottom. When his feet were on flat ground, he called up to Tommy and gave him the all-clear.

Tommy stared at the dingy orange cord. He tentatively picked it up and gave the thing a few test pulls of his own. Satisfied it would hold, he started inching his way down the hill.

Sean watched as his friend methodically descended the slope like a sloth climbing down a tree.

"Take your time, buddy. We have all day."

Tommy's forearms burned from the strain. He couldn't imagine doing this same stunt six months prior. "Shut up. I don't exactly trust your rope thingy. Feels like it could break loose any second. And don't make any jokes about me being out of shape, either."

"I wasn't going to. You're in the best shape of your life, probably fitter than me. Seriously, you're doing fine. Just a few more steps."

Tommy's feet touched the dirt in front of the cave, and he let the cord fall to the ground. He clenched his fingers into a fist several times to get the feeling back and to help with the tightness in his forearms.

"That sure is a workout," he said.

"No kidding," Sean said with a slap on his friend's back. "I doubt you could have done that last year."

"No way I could have."

Tommy looked up at the cave entrance. Then, he took out his phone and switched on the light. "Well, let's take a gander inside. After you."

Sean switched on a flashlight and started into the cave.

The first twenty feet were easy enough. The floor was covered in sheets of rock that—at one point in time—had been on the cave roof. Years of erosion and occasional seismic activity had caused the layers to break away and collapse to the floor.

"If there was anything in here on the ground, it's underneath tons of rock now," Sean said, shining his light around on the broken stone.

Tommy scanned the room. "Yeah. I wonder how much of the ceiling fell. The actual cave floor could be ten feet farther down."

"It's possible."

Sean flashed his light ahead where a short wall appeared to block the way. "We have to climb up to that opening," he said, pointing at a passage above the blockage.

"Was it always like that?"

"As far as I know. Had to do the same thing twenty years ago when I came down here. Although it does appear more of the ceiling has fallen in since then. Seems like the floor is closer to that corridor."

Tommy didn't like the sound of that. "How often does the ceiling fall in this place?" His eyes darted around as if the rock above could crush them at any given second.

"No idea," Sean said as he reached the wall. He stepped up on a smaller boulder and pulled himself up easily to the opening. It was only seven or eight feet up, and the rocks had fallen in such a way that getting up was no problem. "I'm not a geologist."

Tommy started climbing the boulder once Sean was out of the way and into the passage. "Yeah, I just thought since you'd been here a few times maybe you could gauge it."

As Tommy's right foot touched the top of the boulder, something brushed by his face and knocked him off balance.

He shrieked, waving his hands around like a bird trying to fly for the first time. His weight shifted backward, and he lost his footing. Tommy desperately reached out to keep his balance, but gravity was working against him.

He felt Sean's hand slap him in the chest and squeeze his shirt. A split second later, Sean jerked his friend away from the ledge and into the safety of the narrow corridor.

Tommy panted for a second, still feeling panic course through his veins. "Something flew past my face," he said, swiping his hand around like he could feel an insect crawling on his skin.

"Probably just a bat," Sean said. "Keep moving."

Sean pushed forward while his friend gave a few

more precautionary brushes on his arms and neck.

"There are bats in here?" Tommy asked.

"It's a cave," Sean said, keeping his eyes forward. "Of course there are bats in here."

Sean couldn't see his friend blush in the darkness.

"I guess I didn't really think that one through."

Sean pushed forward with bent knees, staying low so he didn't hit his head on the low ceiling.

The narrow corridor stretched deeper into the cave for about thirty feet before coming to a sudden end that dropped back down to the main cavern floor.

Sean unfastened his gear bag and fished a pair of glow sticks out of it. He cracked the sticks, shook them up, and dropped them to the bottom to shine a little light on the climb down.

Carefully, Sean made his way down the wall until he was back on the ground and stepped back to give Tommy some room.

"Are there many more climbs like this?" Tommy asked as he worked his way down the wall. "Will make for some pretty slow going."

"No," Sean said. "Just this one. It goes downhill from here."

He took off again, trudging through the mud and across the wet rocks, leading the way down the gradual slope. The damp air smelled, well, slimy— like a hundred years' worth of mildew had built up on the stone. The temperature remained constant in the high fifties, warmer than aboveground but still chilly enough to warrant a jacket.

The two friends pushed on, navigating their way deeper into the cave until they arrived at a spot where the tunnel ended in a small circular room. The ceiling shot high into the rock, much taller than in the passageway.

An empty milk jug sat on the muddy floor next to a couple of old beer cans. Several loose stones were arranged in a circle close by with charred black wood in the center.

"Looks like we're not the first ones down here," Tommy said.

"Nope," Sean shook his head. "The funny thing is that stuff was here when I came down twenty years ago."

"Seems like having a fire down here isn't a good idea. Would get awfully smoky."

"Yeah. I was wondering about that, too."

The two men looked around the room but quickly realized there wasn't much to see.

"So...what are we looking for down here?" Tommy asked.

Sean set his gear bag on the floor and dug out some larger lights and mounts. A minute later the powerful bulbs bathed the cave in bright light.

"The times I came down here before, I never noticed anything unusual," Sean said. "But I didn't have much light, either."

He tilted his head back and looked around the upper reaches of the room. The rough rock walls almost had the feel of being hand-hewn. Unlike most natural caves, this one had no stalactites or stalagmites.

"I wonder how many people have been in here through the years," Tommy said as he ran his fingers along the wall's surface. He bent down and picked up a loose rock and then tossed it aside.

Sean was still searching the upper reaches of the cave walls for anything out of the ordinary.

"Always weird to think about it like that. You never know whose footsteps you're standing in when you visit historic places, or any place for that matter."

Tommy kicked one of the beer cans, sending it rattling along the hard floor. The sound echoed in the room, amplified by the high ceiling's natural dome shape. He looked up to the wall opposite of Sean. Spotting something that seemed out of place, he paused, cocked his head to the side, and then got Sean's attention.

"Hey, what's that up there?"

Sean turned and followed Tommy's finger to the spot.

High up on the wall, about fifteen feet off the ground, was a collection of stones stacked on a ledge. At first glance, they were nearly impossible to discern from the rest of the wall. The stones matched the rock from the wall and were packed tightly in the shadows. Unless someone was looking for it, the little arrangement of rocks would easily be missed.

"It's definitely something," Sean said.

"Yeah. No way that's natural." He turned to his friend. "You think we can get up there to check it out?"

"Maybe," Sean said, his voice full of hesitation.

"It's not that high," Tommy said. "You usually only get freaked out by things higher than twenty feet. That's maybe sixteen feet, tops."

Sean's rabid fear of heights had been an issue as long as he could remember. Usually, the phobia manifested itself in tall buildings or on mountains where a steep drop-off was nearby. When Sean found himself in a high place, it was paralyzing. His muscles tensed, and he could barely make his body move.

"The height isn't the problem," Sean said. "I'm just not sure about how to get up there."

Tommy searched the wall for a moment and then stepped closer. He put his hand up and grabbed a narrow ledge. His fingers strained as he pulled himself up. Next, he put the toe of his right shoe on a thin lip and reached up with his right hand to another handhold.

Sean watched, mesmerized, as his friend expertly navigated the climb. Tommy was ten feet up when he hit a snag. There was a solid piece of rock jutting out from the side of the wall. Climbers would have called it a chicken head due to the shape. Tommy could reach the hold, but there wasn't another foothold except for a ledge right under the chicken head.

Sean started to say something but decided not to

break his friend's concentration.

Tommy's legs were spread out in an upside down V as he clung to the wall. He eyed the chicken head, knowing what he had to do next but unsure if he could pull it off. There was only one way to find out.

He stretched out his left hand and took his right foot off the ledge. Grabbing the chicken head—first with his left—he swung his weight directly underneath the hold. His right hand shot up quickly, his fingers wrapping around the rock like a vise grip. The muscles in his arms and back strained against gravity, pulling his body up as he stabilized the movement by walking up the wall with his feet.

Tommy felt his shoes touch the next ledge and dug them in hard to keep his balance as he reached up to the lip where the loose rocks were stacked in a semicircle.

"I'm impressed," Sean said. "That was a tough move."

Tommy didn't look down. He was intensely focused on the target just above his head. "Part of my new workout regimen is doing more functional exercises, like rock climbing and pull-ups. I go down to the climbing gym once a week now."

"Well, it's paid off."

The stack of rocks was only a few feet away from Tommy's face. He reached over and pulled away one of the stones from the top, then another, and another, until he'd removed half of the rocks from their resting place.

"I see something," he said. "Looks like a metal box."

He stretched his hand out and grasped the object, pulling it away from the makeshift shelf.

"What is it?" Sean asked, looking up at the thing.

"Um...it's a metal box, like I said."

"Right, but what is it?"

"Not sure." Tommy said. "I'm going to drop it down to you. Don't miss it, okay?"

"I won't," Sean answered, putting his hands out to signal he was ready.

"Seriously. If you let it hit the ground, it could break whatever is in here."

"How do you know it's breakable?"

"Are you ready or not?" Tommy said, an irritated scowl crossing his face. "I can't hold this grip much longer."

"Yeah. I'm ready. Go ahead."

He held out the box directly over Sean and let go. The object fell straight into Sean's hands. He cushioned the fall and cradled the box carefully to make sure the sudden stop wouldn't harm anything inside.

Tommy lowered himself down the wall, and when he was about six feet up, let go and dropped to the ground. His shoes hit the floor with a thud, and he grunted. He dusted himself off and clenched his fingers. The muscles in his forearms still burned from the workout.

Sean knelt down near one of the lights and

rotated the box a few times to get a better look at it. The metal appeared to be tin, dented and worn out by the ravages of time and weather. Being down in the cave had protected it from some of the elements, but the damp conditions could have ruined anything inside. Sean wasn't about to open the box in there. They'd need to do that in a contained environment.

Tommy stood close, inspecting the thing with his friend as he turned it over in his hands.

"What do you say we get out of here and get this thing to a nice, dry lab?" Tommy asked.

"Good call. Here," Sean handed Tommy the box. "I'll get the lights and gear."

A loud boom rocked the entire cave. Pieces of ceiling broke loose and dropped to the ground, shattering at Sean's and Tommy's feet. They looked up at the same time and saw another large, flat piece breaking free.

Sean grabbed his friend and ducked to the side just in time as the huge piece of rock crashed to the ground. The room dimmed suddenly, one of the heavy sections of ceiling crushing a light in the mayhem.

12. Washington

Adriana sprinted down the hotel corridor, bumping into people and weaving past them as she gave chase. Her heart pounded with every step. Someone had tried to kill the president. Her money was on the guy in the suit running thirty feet ahead.

Amid the chaos, no one had seen her or the man she was chasing as they ran out of the grand ballroom and into the hall. Most of the security teams were flooding into where the president was making his speech. Members of a SWAT team charged forward into the ballroom while other cops started setting up a perimeter just outside the doors.

The guy Adriana was following avoided all that, which told her whoever he was, he had a good sense of procedure.

He ducked to the right, down a side hall, and slowed down as she rounded the corner. His attempt to look casual was a smart move, since a guy running from an assassination attempt on the president would seem a tad on the suspicious side.

She slowed as well after rounding the corner and realizing her target was no longer running. His head swiveled around, and he gave her a short look over his shoulder. Adriana played it cool and flashed her best flirty yet slightly nervous grin.

The corner of his lip stretched for a moment, a feeble effort to return the smile. Then, like a frightened deer, he bolted through the door on the left.

Adriana's instinct was to rush in after him, but that would put her at a disadvantage. The guy could easily be waiting on the other side of the door, ready to pounce or shoot, or anything. Then again, if she didn't pursue, he would get away.

She reached the door and waited a moment. Unarmed, she was still dangerous. That didn't mean she wasn't wishing for a pistol. She looked down the hallway as two more police officers ran by. Her fingers wrapped around the doorknob, and she twisted. The door opened with a faint creak, and she spun around the edge to get a peek inside. Staying on the balls of her feet, she twisted one more step beyond the doorway's threshold and over to the other side.

The quick look revealed an empty maintenance corridor lined with painted cinder block walls and illuminated by sterile fluorescent lights down the ceiling's center.

She poked her head back through the door frame and looked again. She heard footsteps on the thin carpet. He was on the run again.

Adriana hurried into the hallway and turned right at an intersection with another corridor. Her quarry was nearly at the other end. She pumped her legs as fast as she could, but there was no way to catch him before he slammed through the door and out into the street.

Seconds later, Adriana ran into the door, barging the lever to undo the latch. Her body shuddered against the metal, only able to open the thing a few inches. Dull pain radiated through her shoulder from the impact. She looked down through the crack in the door and saw a trash can propped up against the handle.

She stepped back and kicked the door lever. The sudden jarring blow freed the door from the makeshift brace. It flew open and slammed against the wall.

Adriana poked her head around the corner. She was in an alley just off one of the main streets. To the right, the street ended in a brick wall. To the left, cops swarmed into the area, running to the scene of the attempted assassination. Various sirens screamed from ambulances, fire trucks, and police cars.

Something metal clanked from the other side of the brick wall to the right. Adriana frowned. *He went over the wall?*

She didn't stop long enough to debate the possibility in her head. If the guy had gone left, he'd have run headlong into the police. Considering what just happened, they'd be questioning everyone.

"You! Stop right there!" a voice yelled from the left.

Adriana saw a cop stalking toward her with gun

drawn. He was still a good fifty to sixty feet away, much too far for him to be accurate with the weapon.

Her feet shifted toward the right. Her muscles tensed, and she took off.

"Hey! Stop!"

The cop fired.

The round ricocheted off the wall next to her.

She heard him shouting into his radio, calling for backup just before he fired another shot.

"I said stop!" he shouted again.

Adriana bent her run toward the end wall to give her a better approach.

She neared the corner and jumped.

Her right foot planted against the side wall and pushed off. She did the same with her left foot on the end wall, back to the side wall, and once more until she landed on the top. The cop fired one last time as she dropped over the side.

Adriana gripped the concrete top of the wall with white-knuckled fingers, lowering herself to a safe distance before she let go and fell to the ground.

Her feet hit the asphalt hard, and she rolled to a stop on one knee. Her chest expanded and contracted, taking in big breaths of air. She couldn't take a break, though. The guy was nowhere in sight, and if he got away, she feared no one would catch him.

She pushed herself to get up and run again. Her legs felt like they were tied to bags of sand, but she kept going.

Up ahead, the next street was quieter than the last even though the sounds of sirens still echoed through the concrete-and-brick canyon.

There was no sign of the guy, and when she hit the sidewalk, she'd have to make a decision if he was out of sight.

She ran by a blue dumpster and was about to reach the corner when a garbage can flew at her face, striking her square in the forehead.

The blow knocked her onto her back. The buildings, the sounds, the smells of days-old garbage all swirled in her head.

The man she'd been chasing stepped out of the shadows and loomed over her. He was about to speak, but she kicked her foot up and planted the top of her foot right in his groin.

He doubled over with a grunt.

Adriana managed to roll onto her side and kicked again, this time striking the man's heel and knocking him on his back.

She planted her hands on the cold asphalt and spun to a fighting stance as he scrambled to recover. Her next attack was swift, but he was ready, easily deflecting her right jab, left, right again, and then swatting away an attempt to kick him in the gut.

He countered with a right hook that caught her in the jaw and knocked her back a few steps.

Her left ear rang from the blow, and a stinging, throbbing pain pulsed through her face. He charged, aiming to dig his shoulder into her midsection, but she sidestepped the attack and stuck her foot out. It hit his shin and, combined with the momentum, sent him stumbling onto his face.

Adriana moved fast in spite of the aching in her jaw and forehead, rushing to where he clambered to get up. She swung her foot again, this time striking him on the side of the head.

The shot sent him back to the ground, this time with a series of low moans. He scratched at the pavement, desperately trying to claw his way free of the attack.

Adriana pounced, driving her elbow into his upper back then pounding both sides of his face with one hammer fist after another.

He tried to cover his head with both hands like a prize fighter who'd all but lost.

Her arms felt like Jell-O and grew heavier with every punch.

"Stop right there!" a man's voice yelled.

Adriana panted for air. Her heart was racing. Strands of her brown hair had broken loose of the ponytail and hung around her face and ears. She didn't look up immediately, instead just staring down at the groaning man.

"Put your hands up high where I can see 'em," the cop said.

A second later, three more cops appeared around the corner with weapons drawn.

The first one stepped cautiously toward her, approaching as he would a venomous snake coiled under a tree and ready to strike.

Adriana's eyes darted from one cop to the next.

"I said put your hands up!" the leader ordered once more. "Don't make me tell you again!"

Adriana gradually straightened her spine. She raised her hands as smoothly as she could, careful not to make any sudden movements.

"This guy is the one you're looking for," she said. "He was in the ballroom when the shots were fired. I think he's the one who tried to kill the president."

"Be quiet!" the cop yelled.

"But he's the one you want."

"I said be quiet! Now, nice and easy, get off him, and stay on your knees!"

Adriana didn't try to hide the confusion on her face as she moved one leg over the beaten man. Once both knees were on the ground next to him, two of the other cops moved in while the first to arrive and one other officer kept their weapons trained on her.

"Aren't you going to arrest him?" she asked.

The two approaching her, grabbed her by the wrists, and shoved her face into the pavement. The cold, jagged asphalt scratched her cheek. The arresting officers didn't try to be gentle.

They forced her hands behind her back and secured cuffs tightly around the base of her wrists.

"Why aren't you arresting him?" she asked again, pushing the issue. "I've done nothing wrong. He's the one you want."

"If you say anything again, I will put a bullet

through your head."

The threat silenced her for the moment. She'd never heard a cop speak that way and was fairly certain that wasn't standard operating procedure.

"Your car close?" the one in charge asked.

The two apprehending Adriana stood up, lifting her with hands underneath her armpits.

"Yeah, just right out there," the one on her right said.

"Good. Get her out of here."

"Take her to the precinct, sir?" the one on her left said. He was younger, probably in his mid-twenties. His face gave off the appearance he was still a teenager.

The cop in charge shook his head. "No. She's not under arrest."

The young cop looked confused. "I don't understand, sir. What are we doing with her, then?"

The lead cop turned his weapon and fired a bullet through the young man's forehead. His wide eyes froze permanently in shock as he fell over onto his side.

"We have an officer down. Repeat, officer down. Please send backup." He rattled off his location as the cop on Adriana's right tugged her toward the street.

She watched in horror as the one in charge turned his weapon to the gunman on the ground. He tried to push himself up on all fours, but another shot rang out, planting a round in the back of his skull.

He collapsed, prostrate on the pavement, and went completely still.

The lead cop turned to the remaining two. "Johnson, stay here with me. Tulley"—he turned to the other—"get her out of here. Dump the body. Then report back to the hotel."

The men nodded.

Adriana didn't need to ask what was going on. Now it was clear. The police—at least some of them—were in on the assassination attempt. Who knew how deep the rabbit hole went?

Another thing was certain: the second she got in the back of that squad car, she'd be dead.

She knew police procedure. She knew their moves, their defenses, how they would react to resistance from a prisoner. So, she did the one thing they wouldn't expect.

She waited until they were out of the other two cops' view. Just feet from the back door of the squad car, her arms and legs suddenly went limp. The cop handling her felt her body suddenly get very heavy, and he strained to keep her up.

His grip slipped off her forearm as she fell to one knee.

"Hey, what do you think you're doing?" he asked.

He didn't realize he'd already fallen into her trap.

The cop bent down to force her onto her feet, and that's when she struck. Her right heel kicked backward, digging deep into his groin. His head lurched forward from the abrupt and terrible pain. She sensed his head close and snapped hers back, crunching his nose with the top of her skull.

He howled in agony, dropping to his knees with one hand on his man parts, the other on his now-bleeding nose.

"You b—" He started to spit out the insult, but it was cut short.

Adriana spun to her feet and whipped her left foot around, plowing the bone into the side of his head and driving him to the ground.

She worked fast, securing the keys from his belt first and then snagging the weapon from his holster. Sirens wailed from a few blocks away. Reinforcements would be here any second.

She was lucky no one was around, the area having been marked off for the president's visit. On a normal day, the sidewalks and streets would have been flooded with people on their daily commute.

Adriana aimed the weapon into the alley, gripping it with both hands since they were still in cuffs.

The other two hadn't heard the scuffle. She hurried over to the squad car and unlocked it. Next, she removed the cuffs and started to slide into the seat when she realized something. The cop she'd just struck was still unconscious, and the other two were tending to the bodies in the alley.

A crazy thought ran through her head as she stared at the cop on the ground. It was risky, but she needed answers.

13. Ringgold

Clouds of dust hovered for several minutes in the dimly lit cave. Sean and Tommy did their best to cover their mouths to keep as much of the debris out of their lungs as possible.

"What was that?" Tommy said in a loud voice.

The ground and walls around them had stopped shaking almost immediately after the blast. Broken pieces of ceiling were strewn across the floor.

Sean shook his head. "If I didn't know better, I'd say C4."

Tommy coughed. He pressed the bottom of his shirt closer to his nose and mouth to seal out the dust.

"C4? Isn't that a little hard to come by?"

"Not if you have the right military connections," Sean said.

"I guess these guys have them."

Sean nodded. "Seems that way."

He trudged up the slope to the rock wall in the middle of the path. He climbed up the big stones to the top and then crawled back to the other end.

Tommy followed his friend back to the wall and waited at the bottom.

"See anything up there?" His voice echoed throughout passage.

Sean peered into the darkness. He had his phone

in his hand but kept the light off. He wanted to see if any light was coming into the cave from the entrance. It only took him a second before he had a horrifying realization.

The cave was sealed off.

"The entrance," he said, "it's blocked."

"Blocked?" The early stages of panic quivered in Tommy's voice. "How bad is it?"

"Won't know until we go up there and check it out, but from here I'd say pretty bad. No light is coming through, so that can't be a good thing."

"Are you serious? I'm coming up to take a look."

Tommy clambered up the rocks and joined his friend on the other side of the narrow passage. He stared into the darkness after shutting off his light, waiting for his eyes to adjust to the pitch black.

"See anything?" Sean asked with only a sliver of hope in his tone.

"No," Tommy said. "We better have a closer look."

The two made their way down the other side of the wall and across the large room. Dust particles still clouded the air in big pockets while in other spots the debris had already settled.

"More ceiling collapsed here," Sean said, pointing at a giant slab that was cracked in half on the floor. "That wasn't here when we came in."

When they arrived where the entrance used to be, they found nothing but a pile of dirt and rock.

"You don't happen to have a shovel and a bulldozer in your gear bag, do you?" Tommy asked, trying to shake off his fear with a little humor.

Sean clicked his tongue and shook his head. "That's probably what it would take to get out of here. Not the shovel. Definitely the bulldozer."

"Thoughts?"

"Nothing helpful, off hand."

Tommy pressed one of the buttons on his phone and checked the screen. "No signal. I was afraid of that."

"Yeah, I figured."

Sean neared the pile of rubble and picked out a rock, then another, tossing them aside as he worked.

"You realize that could take forever, right? Not to mention it could cause another cave-in."

"I'm not trying to clear it. Just testing how deep it is."

"And?"

Sean stopped after nearly a minute of moving the chunks of rock. "We aren't getting out this way. At the base of this mess it could be twenty feet thick."

Questions flooded the minds of both men. Tommy voiced them.

"Who would do this? I mean, who even knows we're here?"

"I want to know the answer to that as much as you do," Sean said. "But right now, we need to figure out a way out of here."

"Right." Tommy spun around, shining his light around the room. He inspected the walls but soon realized there was nothing to find. "Let's head back the other way. Maybe we missed something that could help us get out of here?"

"Like what?" Sean asked, dubious. "We searched that whole other room. Pretty sure we got everything that was there to find." He held up the metal box for his friend to see.

"Worth a try. It's not like we're going anywhere fast standing here."

Tommy spun around and made his way back to the wall. Sean watched with eyebrows raised. Usually, Tommy was the glass-half-empty type. This new, more optimistic Tommy was a refreshing and slightly annoying improvement.

"Hold up, Schultzie. I'm coming."

When the two made it to the upper passage again, they inched their way forward with Tommy in the lead.

"What's in your head?" Sean asked. "You're moving kind of slow through here."

Tommy was running his hand along the wall when he stopped and looked up.

"What's that?" he asked.

"What's what?"

Tommy pointed his light up above their heads at the corner where the narrow corridor dropped off to the floor below.

"That," he said with a nod.

Sean tilted his head up and saw what had caught his friend's attention. A crack nearly three feet wide and two feet high was opened in the rock.

"I thought I felt a draft when we came through here a minute ago." He aimed his beam to the floor at a big piece of stone, broken in several pieces.

"I guess that was covering the hole," Sean said.

"Where do you think it goes?"

"No idea, but anywhere is better than being stuck here."

"Agreed," Tommy said. "Hold my light for a second. I'm going to check it out."

He handed his phone to Sean and put his hands up to the crack's ledge. His fingers gripped the lip tightly, and he pulled himself up, using his feet to make the job of his hands and arms a little easier.

Sean watched in amazement. His friend couldn't do a pull-up six months ago. Now he was looking like an expert rock climber.

"I have to say, Schultzie, I'm impressed."

"With what?" Tommy asked as he crawled into the cavity, leaving his legs dangling out.

"You're just so much fitter. Old Tommy could have never done that."

"Yeah, that's great. You mind handing me my light? I can't see a thing in here."

Sean chuckled at his friend's ability to ignore the compliment and held the light up high. Tommy stuck his left hand back without looking. Once he felt his fingers touch the device, he grasped it and pulled it inside.

"See anything now?" Sean asked.

"It's another passage. Looks like it goes on for a while. I can't see that far, but it looks like it leads downhill. I'm going to go a little farther. And check it out."

"Okay, I'll be right behind you."

Tommy wiggled his way forward. The gap on either side only afforded him a couple of inches. The ceiling over his head was similarly close, and more than once he almost bumped it.

His light danced back and forth in the tunnel ahead, mingling with Sean's light from behind.

"Seems like we're moving down, all right," Sean said.

"Yeah. I wonder how far this thing goes." Tommy tried to stay cool, but inside, his anxiety was going full throttle. He didn't like being in tight spaces, and so getting out of this squeeze was motivation enough for him to press on a little faster.

The passage twisted slightly, bending to the left and then straightened out, dropping more dramatically downhill.

"My sense of direction isn't always on point," Sean said, "but it feels like we're heading down toward the road."

"Yep," Tommy grunted as he pulled himself along. "Do you know if there's another entrance to this thing?"

"Probably a question you should have asked before we started crawling through a random cave tunnel. It's gonna suck if we have to go backward through here."

"I...yeah, I didn't really think about that."

"Hey, we had to do something. Couldn't sit there in the cave and wait for the cavalry to come rescue us."

Progress was slow for the two friends as they continued to belly crawl down through the tunnel. It didn't take long before their elbows and knees started to hurt from digging into the hard floor. Their winter coats helped cushion the joints a little, but they also caused the men to sweat profusely despite the cave temperature being in the fifties.

Around twenty minutes after leaving the main cavern, the men reached a part of the tunnel where it leveled off and snaked its way forward, bending to the left, right, and back again.

"I wonder how far this thing goes." Sean said.

"Shh," Tommy hushed his friend. "Do you hear that?"

They both stopped and listened closely. There were ten seconds of silence before they heard the noise again. It was a low, rumbling sound that seemed to come from above.

"There it was again."

"Yeah, I definitely heard that," Sean said. He wiped a jacket sleeve across his forehead to remove the sweat rolling down the skin. "Sounds like we're under the road."

"Or really close to it. Maybe there's a way out of here up ahead."

"I hope so. Because I do not want to try to back out of this."

Tommy started crawling again with renewed

strength. "What's the problem? Not enjoying the view back there?"

"Now that you mention it..."

They pushed on, dragging themselves forward until the sounds of the road began to fade and were gradually overcome by a different noise.

"Is that water?" Tommy asked.

Sean wiped the sweat from his nose. "Probably. We must be getting close to the creek. Been a bunch of rain lately, so there's a lot more water than usual."

The two crawled another thirty feet before they were met with an obstacle. Thin cracks of light streamed into the dark space. They were nothing more than slivers, poking through tiny crevices around the edge of what appeared to be a giant stone.

"Someone put this here to block off the cave," Tommy said.

"You think?"

"Yeah. This rock is different than the walls and floor around us. It must have been brought up from the creek bed or maybe from a nearby quarry."

Sean shook his head. "I was kidding, Schultzie."

"Oh."

He inched his way closer to the big stone. He turned his head and reached out his left hand, pushing on the rock as hard as he could. After a minute of effort, he stopped and gasped for air. He rested until his breathing slowed, and then he craned his neck so he could see Sean.

"This thing ain't moving. It's too heavy."

Sean thought for a second and then contorted his body so he could reach his right foot. He'd been dragging his gear bag behind him through the entire tunnel. Inside one of the pouches was something he thought might help their situation.

"Hold on a sec," Sean said. He unzipped the front pouch and shoved his hand inside. He pulled out four little disks. Three were black and the other silver. After putting the three black ones back in the bag, he straightened his body and held the little object out for Tommy.

"Here," he said. "Press this twenty times, and then wedge it into the top of that rock. Try to get it in one of those narrow openings."

"What good is one of your flash bangs going to do here? We need something more powerful to blow that thing out of the way."

Sean swallowed. "That isn't a flash bang. It's high-density RDX with compressed ammonia nitrate."

Tommy's confused look turned to one of fear. His eyes opened wide, and he nearly tossed the thing back to Sean.

"You brought C4?"

Sean sighed and shook his head. "It isn't C4."

"You said there's RDX in this thing. That's what they use in C4."

"It's a modified compound. Much more stable and way safer to use. If you wedge it properly between the mouth of the cave and that stone, the pressure it puts out should knock the stone over from the top."

Tommy was skeptical. He felt like there was something he didn't know but decided to trust his friend—a fact for which Sean was relieved since he didn't tell Tommy that the little device in his hand was twice as powerful as C4. Probably best if Tommy didn't know that.

"Hold it down for three seconds," Sean said. "Then press it twenty times. That will give us enough time to back up to a safe vantage point."

"Twenty times? Why not like fifty times? That would give us a chance to get farther away, you know, to an even safer distance."

"Twenty is the maximum number of seconds this explosive will allow. If you want to give my friend at DARPA some suggestions about his R&D weapons, be my guest."

Tommy took a deep breath and then gave a nod. "Fine. But do me a favor, and start backing up. I don't need you in my way when I'm trying to get clear of this thing."

Sean started scooting backward, pleased to find that moving that direction was easier than going forward. He doubted it would be if they were in the uphill section of the tunnel.

Tommy took a short glance back to make sure his friend was far enough away and then held the button for three seconds. The device gave off a subtle beep, signaling that it was ready for deployment. Tommy blinked rapidly and stared at the explosive before he started squeezing the device.

"You're sure this has been tested and won't explode sooner than expected, right?" Tommy's voice trembled with uncertainty.

"Oh yeah," Sean reassured him while he continued backing up. "They do a ton of testing on all their stuff. We'll be fine."

Tommy wasn't so confident, but he didn't have much choice.

"I'd do it myself, but I doubt I could squeeze by you in here," Sean said.

"I'm fine. Just need a second."

"Shoot. I almost forgot. You'll need to keep squeezing it until you have it in place, otherwise the internal timer will start, which means you'd have less time to get clear of the blast radius."

Tommy swallowed hard again and stared at the device. "You almost forgot?" he said with a tremor of irritation in his tone. "Don't you think that's maybe one of the more important facets of using one of these?"

Sean shrugged. "Hey, we're okay...for now."

Tommy took another in a long line of several deep breaths and looked up at the narrow seams between the cave rock and the stone blocking their exit. One appeared to be just wide enough to allow the disk to slip between.

He squeezed the device, counting carefully every time his thumb depressed the embedded button.

When he reached twenty, he held it down and kept
the thing squeezed tight, pinched between his
finger and thumb as he worked it into the crack.
He had to wiggle the disk to get it how he wanted.
At the last second, he gave it one last shove before
letting go of the button.

His fingers used too much force, though, and the
disk slipped through the slim crevice and out onto
the ground.

"Oops," he said.

"Oops?" Sean shouted. "What oops?"

"I dropped it. It fell outside."

"Get back here! Hurry!"

Tommy shimmied like a worm on twenty cups of
coffee, working his way backward up the tunnel as
fast as he could. His internal clock counted down
the seconds, probably a little faster than reality.

He rounded the first bend in the tunnel near
where Sean was tucked away and covered his head
just as the device blew.

The cave shook violently for a split second, but
the tunnel integrity stayed true. Even the sound of
the explosive wasn't unbearable due to it being
outside the tunnel entrance.

Tommy was about to ask Sean if he had another
one of those disks, but decided to take a look at the
damage first. He crept out of his hiding spot and
pointed his light around the turn. Clouds of dust
hung in the tunnel, illuminated by Tommy's beam
and a greater source beyond the entrance: daylight.

"I've got another one of those in the bag

somewhere," Sean said. "Let's just hope we can get it in a position where it will blow that rock away from the opening."

"Don't need it," Tommy said with a shake of the head. "That did the trick."

Sean wasn't sure what he meant, whether "the trick" was a good thing or a bad thing. He scooted forward and poked his head around the bend, staring through the tunnel just beyond his friend's bulk.

"You blew the whole thing to smithereens, Tommy."

The two crawled the rest of the way to the opening and out into the cold winter air. The sun did little to warm their faces, but just feeling it on their skin again was a huge relief.

Standing next to the new cave entrance, they inspected the damage Sean's explosive device had caused.

The stone that was covering the tunnel mouth lay strewn across the embankment, all the way to the creek twenty feet below.

"I thought it would just be strong enough to topple that thing over onto its side," Sean said, gazing in disbelief at the debris. "I guess it was a little stronger than I realized."

"You think?" Tommy said with arms outstretched. "We're lucky it didn't cause a cave-in."

Sean nodded. His friend was right. They were lucky. And there was no sense in pushing their luck any further.

"Speaking of good fortune, we need to get out of here. A passing car would have seen and heard that blast."

"Not to mention that someone tried to kill us by trapping us in there."

"Right. And they could still be at the top of the mountain, which means we need to take a different way back up. If anyone is up there, they're going to have some questions to answer."

14. Ringgold

"It's done," Porter said into his phone.

He sat in his SUV, staring at the people going in and out of a local diner. No one would think anything of him, not in this little town. If people were nosy, it was with their neighbors, not strangers.

The explosives he and his men set had caused the cave entrance to collapse, trapping Wyatt and Schultz behind a wall of rock and dirt that would take a rescue crew more than a week to get through. With no other means of escape, their death was a certainty, and Porter's employer would be safe, as would his operation.

Porter waited for the man on the other end to say something affirming, a compliment perhaps. It wasn't necessary and Porter certainly didn't need it, though he did expect something along those lines.

Instead, he received more questions.

"Are you sure?" the man's voice said through the earpiece.

"Yes, I'm sure. Our friends Mr. Wyatt and Mr. Schultz had an unfortunate spelunking accident. Those things happen from time to time. I guess they should have had an experienced guide with them."

There was another pause before the other man spoke up again.

"I won't ask for too many details. I just need to know you're absolutely certain they will not be a problem again."

"They won't. I can assure you."

"Good, because after the fiasco in Washington, I'm starting to wonder if I brought on the right man for the job."

Porter frowned. *Fiasco? What fiasco?*

"I'm sorry?" he said. "I'm afraid I don't know what you're talking about."

"You should be. Your man in the castle failed. The piece is still in play."

Porter knew what the code meant. The castle was Washington, DC. And the piece was the president of the United States.

He'd sent one of his best assassins to take out President Dawkins. As far as Porter knew, that asset had never failed a mission before and claimed twenty-three confirmed kills. Sure, taking out the leader of the free world was a tall order, but Porter knew his man was capable.

"What happened?" Porter asked.

"I'm not sure. You tell me. I wasn't there. All I've heard so far is that there was some kind of mechanical gun on site. The weapon fired, but someone dove on the president seconds before bullets tore the podium apart."

That wasn't good. Dawkins would be even more difficult to take out now that someone had made an attempt on his life. The president's security was already top flight. It would be impossible to get close to him for the foreseeable future. One detail about the story stuck out in Porter's mind.

"You said someone got the president out of the way in the nick of time."

"That's right," the man on the other end of the line said. "He was lucky. And that makes us unlucky."

Porter ignored the quip. "Who was the hero? One of his Secret Service men?"

"No. It was a woman. I don't have a name yet. My men are working on it, going through the surveillance footage as we speak."

"A woman?" Porter was surprised.

"Yes. I don't know anything else about her, but we will soon enough."

"I'll figure it out, sir."

"Don't bother. Stay on standby. Now that Wyatt and his partner are out of the way, I'll be handling things from here on out."

The comment blindsided Porter. Up to that point, he'd done everything his employer asked. Now he was being pulled off the job? The notion sent a fire through Porter's veins.

"I'm sorry? What did you say, sir?"

The other man only waited a second to respond. "I said I will be handling things now. Remain on standby until further instruction. I'll call you if and when you're needed again."

Before Porter could say anything else the call

ended. "Hello? Sir?" He looked at the screen, confirming his employer had hung up.

His jaw clenched, and he ground his teeth.

"What's our next move, sir?" one of his men asked.

Porter spun around and faced the two guys standing by the SUV.

"Our friend no longer needs our services. At least for now. Our orders are to stand by and wait."

The two men looked at each other and then back at Porter. "Okay. What about our money?"

Their employer hadn't said anything about payment, a fact that Porter was unable to bring up due to the brevity of their conversation.

"Your money will be deposited in your accounts as usual. I would assume by the end of the week."

He waited to see if they bought the lie. There was no way of knowing if the money would be put in their accounts or not. If it wasn't, however, then there would be trouble. And they would bring it to their employer's doorstep if necessary.

"What should we do, then?" the other guy asked. He had a head of spiked black hair that bristled in the chilly wind.

Porter stared out across the hills and mountains. His eyes narrowed against the biting cold.

"He said there was trouble in DC. I say we go back there to wait. Maybe something will come up. If it does, we'll be close by and ready to go."

15. Bowie, Maryland

The cop stared up from the hole in the ground.

His hands were tied behind his back. His ankles were bound as well. He'd been stripped of his shoes and socks. His feet and toes were almost numb from the cold. The same duct tape used on his appendages had been slapped across his face as a makeshift gag in case the notion of calling out for help went through his mind.

He blinked his eyelids rapidly against the bright light. A figure was standing over him. At first, it was nothing more than a woman's silhouette, looming like a dark apparition in the snowy woods.

He struggled to turn his head right and left, suddenly realizing where he was: a shallow grave in a forest.

He squealed and screamed, but the noises were muffled by the duct tape. He tried to squirm and wiggle his way free, but the binds on his hands and feet were too tight.

After a minute of failed efforts, he let his head hit the dirt. He breathed heavily through his nose and stared up at the ghost hovering over him.

"Are you going to stay quiet?" the woman asked. "Or do I need to keep that tape over your mouth?"

He made several muted sounds that she took to mean he would do as told.

"Because if you start screaming for help or try something stupid, I'm going to bury you alive. Understand?"

"Mmm-hmm," he said.

His eyes dripped with fear.

She jumped into the grave, planting her feet on either side of his hips. When she did, the light shifted, bringing her face into full view.

It was the woman from the alley.

She reached down and jerked the tape off his face like a Band-Aid.

He let out a painful whimper.

"I hope you dug two of these graves," he spat. "You have no idea who you're messing with, lady."

Her eyebrows raised. "Oh? Because from where I'm standing, it looks like I'm messing with a dirty cop."

His head twisted back and forth slowly. "No. You don't understand. The people I work for aren't the types to accept failure. You might as well kill me now because they will. And they'll kill you, too."

Adriana leaned over close enough that he could smell the light, flowery scent of her perfume.

"That's a good start," she said in a cool tone.

The cop frowned. "What do you mean, a good start? Didn't you hear what I just said? They're going to kill you, lady. You're dead. If I was you, I'd get as far away as possible. And even then, that's not far enough. They'll find you. There's nowhere you can go where they won't get to you. Do you understand me? They control everything."

"It's a good start because you're already talking about what I want to know."

"What?"

"Don't stop now," she said, standing up straight. "You're on a roll. Tell me. Who do you work for?"

"You want to know who I work for? Why? So you can go after them? Think again. No one goes after them because they're everywhere and everyone. Just when you think you can trust someone, you find out they're in on it, too."

"Who do you work for?" she asked again. "Tell me everything you know."

He shook his head vigorously. "No. No way. There's nothing you can do to make me talk. Anything you could do to me, they'll do ten times worse. And then they'll do it to everyone I know."

"Oh," Adriana said in a mock sympathetic tone. "You have a family? Wife and kids?"

"N-no," he stammered.

She wasn't sure if she believed him, so she applied a little pressure to his groin with the heel of her boot.

"Ah!" he yelled. "I'm telling you the truth! I don't have any family. My parents died years ago. I was married once, but we never had kids."

She let off the pressure and cocked her head to the side. "I believe you," she read the name tag next to his badge, "Officer Einhorn. That's an interesting name."

"I hope when they find you, they peel the skin from your bones."

Her face contorted to a frown, and she resumed the pressure on his private parts.

He screamed again and tried to turn over, but she was too strong.

"That's not very nice," she said. "And it's an especially terrible thing to say to a lady."

"You can go to—ah!" He yelled as she pressed her foot down harder.

"That's also not a nice thing to say to a lady. For someone so mouthy, you're doing very little talking about what I want to hear."

She climbed out of the hole and disappeared from view for a second.

"Do whatever you want to me," he said, gasping for air. He was momentarily relieved to not have a boot crushing his testicles. "It won't make a difference. You'll never get to them."

Adriana returned with a pair of yellow cables hanging from one hand and a box in the other. When she squatted down next to the grave, the cop could see what she was holding.

"How much do you know about electricity?" she asked.

He wiggled again, fighting against the bonds on his hands and feet.

She didn't wait for an answer. "It's a fascinating thing. I've been shocked by it a few times myself. Nothing major. Mostly just static electricity from touching a doorknob. There were a few times, though, that really hurt. Did you know, for example, a motorcycle spark plug can send a

significant jolt through your body? Feels like a
giant finger flicked you."

As she spoke, she connected the jumper cables
to the battery and then dropped the other ends into
the grave. She reached behind her back and picked
something up. It was a bowl.

She placed it in the grave next to his bare feet
and then stared at him. The pause allowed his
anxiety to build.

"You don't scare me," the cop said, doing his best
to sound brave. "I've been tased before. We all have
to go through that just to carry a Taser."

Adriana pouted her lips, pretending to be
impressed. "Oh. Well, maybe this won't hurt as
much as I thought. Still...I went through the
trouble of getting it at the auto parts store, and I'd
hate to waste money. Should probably give it a try,
just in case."

She took one of the cables and dipped it into the
big bowl. Then she grabbed his feet and dunked
them into the water. The liquid was warm
compared to the freezing air temperatures, but
Officer Einhorn didn't take any comfort from that
fact.

He started shaking violently, trying to get his
feet out of the water and maybe—if he was lucky—
knock the bowl over entirely.

Adriana drew a pistol out of her coat and pointed
it at the cop's knee. "Stop struggling. You're
spilling my water, and I don't want to have to put
more in there. If you don't, I'll blow off your

kneecap, which is probably more painful than the electrocution you're about to endure, and certainly more permanent."

He froze, staring up at her like a chastised child with a frightened look on his face.

"That's better," she said.

Adriana bent down and picked up the tape. Then she hopped back in the grave and stood over him, dangling the silver adhesive strip over his head.

"Before I put this back on your mouth and start shocking you, is there anything else you'd like to say? Anything? Names would be good. Places, bank routing and account numbers, previous atrocities committed by this mysterious *them* you keep talking about?"

The cop's head trembled, but he kept his lips sealed.

"Very well. I guess we do this the hard way."

She crouched over him and started to strap the tape to his mouth when he pursed his lips and spit on her face.

Adriana winced then wiped the saliva on her sleeve. She shook her head. "That wasn't very nice. And to think I was just about to let you go." The last comment was a lie, but he didn't need to know that. It was just one more needle under his skin.

She slapped the tape onto his mouth as he tried to hurl profanities and insults. Soon, the words were muted, coming out as mumbled gibberish.

"Feel free to scream as much as you want," she said. "From what I know about this sort of thing, it's going to hurt quite a bit."

Adriana climbed out of the hole again and picked up the second cable. She held it over the bowl of water while the cop kicked around, trying to get his feet out.

"I thought I told you not to do that," she said. "Oh well. I guess you'll learn with a bit of voltage going through your body."

She lowered the cable closer to the bowl, letting the tension build.

Einhorn screamed as loud as he could. She wasn't sure what he was saying, but the desperate noises sounded like he was trying to say, "I'll talk."

"You ready to talk now? Is that it?"

He nodded his head as fast as possible. His eyes boiled over with terror.

"Good."

She set the cable on the ground next to the hole and tore the tape from his mouth again.

"Yes!" he said. "Yes! I'll tell you everything you want to know. Just...just don't do this." His voice trembled on the verge of sobbing.

"That's much better. Now tell me. Who do you work for? Why did they want the president dead?"

"I...I don't know why they wanted the president dead," the cop muttered.

She tilted her head to the side and pressed the gun into Einhorn's kneecap.

"Honest!" he shouted. "I swear! I don't know why they want him dead. He must have stumbled onto something he wasn't supposed to see.

Dawkins is a puppet, okay? Just like you and me. You think you live this life based on your own free will and your hopes and dreams? Doesn't work that way, lady. They run everything. Everything! You don't cross a street without them knowing about it."

"Who? Who is behind all this?"

"I don't know who is pulling all the strings."

Her finger tensed on the trigger.

"I'm telling the truth. Me and the others, we got a call about the guy who tried to kill the president."

"A call from who?"

His head twisted back and forth. "I don't know his name. We don't know any names. All I know is when they call, I have to answer."

"And this mystery caller sent you to take out the assassin?"

The cop nodded. "Yes."

"Why? Wasn't that guy on the same team?"

Einhorn snorted a laugh. "Yeah, but these guys aren't the types to leave loose ends lying around. Our orders were to take him out, and if any of our own were causing problems...well, you saw what we did."

She did see. For all his talking, though, this cop was being relatively unhelpful. She needed to expedite things.

"Who do you work for?" she said, redirecting the conversation back toward what she hoped would be useful information.

"I don't know who they are."

His words drew her ire, and she reached up to grab the cable. Holding it over his feet, she stared blankly into his eyes. "I can see you don't know anything. Sorry, Officer."

Her fingers loosened on the cable, and it dropped toward the water.

"No! Wait!" he yelled. She clutched the yellow wire coating before the clamp hit the liquid.

"What is it now?" she shouted at him. "You keep stalling like someone is going to come to your aid. We are in the middle of the Patuxent Refuge. No one is around to hear you scream."

A puzzled expression washed over his face for a moment. "What's with the duct tape, then?"

"For my own sanity. Now tell me everything. And no more stalling."

He gasped for air for another ten seconds before he spoke again.

"They're the Knights of the Golden Circle. They run everything, own everything, and everyone. Okay?"

"Knights of the Golden Circle? The same group behind the Lincoln assassination?"

"Yes. Yes," he said with a voice full of desperation. "The very same."

She shook her head. Growing up in Spain, Adriana's knowledge of United States history was scattered at best. She'd read enough books on the subject of Lincoln's murder to know a little about the KGC. The last thing she remembered reading was that they'd ceased to be active in the years following the Civil War.

"That order hasn't been around in more than a century."

A sickly laugh escaped the cop's lips. He shook his head at her like she'd just made the most ridiculous statement of all time.

"That's exactly what they wanted everyone to think. Meanwhile, behind the curtain, they pulled all the strings."

Adriana's head turned side to side. "That doesn't make sense. The KGC was working with the Confederacy."

Einhorn shook his head. "Yeah. Of course they were. But when they saw there'd be no beating the Union...well, you know the old saying."

Things still weren't adding up. Adriana wondered how much of what was coming out of the man's mouth was truth and how much was a lie. She pushed through the doubt and kept him talking.

"Why would they work with the Union? It was against everything the Confederacy stood for, everything the South wanted."

"No," the cop shook his head. "The Confederacy, the KGC, all of them wanted the same thing."

"And what was that? Money?"

"Sure, money. It's the great driver of all things, isn't it? But behind the quest for money is a search for something else."

"Power," she said, realizing where he was going with all this.

"Bingo. The KGC knew the South's cause was done. There was no way they were going to win the war. So, they joined the winning side, infiltrated the government, and spread like a virus."

Adriana let the information sink in.

The Knights of the Golden Circle, an old secret society from the South, was behind the Dawkins assassination attempt and—according to this guy— behind a great many other things as well. If what he was saying was true, their reach could be unending.

"CIA? FBI?" she asked.

"NSA, you name it. They've got their fingers in all the pies. Even the police."

"Why Dawkins? Why kill the president? You said he must have found something."

"Look, lady, I have no idea why they wanted to kill the president. Like I said, he must have found something on them. What that could be, I have no idea. I swear. I'm just a low-level errand boy for them. They don't tell me much, almost nothing. I just get a little bonus money every quarter for doing as they say."

"So, you sold your soul to the devil."

"Did you hear anything I said? They own everything. These aren't the kind of people you say no to. You either get on board, or they erase you. Simple as that."

Adriana crossed her arms. "Like you did with your cop friend and the would-be assassin?"

His eyes wandered away from her, focusing

somewhere in the treetops for a moment.

"Oh, grow up. You think that's the worst thing we've done for them? We all know the score. We know what happens. When you're in, you're in. And you only get out when they say so."

"Sounds like an uncertain way to live life. Never know when the guy next to you is going to stab you in the back."

He returned his gaze to her, his eyes mere slits. "Life is uncertain, sweetheart. You might as well get something for your trouble while you're here."

"Mmm," she said with a nod. "That's a good point. And this whole talk has been great, except you haven't really told me anything. Have you? This entire time you've been jabbering all you've given me is something I could have read on some crackpot's blog. So, you know what? I think we're done here. Honestly, I'm shocked. Actually, that would be you."

She dangled the cable over the water, nearly skimming the surface.

"No! Please! There's one more thing I can tell you!"

"It better be good," Adriana said. "I'm done wasting my time with you."

His lips quivered. She wasn't sure if it was from fear, the cold, or both. Probably both.

"All...all I know is they're trying to hide something. Okay? I don't know what it is, I swear."

"Hiding something?"

"Yeah. Something they found a long time ago.

None of the people in charge have told me what it
is. I've only ever heard rumors. Whatever it is
they're hiding...it's big. Supposedly, it's the source
of the KGC wealth and power."

Adriana narrowed her eyes, sizing up the cop's
story. What could the Knights be keeping from
public view? This guy clearly didn't know much
about it.

"I feel like you're just shoveling myths that you
and your buddies sling around at the poker table."

"No! Please! I'm telling the truth. They found
something in the 1800s, somewhere in Alaska.
Okay? I don't know where it is. Like I said, I've
only heard the rumors myself, but according to
what I've heard, it's how the KGC are what they are
today."

"So, they found a big gold deposit? Some kind of
ancient treasure?"

"All of that...and more."

"More?"

He nodded eagerly. "Yes. They say there's some
kind of power generator, something that makes
gold."

And now they were back in left field again.
"Sounds like you're talking about alchemy,"
Adriana said with a derisive look.

"I know. It's crazy. I'm just telling you what I
know. That's what you wanted."

His eyes suddenly fixed on a spot over Adriana's
shoulders, high in the trees. His body shook
violently. Veins popped out of his forehead and his

neck like he was straining hard against something.

Then his body went limp.

"Officer Einhorn?" Adriana said, bending down to see what was the matter.

She let go of the jumper cable, allowing it to fall into the water bin. She'd been bluffing the whole time. The battery hadn't been charged yet.

She pressed two fingers to the man's neck. No pulse. She pulled up one sleeve on his shirt to repeat the examination on his wrist. At the base of his hand, an eye was tattooed on his skin. She looked at it closely and realized it was covering up a surgical scar. A half inch farther up the forearm was a little bump just under the skin. It was about the shape of a pill. The tattoo was one she recognized: the Eye of Horus. From what she recalled of her studies regarding ancient Egypt, the eye was used as a symbol of protection. What that had to do with this guy, she wasn't sure.

Adriana snapped her head around, scanning the surrounding forest. No one was there, at least not that she could see. Someone had just killed her prisoner from a remote location. She wondered how many people had similar devices installed under their skin.

The rabbit hole had just gotten deeper.

16. Chattanooga, Tennessee

"We have to look at the facts so far," Sean said. He turned his head one way and then the other, eying the other faces in the little coffee shop.

Chattanooga's south side had turned into a trendy place for bars, restaurants, and coffee shops. It was also a great place to lie low since there were few traffic cameras around and he knew relatively few people in that part of the city. That wasn't to say he would let his guard down.

"Right. And we need to get this to a lab," Tommy said, tapping a finger on the top of the metal box.

They'd debated opening the thing in the car, but decided not to risk it. Whatever was inside could be delicate and easily destroyed, especially in a vehicle.

"Honestly, right now we don't know who we can trust except each other."

"Well, and the ladies."

"True. My point is we may not get a better opportunity than right here."

Tommy looked mortified. "You mean open it here? In this coffee shop?"

Sean surveyed the room again. "Yeah. Nothing but a bunch of hipsters and freelancers in here. It's clean enough. Doubt we'll do better anytime soon."

He took a sip of his cortado, letting the nutty

flavors swirl around on his tongue before he swallowed.

Tommy was still hesitant. He panned the room as well to make sure no one was watching or listening. He returned his gaze to Sean and leaned across the table, bracing himself on his elbows.

"It's not the ideal place," he said.

"I know. Here's the other thing to consider. We could walk out that door right now and be scooped up by dirty cops or worse...CIA, NSA, you name it."

Tommy licked his lips as he stared at the box. "Okay," he said. "We do it here. Just do me a favor, and put your coffee on that table next to us." He set his cup on the table to the right. Sean did as told, placing his cortado next to Tommy's drink.

Tommy took a deep breath and sighed slowly as he centered the tin container on the table in front of him. He worked his fingernails under the lid and paused.

"You're sure you want to—"

"Just open it," Sean said. "We might not get another chance."

Tommy swallowed and nodded. "Okay, here goes."

The lid was on tight, sealed not only by the previous owner but also by time. His knuckles turned white as he pulled hard.

"Need me to get it?" Sean asked with a playful smirk.

The top of the box popped free, and they both held their breath for a second.

"No," Tommy said, returning the smirk. "I got it."

They leaned over and stared into the container.

An old piece of parchment was folded inside. The two friends glanced at each other and then returned to the box's contents.

Tommy took a dry napkin from the table and bent it between two fingers. Carefully, he reached into the container and pinched the parchment between the folds of the napkin, lifting it out with delicate precision.

"Spread out a couple of napkins on this table," Tommy said. "We don't know what kind of chemical residue might be on it from cleaning."

Sean did as told and hurriedly spread out two napkins flat on the surface.

Tommy eased the parchment down onto the makeshift tablecloth and let it go. He took another quick look around the room to make sure no one was watching before he picked up another napkin and pinched one corner of the parchment.

"I really need gloves for this," he said.

"I know, pal, but you're doing great."

Tommy had done this sort of thing hundreds of times. Usually, though, it was in a controlled, dry environment in their labs in Atlanta.

He ever-so-gently peeled back the first fold in the parchment, overly aware that the slightest mistake could tear the page or remove a layer that might contain valuable information. When the first fold was done, he sighed with relief and set to work on the next fold.

Tommy repeated the process two more times before the entire parchment was unfolded and laid out on the table.

The two friends stared at it in awe. The ink had faded to near invisibility over the years and was barely readable.

"It's a note," Tommy said. "Looks like some kind of journal entry."

"Without the journal."

"Hard to make out what it says. Cursive is hard enough to read when it hasn't gone through 150 years of fading."

Sean scooted his chair around so he wasn't attempting to read the parchment upside down. He leaned around the table corner, squeezing close to Tommy.

They read the note silently.

The rebs are on our trail, and we're running low on fuel. We have the map and the location of the thing the rebels were looking for. We will have to abandon the mission soon. I've given the map to Knight. Andrews asked Knight and me to split up since we're the fastest runners. I have the difficult task of going back to the South toward Atlanta. There I will attempt to blend in until I can secure transport back to Northern lines.

The plan is simple. Knight is to get the map to Secretary of State Seward. This note is for President Lincoln. If either of us fails, we are to hide our half somewhere safe.

The map Knight carries is useless without this note. Likewise, this note is useless without his map. We did this to ensure the rebs wouldn't easily find the location of the artifact.

I pray we are successful.

Sean and Tommy finished reading the main passage and then looked at a strange sequence of letters at the bottom.

C S E M N

D N L

"Code," Sean said.

"Two lines. Mostly consonants."

"What would you give to buy a vowel right now?" Sean joked.

"Right. Even if we moved all those letters around in a thousand different ways, it won't spell anything coherent."

"I guess that's what the writer meant when he said without the map this note is useless."

"Must be," Tommy agreed. "And what's with the hole here in the middle of the page?"

Offset by a few inches from the parchment's center was a little hole poked into the note.

"I guess it degraded with time. Weak spot in the material?"

"Maybe," Tommy said. "But usually when something deteriorates, it's a lot less uniform. This almost looks like it was done on purpose."

They stared at the parchment for another minute, analyzing every inch of it to make sure they hadn't missed anything. The espresso machine at the bar squealed as the barista made another cappuccino. The door swung open, letting a short burst of cold air into the warm shop. Sean's and Tommy's eyes shifted immediately to the entrance. A blonde woman in a parka stood in the doorway, looking up at the menu.

"This is great reading and all, but we still have nothing to go on," Sean said.

"I know. It would be helpful if we knew who this Knight person was."

Sean pulled out his phone and tapped his search engine app. The Wi-Fi in the coffee shop was free and anonymous. It was highly doubtful anyone would be tracing his search, especially from a temporary phone. That didn't mean he wasn't aware of everything going on around him. Every twitch, every sound, every subtle movement passed through Sean's sensory field.

He typed the keywords into the bar and then hit the search button. It only took a second for the first results to start filling his screen.

"Internet is so fast here," Tommy said. "I wish we had the gigabit fiber in Atlanta."

"Fastest in the world," Sean said with a hint of pride. He scrolled down until he saw a promising link and tapped it.

"So, you searched for Knight and Andrews' Raiders?"

"Mmhmm. Maybe we can see a list of the guys in his unit. If so, we should be able to track down this Knight character."

The website on the screen featured a historical account of the Great Locomotive Chase. It talked about how Andrews and his men infiltrated Atlanta, blending in with the Southerners until the day they stole the train. Sean skipped through all that until he found a chart with a list of several names. One of them was James Andrews.

"There," Tommy said, pointing at one name in the left column.

"That's gotta be him," Sean said. "William Knight."

"Says he was one of the ones who escaped."

"Yep. The question is, where did he go?"

"On it," Tommy said as he whipped out his phone and started searching while Sean continued to read.

"It's crazy how all this happened right in our backyard," Sean said. He hit the back button and tapped on one of the other links, continuing to search for more information about Knight and the Raiders.

"Yep. Lot of history around us from Atlanta to Chattanooga. Pretty amazing." Something caught Tommy's attention, and he held up his screen for Sean to see. "This says Knight is buried in Stryker, Ohio. Must be where he's from."

"Good. Keep looking into that. I'm trying to see if I can find anything about Seward and Knight."

They continued staring at their phones for the next 10 minutes, occasionally scrolling down a page or starting a new search. Patrons of the coffee shop came and went, none paying any attention to the two men buried in their devices.

"Any luck?" Tommy asked, rubbing his eyes.

"No," Sean said. "Nothing. You'd think that one of the heroes of the Civil War would have a picture with the president or something. I can understand maybe nothing with Seward, but come on. College football teams get to meet the president at the White House. You'd think there'd be something about Knight and his comrades with the president."

"Maybe it was too much of a hassle to get them there. Photographs were still in their infancy back then. If there was one taken, there's a good chance it's been lost for a long time. That or people who contribute to the internet haven't thought about putting it up yet." Tommy's theory was probably correct. The internet was full of useful information, but all of it was uploaded by human hands, which meant there were still tons of information out there just sitting around in archives, vaults, and probably waste bins.

"I doubt there are a lot of searches for William Knight with William Seward in the images function," Sean said.

The two continued looking through dozens of web pages for another twenty minutes before Tommy stopped and looked up from his phone.

"I can't find a thing. When you were in Auburn, you didn't see anything like a map in the museum, did you?"

Sean thought about it for a moment. He'd been to the Seward museum several times while he was working on the project. And he'd seen lots of maps. There were a couple on display, but he hadn't thought anything of it at the time.

"Yes, there were a few."

"Any of Alaska?"

Sean lowered his head, giving Tommy a look of haughty derision. "Obviously. The Alaska Purchase was kind of his signature thing in history."

Tommy just stared at him.

"Sorry. Yes, there were maps of Alaska."

"And were any, say, the size of this parchment paper?"

Sean ran through his memory banks, searching for an image of a map that would have been that size. As strong as his memory was, he didn't recall enough details to warrant a firm answer.

He shook his head. "Sorry, man. I know there were some maps there in the museum, but I can't remember the sizes of them. I know there was one or two that probably could be that size. I just didn't pay enough attention to them to really remember. I guess I was too focused on other things." He eyed his friend with suspicion. "Why? What's in your head?"

Tommy moved the parchment around and stared at the center of the note. "I'm just wondering. This message says Knight took a map and was supposed to meet Seward with it. That's kind of a strange decision to make."

"Not if you assume those soldiers knew he was interested in Alaska. More likely, their orders were to deliver it to Seward in person."

"Right. So, for a second, let's assume that the map Knight took Seward had similar letters as these in the bottom corner."

"Would make sense," Sean said, following his friend's logic. "Then the letters could be combined to make a coherent message. I'm guessing there are more vowels on the map than on this thing."

Tommy agreed with a nod. "Yes, and I'm betting there's something else about this document and the Seward map."

"I'm enthralled."

Tommy ignored the barb. "What if this parchment fits over top of the map and that hole points to the exact location?"

He waited to hear his friend lambaste the notion, but the insults never came. Sean leaned back and crossed his arms, staring with new eyes at the parchment. Slowly, his head began to rock back and forth.

"Yes. I think that is exactly their intention," he said. "It makes perfect sense."

"Really?"

"Absolutely. That hole could be like the X that marks the spot on a treasure map. And the letters must be a name of a mountain, a river, some sort of way point they could identify."

The two went silent for a second.

They continued gazing at the parchment for a

moment and then simultaneously looked up at each other.

"We need that map," they said together.

"How much cash you have on you?" Sean asked.

"Few hundred bucks. You?"

"About the same."

"That should be enough to get us up to New York, but after that we'll have to wash dishes to get anywhere else. Or shovel snow."

Sean raised an eyebrow. "Won't be a problem."

"Really? You don't mind doing a little manual labor to get some travel cash?"

A snort escaped Sean's nose. "No, dummy. I keep an extra stash of money, passports, that sort of thing in my condo here in the south side. I'll have more than enough to get us where we need to go. That is, if you can accept driving in a car all the way to western New York. I know you've grown accustomed to the plush life of flying around in your private jet."

"I never heard you complaining about it."

Sean laughed again. "Fair enough."

Tommy had another question. "About the car," he said. "Should we ditch it? I mean, those plates are probably on some kind of watch list."

"Not to worry. We can take my spare. I keep it in the garage at the condo."

"Yeah, but it's registered to you. We'll end up having the exact same problem."

Sean's head turned side to side. "Nope. I've got spare plates, too."

Tommy eyed his friend. "Sometimes I wonder if I even know who you are."

Sean's lips stretched to both sides. "I'm your buddy the spy, that's who."

The two packed up their few belongings and walked out the door onto the sidewalk. Main Street was full of busy people driving in both directions to their morning appointments and destinations. The sidewalks were less crowded, dotted with only a few pedestrians here and there, bundled in thick coats and scarves as they walked hurriedly along in the cold.

The two friends made their way over to the car and a moment later drove off, heading to Sean's condo three blocks away.

They never saw the blond Russian sitting in the corner of the coffee shop, listening to their conversation.

As they revved up the car, Yuri stepped outside and casually slipped into his vehicle near the curb. He started the engine and watched them drive away, turning left on the next street up.

Yuri wasn't in a rush. They weren't going far, and he'd be able to find the car again in the small south side area. While the two Americans were in Wyatt's condo, he'd place a homing device on both cars just to make sure they could be tracked no matter which vehicle they chose to use.

He stepped on the gas and merged into traffic, turning left on the same street Wyatt had taken.

Yuri's plan was working perfectly.

17. Washington

Adriana stepped through the door of her hotel room. None of the lights were on, so the room was blanketed in near total darkness. The curtains covering the windows only let in the slightest glimpse of streetlights below.

She tossed her keys onto the chair at the corner near the bathroom and collapsed on the bed. Her lips flapped as she blew air through them.

It had been a crazy day.

The president had nearly been killed, and in the process so had she.

Then there was the issue in the alley with the dirty cops, the double homicide, and then her narrow escape that ended in another cop being killed, though how that one happened she still wasn't sure. Her best guess was a device implanted in Einhorn's skin released a poison into his body.

But who pressed the button to make that happen?

There were more questions than answers at this point, and she needed some rest. Traveling from Spain to the United States on top of all the other activity had worn her out.

Adriana stared at the ceiling and then closed her eyes. She needed to take a shower, a long hot one. Her eyelids, however, begged her to forgo the shower and just fall asleep right then and there.

The temptation along with the fatigue pulled on her consciousness.

She let out a long sigh and opened her eyes, deciding to get up and take the shower tonight rather than wait until the morning. She'd sleep better if she was cleaned up a bit.

She saw a shadow move across the room.

Fear surged through her. She shot up out of the bed, but it was already too late. Another shadow zipped by in the darkness.

"Who's there?" she asked as she jumped off the mattress.

The only answer she received was a black bag slipping over her head.

She struggled to pull it off, but the hands holding it were too strong.

"What do you want?" she shouted. "Let me go!"

Adriana remembered her training. She'd been in situations like this before going all the way back to when she learned to defend herself as a child. Her martial arts instructor had put her in a scenario much like this one, where she couldn't see anything and had to fight her way out.

She sensed the figure directly behind her and drove her elbow back. The bone dug into the man's abdomen, and he grunted in pain.

She felt someone approaching from her front and, as she felt the footsteps draw close, fired a jab at what she approximated was neck or face level.

Her fist landed on something smooth and hard—

the other attacker's jaw. Another hand grabbed her right arm, and she whipped the left one around to strike the next assailant but someone else grabbed the wrist and jerked it behind her.

"Too afraid to fight a woman?" she spat.

"Calm down, Miss Villa," a sinister masculine voice said. "You need to get some rest."

She heard something that sounded like the opening of a can of tennis balls, then everything started spinning. She couldn't see the room, but her equilibrium failed. Her eyelids immediately began dragging across her eyes, and there was nothing she could do to stop it.

Adriana started to fall back on the bed. She never felt the hands catch her in the darkness.

* * *

"Ah!" she said with a start. She woke up in a dimly lit room on a cot pressed up against the corner.

The concrete walls were painted a redundant gray, and a single fluorescent light stretched across the center of the ceiling. Her head ached, though she didn't feel a bump or bruise. It was more like a hangover from too much wine.

She winced as she rubbed her eyes. Sitting up in the cot, she took inventory of the sparse decor. The makeshift bed was the only furniture in the room. The metal door to her right looked like it was made for a prison, or an asylum. She hoped it wasn't either.

A camera hung from the far corner, pointing

right at her position. She looked up at it with a disdainful scowl. "Where am I?" she asked.

The door unlocked and opened.

Four men in black suits, white shirts, black ties, and sunglasses walked in. Two stood by the door. The other two positioned themselves close to the cot, one on either end.

"You the guys who knocked me out and brought me here?" she asked. Her Spanish accent grew stronger when she was angry.

None of them answered.

She swung her legs off the bed, bracing herself with her hands pressed into the mattress. Even though her brain was still in a fog, she was ready to put a beatdown on these guys.

"Don't feel like talking? Fine. Maybe you're ready for a fair fight after all. Which one of you got the elbow to the midsection? I'll let you throw the first punch."

"Please don't hurt any of my men," a familiar voice said from the hallway. "They are some of the most highly trained and skilled fighters in the world, but I'm not sure they're ready for what you can do."

President Dawkins stepped around the corner and into the room. He flashed a warm smile at Adriana.

"Mr. President," she said. Relief washed over her and filled her voice. "You're okay."

He strode across the room and wrapped his arms around her, embracing her in a big hug. He let go and put his hands on her shoulders. "I'm glad to see you're okay, too. When you disappeared, I feared the worst."

"I'm okay," she said. "Head hurts from whatever drug your guys here gave me, but I'll be fine." She twisted her head around, taking in the surroundings. "Where are we?"

"Ah, this is one of the secret bunkers under the White House. We're underground here. Way underground."

She heard what he said, but her face belied her confusion. "I don't understand. Why the secrecy? And why did you bring me here?"

"For your protection, of course."

"Protection?"

He nodded and then looked at the Secret Service man next to him. "Take your team out into the hall and wait. Oh, and Jimmy, send her in."

The bodyguard nodded. He and the other three stepped out into the hall.

"Her?" Adriana asked with a raised eyebrow.

"Yes," Dawkins said. "We needed some assistance locating you. So, I called on an old friend. She flew up from Atlanta after the shooting at the ballroom."

Adriana knew who it was before the woman appeared in the doorway.

"Hello, Adriana," Emily said, stepping across the threshold and into the little room. She shut the door behind her and crossed her arms while wearing a thin smile. "I came up as soon as I heard what happened." She pointed at the president. "John said he needed help finding you. So here you are."

Confusion still filled Adriana's face. "Why all the secrecy with the pillowcase over my head and all that?"

"We weren't sure if your room was bugged," Emily said. "If you were being watched we had to make it look like someone was taking you. My men swept the room once you were gone. There were no traces of any clandestine devices, so you should be fine. Still, we didn't want to take the chance. I apologize for the headache."

The reminder made the pain more prominent. "Thanks. That makes sense now." She turned to the president. "Sorry I attacked your men."

Dawkins chuckled. "They'll be fine, although you did give Jimmy a pretty good contusion."

"We were concerned when you disappeared for several hours after the shooting," Emily said. "No one seemed to know where you went."

Adriana nodded. "Get me an ibuprofen, and I'll tell you all about it."

As if reading her mind beforehand, Emily reached into her back pocket and pulled out a packet containing two pills. "I thought you might need that since the drug they used tends to have that effect on people."

Adriana gratefully took the pills, popped them in her mouth, and swallowed.

The president held out a bottle of water he'd

brought in with him, but Adriana waved it off.

"Thank you, I'm good," she said.

"Tell us what happened," Emily said. "We need to know everything."

Adriana nodded and looked around the room. "This room is clean, right?"

Emily and the president exchanged a knowing glance and then both nodded.

"Cleanest one you'll find."

Adriana sucked in a long breath through her nose and looked down at the floor, trying to collect her thoughts and all the information she'd gleaned from Officer Einhorn.

"What do you know?"

The president answered. "We saw the footage from the hotel security cameras. They caught you chasing a man out of the building. Street cameras weren't able to catch anything. There was a glitch in the system. They're trying to fix it now. We lost you as soon as you left the building."

Adriana bit her lower lip and nodded. "Interesting." She considered what to say first and decided to relay her story from the beginning.

"You're right about me following that guy. I don't know who he is. I just know he looked suspicious. So, I went after him. He saw me and took off down an alley. Cops cornered us. They killed him and one of the other cops."

"Wait a minute," Emily said, interrupting. "They killed one of their own."

"Mmhmm. They did it to make it look like self-defense." Saying it out loud caused her to have another thought. "That means they don't own everyone," she said to herself more than to the others in the room.

"What was that?" Dawkins asked.

Adriana snapped back to the present. "One of the cops—a guy named Einhorn—was going to take me somewhere, I assume to execute me. I'm not sure why they didn't just do it right there. I managed to escape, took the cop and his car out to the woods, and there I questioned him about everything."

"And?"

"He said he and the others...they're working for the Knights of the Golden Circle. He wouldn't tell me who he works for directly, said he didn't know any names. The only thing he would say about the KGC is that they're everywhere and own everyone."

The room fell silent. Dawkins and Emily eyed each other, probing for answers neither had.

"The Knights of the Golden Circle? That's an old secret society from the South," Dawkins said, breaking the silence. "They've not been around for over a century."

"Weren't they the ones behind the Lincoln assassination?" Emily asked.

"Yes," Adriana said. "And according to the late Officer Einhorn, they're still operating inside the government. He claimed that after the war, they decided they could do more working *with* the federal government than against it. He suggested they have connections in every branch of the government."

The president's right eyebrow lifted an inch. "You said the late Officer Einhorn. Did you—"

"As much as I may have wanted to, no, I didn't kill him. He had some kind of device embedded in his forearm, just under the skin. Must have been some kind of poison. The only thing I can figure is the device was activated remotely. One of the other cops must have had him killed when he didn't report in."

Dawkins and Emily exchanged a worried glance.

"There was something else he said, too," Adriana went on. "I couldn't get many details out of him, but he said there was some kind of ancient treasure in Alaska."

"Treasure?" Emily said.

"Yes. And he claimed there is a device that can create gold. Some kind of alchemy engine, I guess. To be perfectly honest, I don't know how much of what he said could be true or not. But he was very clear about one thing: they wanted you dead, Mr. President."

Dawkins's face was long. His cheeks sagged, and his eyes looked more droopy than usual. It was understandable. Someone had just tried to kill him with a big mechanical gun.

Emily diverted the subject to the assassination attempt. "We're still investigating, but are coming up with very few leads. The weapon found at the hotel was a remotely operated, modified AR-15 attached to a rotating tripod. They used 223 Remington rounds, otherwise known as 5.56 NATO. Those rounds are common now. No way we can trace where they came from. We hoped ballistics would tell us the rounds were exotic, but sadly that wasn't the case. No prints were pulled off the weapon. And as far as a motive is concerned, we got nothing."

"It must have something to do with what Sean's looking for," Dawkins said in an almost absent tone. "I asked Sean to look into something for me. He's been in western New York and New England the last few months investigating a letter I found in...in the Presidential Archives."

That was the first time Adriana had ever heard of such a thing. "Presidential Archives?"

"Yes," Dawkins said. "There are rumors about a secret book that the presidents pass down to their successor. The legends suggest that book contains secrets of all the presidents for the last few hundred years. I can tell you that if there is a book like that, I've never seen it. But the archives do exist, and they contain quite a few secrets. That's where I found the letter."

"Letter?" Emily asked.

"Yes. I enjoy looking through the archives. I find that going through the words and thoughts of past leaders often helps lend me wisdom to tough decisions I have to make. I'll spend an hour or two in there every week. A while back, I was looking through some documents from Abraham Lincoln when I discovered a note that seemed a bit out of place. The page was a different color than the rest and had been written in someone else's handwriting. I read the note and realized why. It was a letter from Lincoln's secretary of state, William Seward."

Emily shook her head. The president said it like reading through Abraham Lincoln's personal diary was no big deal. She moved past her amazement and stayed on topic.

"This letter, sir, what did it say?"

Dawkins looked bewildered. He waved his hands around and shook his head. "I don't remember all of it exactly. It was a few months back."

Adriana stepped closer to him. "What do you remember?"

He stared at the base of the wall, scouring his memory for details. "It said Seward's explorers had found something important in Alaska, something he called *the anomaly*. The letter didn't say what it was or exactly where it was. Whatever it was, Seward thought it was big enough to spend over seven million dollars to keep it from anyone else."

"The Alaska Purchase," Adriana said.

"Precisely. Whatever is hidden out there was scary enough to spend seven million they didn't have in the national coffers. They were still paying for the war by the time the purchase went through. The country was in a recession. The last thing we needed to do was blow a bunch of money on a giant icebox."

"There must have been a pretty convincing reason, then," Emily said.

Dawkins thought for a second. "National security," he said.

"Sir?"

"Seward suggested that the security of the nation rested upon the purchase of Alaska, that if the anomaly were to fall in the wrong hands, it would be a threat to the safety of the entire country."

His words hung in the air for a moment.

"The KGC...if they're really behind this like you said, would have their fingers in more places than we know," Dawkins said in a grave tone. Then he remembered something else. "The letter...it mentioned something about the KGC knowing about the anomaly. Seward didn't just want to hide it from the Russians or the South. He wanted to keep it safe from them, too."

"And now it would appear they have reared their ugly head and attempted to kill you, sir," Emily said.

"And burned Sean and Tommy," Adriana added.

Emily turned her head and faced Adriana with a confused expression. "What? What are you talking about?"

"Sean and Tommy," Adriana went on. "Their bank accounts have been wiped out. Sean tried to call you at Axis HQ, but they said his code didn't check out and they had no record of him being affiliated with the agency."

Emily's face turned ghostly white. From her

reaction, the other two immediately realized she had no idea what Adriana was talking about.

"Sean's been burned?"

"Yes. He has a temporary phone, as does Tommy. The kids and June also purchased burner phones in case they needed to reach out, though those three are lying low right now."

"Where are they? We need to make sure they're all right."

"Sean and Tommy or the other three?"

"All of them."

"Sean likely won't give away his location at the moment, but last I heard he was in Atlanta. I'm guessing he and Tommy are trying to figure this thing out."

"With no resources," Dawkins jumped in. "They won't get very far without money. And their cars are probably being tracked."

Adriana shook her head. A wry grin crossed her face. "I think you forget: Sean can be...resourceful."

18. Auburn, New York

The overnight drive from Chattanooga to Auburn, New York, took a little over thirteen hours. Sean and Tommy encountered little traffic in the early morning hours and were able to make better time than they expected.

It was just after 7 in the morning when they arrived. Most of the small town's citizens were headed to one of the local diners or coffee shops to get their day started with a cup of joe or plates full of eggs, pancakes, and sausage.

Sean and Tommy did their best to blend in, opting to grab breakfast at the counter of one of those local diners. No one seemed to pay them any mind, treating them as they would any out-of-towners.

After a quick breakfast of eggs, hash browns, and oatmeal, the two friends killed time milling about the village for a few hours. The museum didn't open until 10 in the morning, which was less than optimal for a couple of guys in a major hurry.

They found the town had several shops, quaint little boutiques, and some mom-and-pop restaurants, but other than that didn't have a lot going on.

When they'd exhausted the town's entertainment options, they went back to the car and waited, keeping it parked in a shaded area a few hundred feet from the museum.

The views of the town and surrounding countryside were straight out of a wintry Norman Rockwell painting. The roads had been cleared with plows and salt, but everything else had a fresh, snowy look to it. Tree branches bent under the weight of white powder. Long, pointy icicles hung from gutters, awnings, and eaves.

There were few children out and about, which told Sean and Tommy school was probably still in session.

Back in the South, school got canceled if there was a 30 percent chance of snow in the forecast, often without seeing a single flake.

Up north, they dealt with it. Life had to go on, after all.

Tommy took a nap in the passenger seat while Sean kept a lookout. It was only fair. Tommy had done most of the driving during the night since he was better at it than Sean.

After sitting in the car for nearly an hour, he looked at the clock and saw it was 10 minutes to 10.

"Hey, buddy," he said and nudged Tommy on the shoulder. "Time to go."

Tommy squeezed his eyes and then opened them wide. He rubbed his face for a second and then propped his seat upright.

"Man, I guess I was tired."

"Well, you only drove for, like, nine hours last

night, so..." Sean opened the door and stepped out onto the wet pavement.

Tommy slumped out of the car and zipped up his coat. "Yeah, I know. Back when we were in college and high school, I could do a drive like that and be ready to go the next morning, no problem. Remember that time we drove out to Colorado to go snowboarding?"

"How could I forget? We took a wrong turn and ended up in the middle of nowhere Kentucky at one point." Sean laughed and stepped onto the sidewalk. "Yeah. It was dark out, and we missed a turn."

"And snowing. It only delayed us, like, two hours."

"Ugh, I know. That was my bad."

"You looking for an argument?"

Sean shook his head. "Come on. The sooner we get in there, the better chance we have of getting a few minutes of the curator's time before the rest of the tourists."

The Seward House was originally built by a local judge, Elijah Miller, in 1816. When Seward married Miller's daughter, the judge required the newlyweds to live in his house, a requirement Sean thought strange when he first read it.

It was a beautiful, stately home and on immaculately kept grounds, though the landscaping and gardens were covered in a blanket of snow. The home's light brown walls were accented by dark brown window shutters, railing, roof and doors, giving it a look that tiptoed between Spanish villa, Mediterranean, and colonial.

The interior smelled like a museum, which made sense since most of the furnishings were original, straight from the Seward family collections passed down through the decades.

A woman in a cherry-red cardigan and a black dress stood just inside the entrance. Her name tag said she was Janice.

"Hello, and welcome to the Seward house," she said in a nasally accent. It took her half a second to realize who Sean was. "Oh, welcome back, Sean. Back for more investigations on your little project?"

"Morning," Sean and Tommy said. Their Southern drawls weren't always prevalent, but whenever they went up north the accents seemed to deepen a bit.

"Yes, ma'am," Sean said. "And I was wondering if I could meet with Mr. Johnstone for a few minutes. I have some questions regarding a few items you may have here."

"Sure thing," she said with a polite smile. "He just arrived a couple of minutes ago. He's in the office in the back. You remember where it is, right?"

Sean nodded. "Yes, ma'am. Thank you."

"Happy to help."

Sean led the way through the foyer and into the hallway where it split off in different directions. A great room with tall, ornately decorated drapes, fancy wallpaper, and plushly upholstered seats was off to one side. On the other side was a smaller sitting room with the original hearth and more chairs circling around the fireplace.

"This place is awesome," Tommy said as his head turned from side to side. He took in the splendor of the 1800s architecture and design.

"Pretty cool, huh?" Sean said. "Kind of can't believe you've never been here."

Tommy rolled his shoulders as he followed his friend back through the corridor toward the rear of the house. "Never had a reason to until now."

They arrived at a little room that was previously a pantry when the house was still used as a primary residence. Now, the door hung open revealing a small desk, chair, a few bookshelves, and a man sitting inside checking his email on a laptop.

Mr. Johnstone heard the two approaching and turned to look out the door. His head had a rim of hair around it from one ear to the other, encircling a shiny bald pate. His thick mustache bristled when he twitched his lips. He wore a tweed jacket like so many university professors might.

"Ah, good morning, Sean. Back again, I see?"

The slim museum curator stood up and shook hands with the two visitors.

"Who's your friend?"

Sean slapped Tommy on the back. "This is my friend Tommy. He's the founder of the IAA."

"Oh my. I'm so sorry. I should have known that.

You've done so much incredible historical work all over the world. I apologize."

"Trust me, it's fine," Tommy said. "I usually try to stay out of the spotlight, except when we find something big. Very few people know who I am."

"Well, I think your agency has done so many wonderful things, and I appreciate everything you do. So"—Johnstone looked from one to the other—"what brings you back to the Seward House?"

"Same reason I was here before," Sean said.

"Still looking for that lost Seward treasure?" Johnstone said with a mischievous grin.

"Sort of. I mean, we still don't know what it is we're looking for in that regard, but there's definitely something out there."

"We were hoping to take a look at any maps you might have on display, or even if you have a few in some archives that aren't available to the public," Tommy said.

"Certainly," Johnstone said, beaming with pride. "Although I don't believe we have any maps tucked away in a secret place. Our archives are relatively small. I'd be happy to check our catalog, though. Follow me. I'll show you the ones we have on display, and while you're looking at those I'll see what else we have."

"That would be great," Sean said. "Thank you so much."

Johnstone led the two through the home and up the stairs near the foyer. When they reached the top, they turned left and walked down the hall, turning right into a small room that looked like it was once an office.

"This is where Secretary Seward did most of his work. The desk and other furnishings are originals, as are the maps encased in glass over there, and there." He pointed at two display cases sitting next to each other. "You can see we had to block off the windows since sunlight would have faded everything on paper."

Sean and Tommy noticed the window on the far wall had been covered with a solid sheet of wood and then disguised with a painting of the Appalachian Mountains.

"Good thinking," Tommy said.

"Make yourselves at home. I'll be back up as soon as I find anything...or not."

"Thanks, Mr. Johnstone."

"Please, call me Gary."

The slim man strode out into the hallway with his blazer flapping behind him.

"Nice guy," Tommy said.

"Yeah, he's been very helpful. Let's take a look at these maps."

They sidled over to the display cases against the interior wall. The maps inside were clearly originals, the paper brown with age. Some of the lettering had faded a bit but not so much that the words were illegible. One of the maps was of the United States as it existed during Seward's time. Sean and Tommy noted the date in the bottom corner: *1866.*

Next to the map of the country were three additional maps, all showing the Territory of Alaska.

"It's amazing how detailed cartographers were so long ago. I have no idea how they got things so accurate," Sean said with admiration.

"You're right about that. I've always thought that was an incredible talent."

Sean pointed at the maps. "None of these would fit that note we found," he said with a hint of disappointment in his voice.

Tommy shook his head. "Nope. They're all too big. Is this all of them?"

There was one more display case in the corner. They stepped over to it and looked inside. It housed a map of Alaska, but it was much smaller than the others and too small to be the one to match the note.

They searched the rest of the room, wandering from one corner to the other until they'd exhausted all possibilities.

Tommy stared at the desk. "You don't think there's something hidden in this, do you?"

"No," Sean said with a shake of the head. "I already checked it the last time I was here."

"Johnstone opened it for you?"

Sean's cheeks flooded with red. "Something like that."

Tommy snorted. "You looked without his permission, didn't you?"

"Maybe. Doesn't matter. The point is, none of

these maps work. Let's hope Gary can find something. Otherwise, this trail is going to come to a sudden and disappointing end."

"Not to mention a wasted long drive all the way to western New York."

They hung out for another few minutes in the office, reading over some of the documents encased in glass and inspecting the desk to make sure they weren't missing a secret compartment.

When the sound of Johnstone's shoes on the wood floor began tapping their way down the hall, the two friends moved away from the desk and back to the maps, pretending to inspect them.

"Find what you were looking for, gentlemen?" Johnstone asked as he entered the room.

"No, sir." Sean shook his head. "Any luck in your archives?"

"Sadly, no. We don't have any maps tucked away in the vault. Do you know what it is you're looking for? Maybe you could give me some more details."

"I wish we had details to give," Tommy said. "All we know is it's about the size of a standard letter, maybe eight by eleven."

Johnstone thought for a minute, biting his lower lip as he looked up to the ceiling. After his momentary deliberation, he returned his eyes to the guests. "Sorry, I can't think of anything that size, and I've worked here for nearly ten years."

"Don't apologize," Sean said, pushing aside the disappointment lumping in his throat. "It's not your fault."

"Will you be needing anything else right now? I have a phone call to make."

"No, sir. Thank you," Tommy said.

"Happy to help. Wish I had what you were looking for."

Johnstone spun around and stepped out into the hall. Sean and Tommy followed, dragging their feet along the way.

They passed paintings of Seward family members down through history hanging from the walls. There were women in beautiful dresses, smartly dressed men in pristine suits and hats, and even a few of children. As the three neared the staircase, Sean caught something out of the corner of his eye and stopped.

He turned and looked at a painting that was different than all the others.

It depicted a man running out of the house, looking back over his shoulder as if afraid someone was chasing him. The home was clearly the Seward house, but the man was unidentified.

"Gary?" Sean said, stopping the curator before he took the first step down the stairs. "What's this painting?"

Johnstone did a pivot, keeping one hand on the banister. "Oh, that's a painting of the night Secretary Seward was nearly killed."

Sean took one step closer to the painting to where he stood within an arm's length of it. Tommy was next to him now, also mesmerized by the picture.

"I didn't really notice this on the way in," Tommy said.

"Me, either," Sean agreed.

"I'm sure both of you are familiar with the assassination attempt on the secretary's life the same night Lincoln was shot," Johnstone said, keeping his place on the top step.

"I know the story," Tommy said. "It was crazy how well planned the entire thing was. So many moving parts, the timing had to be perfect, and then there was the problem of security."

"Yes. The secretary actually had more security on hand than usual that night. He was in his bed recovering from a carriage accident. The would-be assassin severely hurt some of his guards and scared his wife half to death. It's a miracle Secretary Seward survived."

"Stabbed in the neck, right?" Sean asked, already knowing the answer.

"Correct. They said the knife barely missed the arteries and veins. Difficult to believe back then, with the lack of medical knowledge and technology, he was able to survive. Perhaps that's a tribute to the way people were back then. They were tougher, hardier."

"Survivors," Sean said.

"Exactly."

Johnstone turned to continue his descent with Tommy right behind him when Sean stopped them both again.

"I'm sorry, Gary. But what's this in the

painting?"

"What's what?"

Sean leaned in close to the image to stare at something in the fleeing man's hand. It looked like a rolled-up piece of paper.

"That," Sean said, putting his finger an inch from the canvas. He was careful not to touch it.

Johnstone stepped back up onto the second floor and wedged between the two visitors. He leaned in like Sean was doing and narrowed his eyes. "Oh, that. Yes. That night, witnesses said that the assassin stole something from Seward's study. No one is really sure what it was. We assume it was valuable, perhaps some bonds or a property deed. It's all conjecture at this point. Anyone who knew any details about it has been dead for a long time."

Sean straightened up and twisted his head, facing the other two. "Seems a little strange, doesn't it?"

"Strange?" Johnstone asked.

"Yeah. I mean, this guy came up here to western New York, all the way from Washington, to kill Seward. Just seems a bit odd that during what must have been a pretty rushed getaway that he'd take the time to swing by the study and steal something."

Tommy nodded. "That *is* weird."

Johnstone was the last to put the pieces together. "Are you thinking that piece of paper in the assassin's hand is the map you're looking for?"

"It's just an odd piece to the story. These guys

plan out the assassination to a T. They get all the details, know where their mark will be and when. Then one of them goes in, doesn't manage to kill a bedridden guy, hurts some of his guards, and then you would imagine flees into the night in a panic. But no, he stops on his way out and grabs something."

"Or maybe after he took out the guy at the door, he went to the study first and then attempted to kill Seward," Tommy said.

"Either way, it's fishy." Sean turned his head and faced Johnstone. He was so close he could smell the cheap aftershave on the guy's skin. "And you have no way to know for sure what that was?" he asked, pointing a finger at the painting.

"Sorry, Sean," he said, shaking his head.

Sean sighed.

"Another dead end," Tommy said.

"Unless..." Johnstone let the word linger in the hallway. The other two looked at him as if their gaze could pull the words out of his mouth.

"Unless what?" Sean asked.

The two visitors could see the wheels turning from the look in the curator's eyes. "Unless he took it back to Washington."

19. Auburn

"Back to Washington?" Sean asked.

"Yes," Johnstone said with a nod. "After Lewis Powell tried to kill the secretary of state, he took off on foot since his partner got scared and left with the horses. Somehow, Powell found a way back to Washington to their rendezvous point at Mary Surratt's boarding house. That's where he was arrested the next day. It's possible that whatever he took from here might—I reiterate, might—be hidden somewhere in Washington. Possibly even in the Surratt house."

Sean and Tommy exchanged a knowing glance.

"Yeah, except the Surratt house is a Chinese restaurant now," Sean said.

"Yes." Johnstone hung his head. "Sadly, not every historically significant building can be saved from being destroyed or turned into a sweet-and-sour palace."

The two friends chuckled.

"Most buildings like that have already been torn down or repurposed. Such a shame."

"That doesn't mean Powell didn't hide something there," Tommy said. He had a tone of hope in his voice. "If it was hidden well enough, maybe it's never been found. There's got to be a chance, right?"

Sean shrugged. "I guess so. Normally, I wouldn't have a problem with going down to DC and probing someone's restaurant for a hidden map. In this instance, though, it's going to be tricky."

"Tricky?" Johnstone asked.

"Because," Tommy quickly jumped in, "we've driven so far and haven't really slept. It's several hours back down to Washington."

"Oh. Well, in that case, you two should get a room at the inn nearby. I'm sure they'll have vacancies during this time of year. We don't get too many tourists in the dead of winter."

"Thanks," Sean said. "We'll look into it. And thank you for all your help, Gary. We really appreciate it."

"Not a problem, fellas. I need to get going. Don't hesitate to drop by again if you need." The curator started back down the steps but once more stopped and looked back at the two visitors. "You know, it's weird us talking about the Seward and Lincoln assassination, seeing what happened yesterday and all."

Tommy and Sean exchanged puzzled glances.

"What do you mean?" Sean asked.

Johnstone searched both men's faces to make sure they weren't messing with him. "The assassination attempt on President Dawkins. Everyone's talking about it. Surely, you heard."

"Someone tried to kill the president?" Tommy asked, a sudden fleck of concern seeping into his voice.

"You two really don't know?"

They shook their heads at the same time.

"We were on the road," Sean said. "Took a while to get here."

Johnstone's eyes went from one to the other and back again like he was watching the fastest tennis match ever played. "You don't listen to the radio?"

"Satellite. No commercials. No interruptions."

The curator sighed. "Well, apparently someone set up a gun in the ballroom where the president was to give a speech. They used some kind of mechanism to fire the weapon remotely. The police found a suspect in an alley not far from the hotel where it went down. Seems he was trying to get away, shot a cop, and then the other police took him down."

"He's dead?" Tommy asked.

Johnstone nodded. "Yep. He shot a cop. They took him down. Sounds like that was their guy. They found evidence on the scene that linked him to the attempted assassination along with more evidence in his apartment."

"What about President Dawkins?"

"It was the wildest thing. He was rushed out of there unscathed. Didn't even get a scratch. Some brunette charged the stage and tackled him. She saved his life. There's video footage of it on the internet. Everyone's talking about it, and no one knows who she is or where she went."

Sean's immediate thoughts went to Adriana. It had to be her. Sean and Tommy knew about the threat. So far, they'd played the ignorant role perfectly with Johnstone. That was due, in part, to the fact that they really didn't know the attempt to take the president's life had already happened. Sean was surprised at the speed with which these men operated, in spite of years working on the inside of the government. Axis always took care of things with calculated speed. Not all the other pieces were so efficient.

One thing was certain: whoever was running this operation knew exactly what they were doing.

After saying their goodbyes, Sean and Tommy returned to the frigid outside. The sun was climbing into the clear blue sky, but it did little to warm the cold town.

"Good one," Tommy said as they marched back to their car.

"Yeah, I know. Happens to the best of us."

"True, except your timing couldn't be worse."

"It won't happen again," Sean reassured him.

Tommy let the incident go. "So, the real question now is, what are we going to do? I don't exactly like the idea of going to Washington."

"Into the lion's den."

"That's what I was thinking. Seems like whoever erased all our money, our identities, whatever, is probably operating out of Washington.

"And they're on the inside, which will make things even more difficult," Sean said.

Back inside the car, the seats and steering wheel were freezing to the touch. Tommy couldn't turn on the engine fast enough.

"It's our only lead," Sean said as he rubbed his hands together to fight off the cold in his fingers. "I really don't see what other choice we have."

He took his phone out and pulled up Adriana's number. He tapped the call button and listened to the phone ringing.

"Calling Adriana?" Tommy asked.

Sean nodded. After twenty seconds, he got an automated message telling him the phone's user hadn't set up voice mail yet.

"No answer," Sean said, his voice smothered in disappointment.

"I'm sure she's fine," Tommy offered. "Sounds to me like she saved the president's life. Congratulations, buddy. Your girlfriend is a hero."

The comment did little to cheer up Sean. "I hope she's all right."

"Gary didn't say anything about her being hurt. I'm sure that would have been included in the news reports if the person who saved the president was injured."

Sean relented and gave a subtle nod. "I guess you're right."

"Of course I am." Tommy rubbed his hands together. "So, what are your thoughts on Washington?"

"The Surratt House?"

"Yep."

"I don't see any other option. I guess we have to go down there and check it out. It's not exactly my first choice. But what else can we do?"

Sean shifted the car into gear and looked back in the mirror to make sure no one was behind him. They hadn't seen many other cars since leaving the diner. Most of the town was busy at work so the streets were largely vacant. Sean started to ease the vehicle out of the parking spot and then stopped suddenly.

Tommy's head bounced on the headrest. "What?" he asked, looking over at Sean with wide eyes. "Why'd you stop?"

Sean narrowed his eyes as he stared into the mirror. His jaw clenched. "That car back there," he said. "It was there when we went in."

Tommy leaned toward his friend and peeked into the mirror. He noticed the black sedan with a figure of a man inside. "So? There are lots of cars that were probably there when we went in. People are at work or eating a late breakfast."

"No," Sean said with a shake of the head. "That guy has been sitting there longer than that. He was there when we were walking around. I noticed him in that same spot when we went to eat. He's been there all morning."

Tommy bent toward the middle of the car and looked back again. "Maybe he's reading a really good book."

Sean twisted his head, wearing the most derisive expression he could muster.

Tommy did his best to look innocent. "What? Sometimes people get lost in books. I know I do."

"For four hours in a car, in the freezing cold?"

"Okay, you may have a point. But who is he?"

Sean frowned. "That, I don't know. And I don't know why he's following us."

"Strange he hasn't tried to engage."

Sean turned his head slowly toward his friend again. "Engage?"

"Yeah, you know. He hasn't tried to get in the way of what we're doing."

"Since when did you start using words like that?"

Tommy blushed. "I don't know. About ten seconds ago, I guess."

Sean returned his gaze to the sedan. It was parked on one of the main streets. From their current vantage point, the vehicle was barely visible through the trees, bushes, and a wrought-iron fence along the property.

"Keep your eyes behind us," Sean said as he backed up and then shifted the car into drive. "Let's see if he follows us."

20. Washington

Adriana sat across the boardroom-style table, probing Emily and President Dawkins with a questioning gaze.

"I'm sure you have thought of this, sir, but how in the world did that guy get that weapon into the ballroom?" Her query was one the president had, indeed, thought about. "I figured your security teams would have gone through everywhere, checking everything multiple times."

They'd moved from the room with a cot to a makeshift boardroom. It looked much like the other, the major difference being there was a television hanging from the wall and a table in the center. Other than that, the same sterile lighting and cinder block walls were standard decor.

"They do that everywhere I go," Dawkins said. "No way they wouldn't have done it this time as well."

"That means someone on the security team either screwed up or was in on it," Emily said.

"None of my Secret Service men would have been involved. I trust every single one of them like they were my own children."

"Sometimes children disobey their parents."

The president sighed. "I see what you're saying. Believe me, I do. But these men wouldn't have had anything to do with it."

"Okay," Adriana said, "then who else was involved with making sure the ballroom and hotel were secure?"

Dawkins shook his head, bewildered. "I don't know. Maybe they had some people from the CIA and FBI go through and check it out. That would have been out of the ordinary, but not impossible."

"We need to know the names of everyone who went through that building," Emily said. "And I want to see the surveillance tapes from the previous two days before your speech."

"They're already looking at the footage," Dawkins said. He put his hand on Emily's shoulder in an attempt to ease her temper.

A knock came at the door.

"Yes?" Dawkins said.

"It's Agent Caldwell, sir."

"Come on in."

The door opened, and a tall man with mocha skin wearing a black suit and tie stepped in. He set a file down in front of the president.

"The man the police shot in the alley. He's the one behind the shooting, sir."

Dawkins opened the folder and flipped through a series of black-and-white photos.

"These from the security cameras?"

"Yes, sir," Caldwell said with a nod. "You can see he snuck into the sound booth carrying this case." He tapped on the image of the suspect carrying what looked almost like a musical instrument case.

"This was taken the morning of the shooting."

"Who is he?"

Adriana and Emily leaned closer to get a look at the images.

Caldwell hesitated.

Sensing his bodyguard's reluctance, Dawkins reassured him it would be okay. "Speak freely, Son. I trust these two every bit as much as I trust you. They'll be fine."

Caldwell nodded. "Yes, sir. His name was Special Agent Terry Kendricks."

The three at the table raised their collective eyebrows. Dawkins turned his head to look up at Caldwell.

"Which agency?"

"CIA, sir. Our team is on the phone with Langley as we speak. We'll know more in the coming hours."

Dawkins flipped the images back onto the table and leaned back in his chair. He put his hands behind his head and looked into the ceiling. "So, now we have CIA agents working against us."

"He had clearance, sir. That's how he was able to walk right into the ballroom. We still don't have a motive."

"I don't care about motives," Dawkins said. "Keep up the good work, Caldwell. Thank you."

The agent nodded and slipped back out into the hallway.

Emily and Adriana stared at the president, eager to hear what he would say concerning the new revelation.

He thought for a minute before speaking. "What we really need to know is who this guy was working for."

"Didn't your bodyguard just say he was CIA?" Emily asked.

"Yes, that's where he worked. There's more to this than meets the eye, though. CIA agents don't usually just go rogue like this. Someone else put him up to this."

He slid the images and file over to Emily so she could take a closer look.

"This was sloppy," she said after poring over the pages. "Really sloppy."

Adriana looked at the images as Emily finished each one. "Looks like he didn't care if he was spotted by the cameras."

"Right. He made no effort to hide his face or anything."

"Almost like he wanted to be caught."

"Wanted to be caught?" Dawkins asked.

Emily nodded. "Sometimes we come across those types. They commit crimes in such a way that they have almost no chance of succeeding. Have you done anything recently that would have angered someone in the CIA, perhaps given them a reason to come after you?"

"Not that I know of."

Adriana flicked her eyebrows. "I suppose it could be politically motivated, then. Maybe he just didn't like your policies."

"Could be," Emily said. "But these guys go through a number of psychological assessments before they're given a job. Their training is also extremely rigorous. If Kendricks had a screw loose, someone would have picked up on it by now."

Adriana picked up one of the photos and stared at it for a long moment. "There's a distant, vapid look in his eyes."

"Evil," Dawkins said.

"Maybe. It's also a look of someone who knows their number is up."

Emily read through his dossier and looked up at the other two. "No family. Parents are both dead. Wife left him six years ago. Never had any children."

"Sounds like the perfect trigger man," Adriana said.

"For who?" Dawkins asked.

Emily jumped on the question. "I know you have a team in place trying to figure that out, sir. If it's the same to you, I'd like to put a few of my own agents on it. I know they can be trusted. My unit is tighter than—"

"Thank you for the thought," Dawkins cut her off. "But we aren't sure Axis hasn't been infiltrated yet, either. Remember the issue with Sean?"

She'd almost forgotten. Emily blushed, embarrassed by the issue.

Dawkins reached out his hand again and put it on her shoulder. "Don't worry. I'm sure it will all come out in the wash sooner or later."

Adriana knew the relationship between President Dawkins and Emily was beyond the point of professional. They'd been seeing each other—as time allowed—for the better part of a few years. Somehow, they'd managed to keep it out of public view. Adriana wondered if they would ever take the relationship out for a spin. She had a feeling the American public wouldn't mind.

"Still, sir," Emily said, "you need someone else on this. I would be happy to investigate myself."

Dawkins looked surprised at the offer. He pursed his lips as he considered. "Very well, but take Adriana with you. You may need someone to have your back."

"Thank you, sir. We'll figure out who is behind this and bring them to justice."

"I'm sure you will."

Adriana and Emily left the room and walked down the corridor. It was lined with Secret Service on both sides every few yards all the way to the steel elevator doors at the end.

When the two women got on the elevator, Emily pressed one of the buttons. A moment later, the lift began going up.

"So, where do we start?" Adriana asked.

"I already have. Kendricks's file was clean, for the most part. He had a couple of ordinary bank accounts, a home in the suburbs, even a gym membership in spite of the fact he could work out at Langley whenever he wanted."

"You said for the most part."

"Mmhmm. I did a little digging before I came in. He had two other accounts that were less on the up and up. One was in Costa Rica. The other in Nicaragua."

"Not the Caymans?"

Emily shook her head. "That's usually the first place people think of when they want to hide money from the federal government. After the big takedown of all those guys a few years ago with accounts in Switzerland, Cayman, and Lichtenstein, it seems the new trend is to dump money in lesser-known locations."

Adriana processed the information. A dozen ideas ripped through her head. One stood out more than the others. Sean had offshore accounts. Tommy may have as well, though she knew less about his personal finances. While Sean kept a stash of money in his Chattanooga safe house, he also had a significant portion of money deposited in a Swiss bank account. She stuffed that thought back in her mind. Getting Sean's money wasn't the most important item on the docket. Finding out why Kendricks had offshore accounts was higher on the priority list.

"Can you access the Kendricks accounts?" Adriana asked.

"That's just it. Those banks are super tight when it comes to giving out access to their customers' accounts. It's why people go to them. Everyone knows that if you put money into one of those banks, they're going to keep it a secret. At least they'll do their best. That means we really have no way of figuring out where the money came from. And I'm sure whoever made the deposits—if it wasn't Kendricks—did a thorough job of cleaning up the paper trail."

"So, you don't have any way of figuring out who made the deposits?"

"I didn't say that." Emily turned her head and flashed a mischievous smirk. "Kendricks would have had associates, coworkers, maybe even some drinking buddies. First, we'll interview those people, find out more about the man. Then we can start to break down any clandestine meetings he may have had before the assassination attempt. If someone is pulling the strings, there will either be a paper trail or a list of people he had to meet. Sooner or later, the house of cards will come tumbling down."

"What if there was a way to make all that happen faster?" Adriana asked.

The elevator came to a stop, and the door opened. They stepped out into a long corridor lined with big white-framed windows. Heavy golden curtains hung on either side of each.

As they walked forward, Adriana turned her head and looked outside. The pristine White House lawn stretched down to a row of bushes and trees surrounded by a black wrought-iron fence. The grass looked like lush green carpet.

"Hold that thought until we're in my car," Emily said.

She led the way through the halls, security checkpoints, and back out to where she'd parked in a secret lot behind the presidential mansion.

Once they were in her car, she reached under the steering wheel and pressed a hidden button. A few seconds later, a voice came through the speakers. "Device check complete. No threat detected."

Adriana's eyebrows stitched together. "Was that an onboard bug detection system?"

Emily flashed a grin. "Yep. You can never be too careful. The car is clean. Finish your thought from the elevator. You were saying something about getting the Kendricks investigation done faster?"

Adriana snapped back to what she was saying. "Yes. There may be a way to hurry things up a bit."

"How do you plan on doing that?"

"Tommy's lab assistants."

Emily's interest piqued. "The kids?"

"They typically specialize in doing historical research, forensics, things like that. But they might be able to hack into one of those systems and find where the money came from."

"Sounds like a long shot."

"It is. They may not be able to help, but while we're tracking down leads, they could at least give it a try. We don't even have to tell them what it's for. I'm sure they'll be happy to help. After all, they're lying low right now and probably bored out of their minds."

Emily eased the car out onto the street and accelerated. She didn't like the idea of having

ordinary civilians help out with a case, especially
one that involved a presidential assassination
attempt.

After deliberating on the issue for a minute, she
nodded. "Okay, do it. But remember, this has to
stay quiet. No one can know they're doing this for
me or the president. Understood?"

"Absolutely. All the kids need to know is what
we're looking for. I won't tell them anything else."

Emily sighed. "Let's just hope they can find what
we're looking for before anything else happens."

21. Auburn

Yuri watched the two Americans leave the Seward museum and return to their car. He'd turned on his car's motor three times while they were inside just to warm the interior. The gauge on the dashboard said the temperature outside was only 18 degrees Fahrenheit.

He hated the cold.

Growing up in Russia, he'd spent much of his life in sub-freezing temperatures. One of the benefits of working for the government was that he got out of the country to warmer climates, occasionally even to tropical places, though those were few and far between.

Some people thought that since he'd spent his life in the cold, he would be used to it. The truth was he never grew accustomed to it. As a child, seeing his mother and sister freezing on what passed for a bed in their tiny Moscow apartment had only served to build up his distaste for winter.

There were times when snow would blow through cracks in the windows and form little piles on the creaky wooden floor. After the fall of communism, things didn't get better for many years. Food was scarce, heating fuel was even more so, and no one had much hope for anything better. And then there was his dad's reckless spending on booze.

The Western world had applauded the Russian people for dismantling the Soviet Union. It had welcomed Russia into the family of nations with open arms and promises of riches and prosperity.

Those two things never came for most Russian citizens.

Now, both of his parents were dead, and his sister was lost on the streets of Moscow. She'd never had a chance: a poor, pretty blonde girl with a toned body made an easy target for the city's seedy underworld.

The Americans' car stopped as it was backing out of its parking spot, and Yuri's attention snapped back to the moment. He kept facing forward toward a small cinema at the end of the street, carefully eying the other vehicle.

Why had the driver stopped so abruptly? Did one of the Americans forget something inside the museum? Or worse, had he been spotted?

Yuri knew that if he panicked and took off, that could send a signal to the Americans that he was watching them. So, he sat perfectly still and waited. After nearly a minute, the other car pulled out of the parking area and drove away.

When the Americans were out of sight, he picked up a tablet from the passenger seat and pressed a button. The screen flashed to life, and after a couple of seconds a map appeared with a blinking blue dot in the middle.

The dot moved down one of the streets and hung

a right, heading toward the interstate highway.

The tracking device was working perfectly. That would make following the Americans much easier. The question was, what did they find in the museum? And why did they leave after such a short visit? Yuri didn't need to know where they were headed. That answer would come soon enough.

He started the car and was about to shift into gear when he noticed the dot on the screen make another right. It was coming his direction.

Yuri frowned. *Why would they come back this way?*

The blinking dot grew closer. He considered pulling out onto the street and driving away. He calmed his panicked thoughts as his training had taught, and picked up the tablet once more. Staring at the screen as if watching a movie, he only watched the Americans drive by with his peripheral vision.

Yuri never saw their faces and whether or not the other two were looking at him. For the moment, he didn't care. He just focused on the tablet.

A moment later they were gone, turning back onto one of the other streets and disappearing from view.

Yuri waited until they'd turned again toward the interstate before he pulled out onto the street and drove off.

He swallowed hard, driving the lump in his

throat back down into his gut. His chest rose slowly, taking in a deep breath. "Stay calm, Yuri," he told himself. "They don't know you're here or who you even are. Just complete the mission."

At the street where the Americans turned right, Yuri hung a left onto a side street and drove until he found an old church. He turned into the parking lot and steered his vehicle back behind the building—out of sight from the main road.

There, he waited and watched the tablet as the blue dot circled back around through the downtown square one more time.

"Stupid Americans," he thought. "So predictable."

The blue dot passed by where he'd been sitting for the last several hours and then made the same turns again, only this time the other car finally stayed on course down Highway 20.

Yuri waited patiently for another five minutes until he was certain the Americans weren't coming back around again and then took off on the same route. If they'd found something at the Seward museum, he didn't know. Sooner or later, he'd make his move, but only when the timing was right.

22. Washington

Drew Porter took a bite of his Reuben. He stared out the foggy window of his favorite DC deli as he slowly chewed the corned beef, sauerkraut, and rye. He'd released his men to go and do as they pleased until they heard from him. They understood that could mean hours or months. With this particular mission, his only request was that they stick around the area and not wander off too far.

Porter couldn't explain it, but he had a feeling he and his team would be needed again soon.

The television on the wall in the corner was stuck on the national news network. The anchors had been talking about the assassination attempt pretty much nonstop since Porter walked in. They kept showing the video of the mystery woman as she tackled the president just before the bullets shattered his podium and would have surely killed him on the spot. Porter lost count of how many times they cycled that footage through.

He took a sip of his drink and swallowed the bite of sandwich before taking another.

His phone suddenly started ringing, vibrating on the table next to his plate. Porter checked the screen and shook his head. He hit the red *Decline* button and finished chewing his food.

A moment later, the device started ringing again. After he swallowed the next bite, Porter picked up the phone.

"Calling again so soon?" he said. "I thought you didn't need me."

"That was before I found out Sean Wyatt was still alive."

Porter flushed red. "What are you talking about?"

"Your mark? The guy you were supposed to kill? The guy you said you *did* kill? Turns out he's not so dead after all."

"Where did you get that information?" Porter asked after he took a long, deep breath.

"Oh, I don't know. A little birdie in Auburn, New York, called me. I was in meetings and briefings all day, so I only got the message a few minutes ago."

"Auburn?"

"Yes, Auburn. I put someone on the Seward House when I found out Wyatt was snooping around. She called and said he and his friend Schultz came in this morning to talk to the curator. Now, how do you suppose that happened? I mean, one minute, the guy is dead in a cave somewhere in North Georgia. Next thing I know, he's walking into the Seward museum. I don't suppose you have any theories as to how in the world he did it. Do you?"

Porter didn't appreciate the condescending tone from his employer. More than that, however, he was infuriated at the fact that Wyatt was still alive, not to mention his friend as well. He ran through the scenario in his head.

Wyatt and Schultz were down in the cave. Porter and his two men rigged enough C4 over the entrance to take down a small fortress. After the dust settled, he checked to make sure there was no way the men could escape. Even if rescue crews had shown up immediately, it would have taken a day or two to clear the debris for the simple reason that there could be another cave-in if the rescuers weren't careful.

If what his employer was saying was true, the only explanation would be another entrance to the cave. Porter and his men hadn't seen anything like that while they were there, but it wasn't out of the realm of possibility. His knowledge about cave systems was pretty limited. He'd heard of caves with multiple points of entry, so it was certainly possible.

Instead of offering an answer to his employer's question, Porter changed the conversation's direction.

"Where is he now?"

"Right now? At this very moment? I have no idea. My contact in Auburn said all she heard was that Wyatt and Schultz were heading back to Washington."

The comment caused Porter to perk up. "Washington? Why?"

"She didn't know exactly. Something about the Mary Surratt house. They may be looking for something there."

"Good thing my men and I are already here in Washington." Porter hoped the news would change his employer's demeanor.

A silent pause passed for a moment before the man on the other end spoke up again. "Washington? You're here? Why?"

"I thought you might need us again, sir. Although I have to admit, I didn't think it would be to deal with Wyatt. I apologize for the trouble. We'll take care of it."

"You said you took care of it last time. I'm going to get someone else to handle it now. Consider yourself lucky."

Consider myself lucky? What does that mean?

Porter didn't respond well to threats. He was the one who threatened people. The fact that a guy in a suit with no experience in the field actually had the guts to say something like that to him caused Porter's blood to boil.

"I said I will take care of it, sir. You don't have to get someone else on it."

"No, Porter. Do you not understand? You are off the job. Don't make the mistake of crossing me. That will not end well for you."

There it was again, another threat.

"Okay, sir. We're done here. I wish you the best of luck."

"Was that sarcasm? Do you have any idea who you're talking to, Porter? You caused this, not me. You're the one who failed in your assignment."

Porter ended the call without saying anything else. He'd had enough. If his employer thought he could just bring someone else to finish the job he'd started, he'd have to think again.

A plan began formulating in Porter's mind. Whatever his employer was looking for must be something of tremendous value—potentially priceless. Porter snorted at the thought. Everything had a price. Everything.

He flipped through the contacts in his phone and found the number he was looking for.

It was a guy he only used now and then when he didn't care if things got messy. Porter didn't know his real name. He went by an odd alias: Anhur, after the Egyptian god of war. The man had Egyptian tattoos all over his arms and neck. Porter assumed there were more, but he'd never been interested in asking.

Anhur had the reputation of being incredibly thorough in his tasks. The only problem was he usually left a swath of destruction and carnage. He was relatively cheap, though, and Porter didn't care how sloppy the job was done so long as Wyatt and Schultz were out of the way. Then whatever treasure they'd found would be in Porter's hands.

He'd sell it to the highest bidder, of which there would likely be only one. Porter clenched his jaw as he thought about the price tag. He'd make his now-former employer pay dearly. From the boasts the man had made, he likely had billions to spend.

As Porter dialed Anhur's number, his mind

drifted to the beach house he'd buy in the Caribbean, the chalet in France, and the countless other material possessions that filled his desires.

"Yes?" a gruff voice came through the earpiece.

"Anhur, it's Porter. You wouldn't be interested in making a quick five thousand, would you?"

The man's breathing was loud in the phone. "Depends on how quick?" he grunted.

"You still in Washington?"

"Where else would I be? Best place for a bear to catch fish is in the river."

Porter had only talked to Anhur on a few occasions, but he found the man loved metaphors. Porter attributed it to a psychological issue in which Anhur saw himself as some kind of wise spiritual guide. Ironic because when he killed people, he did so in often gruesome ways.

"Good point," Porter said.

It actually was a good point. If a mercenary hit man wanted to make a good living, there were several markets to choose from, both domestic and international. New York was a honey pot, but overrun by the mob. Finding work could be tricky and getting paid even more so. Same with Boston and the Irish.

Chicago was a huge city, but more organized crime and a saturated base of talented hitters made it a poor choice.

Washington, however, was a goldmine of opportunity if you had talent. To get work in that town, one had to be a cut above the rest. The men and women who sought hired guns didn't settle for anything less than the best. After all, their reputations and political careers were on the line.

Anhur's penchant for cruelty made him stand out.

"What's the mark?" Anhur asked.

"There are two marks, actually. They'll be in town later today, barring anything unusual on their journey."

"Where?"

"I'll send you the address along with everything you'll need on these two men. Oh, and Anhur, there's one more thing."

"What's that?"

"Make sure you take them out as they're leaving, not before. They'll have something in their possession that I want. And it's in that house."

23. Washington

Adriana followed Emily through the airport, walking swiftly by other travelers, careful to not make eye contact.

She wore a baseball cap and sunglasses to keep her identity safe from any gawkers who'd seen the viral video of her diving into the president to save his life. The last thing she and Emily needed right now was attention. If someone recognized her, they'd be inundated with questions, maybe even requests for autographs. Neither were things the two women wanted.

They found the gate for their flight back to Atlanta and found seats in a corner against the wall. Boarding would begin in twenty minutes. Until then, Adriana and Emily had plenty of work to do.

Once they were situated, they both took out their phones. Emily called the office to check on why Sean's call hadn't come through to her. Adriana made a call to Alex and Tara.

"Hello?" Tara said after two rings.

"How are you three?" Adriana asked.

"We're good," Tara said. "June picked us up from the office and brought us to Joe and Helen's place. I gotta say, it sure is relaxing being out here in the woods. We need to visit more often."

"You haven't noticed anything unusual, have you?"

"No, everything's fine down here. I think Alex is getting a little bored, but June and I are enjoying the R&R. By the way, thanks for looking out for us with the tip on the burner phones."

"No problem," Adriana said. Her eyes flitted from one traveler to the next as they passed. She feared at any second someone would recognize her. "I was wondering if you could help us out."

"Us? Are Tommy and Sean with you?"

"No. Emily is. This may be outside the realm of your expertise, but we thought we'd give it a try and ask since you and Alex are usually pretty handy when it comes to cyber stuff."

"Oh, sounds interesting."

"You could say that. We're investigating a few offshore bank accounts and were hoping the two of you could figure out a way to tell us where the deposits came from."

Adriana waited as the phone fell silent. She pulled it away from her ear and checked the screen to make sure the call hadn't been dropped.

"That is an interesting request," Tara said. "We don't usually do hacking-type stuff."

Adriana sighed. She was disappointed, but it was also the answer she'd expected.

"I figured you didn't. Had to try, though."

"Well, Alex and I don't really do anything like that, however, we do know someone who does."

Adriana perked up. "You do?"

"Yeah. His name is Clyde. He's an older guy. Might even be retired by now, not that he ever worked a real job that I know of. He's busted into more systems than anyone I know. Doesn't really steal anything like money or identities. He just likes to know the truth, see what's truly going on."

"What's going on?"

"Like in the government or with politicians."

"Oh." Adriana looked puzzled. "Do you think he can help us?"

"Definitely. I'll reach out to him immediately and see what he can do."

"Thanks, Tara. That would be awesome. Let me know what you find out."

"Will do. I'll be in touch soon." She started to end the call and then stopped herself. "Oh, Adriana?"

"Yes?"

"Send me the account information on this person you're investigating. If Clyde agrees to do the gig, he'll need whatever it is you're wanting him to look into."

Adriana reached into her bag and took out her notepad. She'd written down the account information beforehand for this exact purpose. "I'll text it to you right away."

"Sounds good."

After they said their goodbyes, she texted Tara and looked to Emily, who was just getting off the phone with her people at Axis HQ in Atlanta.

"What's the word?" Adriana asked.

Emily bit her lower lip for a second before answering. "They said no call ever came in from Sean."

"You mean they didn't remember getting a call from him?"

"No." Emily shook her head. "The call never came through. They ran a check of all the calls we received for the last several days, particularly the day Sean supposedly called. We never received one."

"That's odd," Adriana said, scratching the side of her head. The hat wasn't the best fit and irritated her scalp.

"What's really odd is that for a brief period of time one day last week, we received far fewer calls."

"Fewer calls?"

Emily shrugged. "A dozen or so. We work with a number of different entities, so the phones are usually busy."

"Maybe it was just a slow day?"

"Possibly. I have another theory. If someone had the resources and capability to burn Sean and Tommy, effectively wiping out their entire source of funding and all that, then those same people would more than likely be able to orchestrate a phone line redirect."

"You mean they took calls from that specific period of time and rerouted them to another phone?"

"Exactly," Emily said with a nod.

Adriana thought for a moment. Even though she'd spent much of her life in the United States, she still didn't have a handle on many of the whos and hows involved with American politics, government, and power.

That first one lingered in her mind: the who. It would have to be someone with a great deal of power to pull off what happened to Sean and Tommy, as well as what Emily was suggesting with their phones.

"Who has the capability?" Adriana asked.

"That's just it," Emily said. "There are any number of agencies capable of pulling off a move like that for a residence or a business. But we have fail-safes in place, security measures."

"You think it was someone on the inside of Axis?"

Emily shook her head. "No. None of my agents would do something like that."

"Are you sure?"

"Yes, I'm sure. The list of people working for me is only known to me and the president. Some of my agents don't even know each other. They often work alone, save for certain, more extreme cases."

Adriana didn't press that issue any further. "So, if it wasn't someone on the inside, who?"

Emily didn't answer right away. Her eyelids blinked rapidly as her brain worked in overdrive to find the solution. She looked up at the ceiling on the other side of the terminal. Two cameras were mounted against the wall, pointing in opposite

directions. The little red lights on the sides of the
devices indicated the area was being monitored.

Emily cocked her head to the side. "Cameras,"
she said.

"What?"

"The cameras," Emily pointed at the two security
devices. "Downtown Atlanta has cameras
everywhere. If we can track down the source of the
phone line redirection, we might be able to figure
out who was behind it."

Adriana still didn't follow. "I don't understand.
How will cameras be able to help you figure that
out?"

Emily licked her lips. Her heartbeat quickened.
"Phone lines coming into a building have
junctions. You see linemen working on them
sometimes in those white buckets that go up and
down."

Adriana nodded that she was keeping up.

"So, to pull off a redirect, the most common way
would be to climb the last telephone pole going
into the building, patch into it, and redirect it.
Someone could have put a person up on one of the
poles outside our building and sent incoming calls
to their own line."

Things were starting to make sense now. "So, if
there's a camera anywhere close to where the patch
was created—"

"We'll be able to identify who did it."

"The people who tried to kill Sean must have
ordered the redirect when he managed to escape."

Adriana rubbed her head. The intrigue was getting deep.

"Yes. Hopefully we can get a visual on who might have been involved. If we can track that person down, we may be able to figure out who they're working for. Speaking of tracking, what did the kids say?"

"Just as I thought. They don't know anything about computer hacking."

"I was afraid of that."

"But they said they know someone who does. An older guy who does some ethical hacking. He does it to get information and keep tabs on the government."

Emily raised an eyebrow at the term. She'd heard of it. She'd even used some people to test their own security at Axis, but she'd never heard of someone doing it just for the sake of learning about what's going on behind the scenes of world events.

"Is he some kind of conspiracy nut or something? Because I gotta be honest, the last thing we need is some crackpot trying to dig up bank account information for us."

"If Tara and Alex trust him, we can, too. I just sent them the information with the accounts. It's a long shot, I know, but let's see what this guy can do. Maybe we'll get lucky."

"I don't believe in luck," Emily said. "I like to make my own."

"Isn't that what we're doing?" Adriana said with a grin.

Emily's head rocked back and forth. "So it would seem."

24. Washington

Sean and Tommy pulled their coats tight as they stepped out of the car and onto the sidewalk. The bitter winter wind rolled through the district, cutting through their clothes and stinging their skin.

Sean pushed his sunglasses closer to his eyes. Tommy did the same.

They were bundled from head to toe, partly due to the cold and partly due to the fact that they'd rather not be caught on one of the thousands of cameras watching over Washington's city streets.

They stared down the sparsely populated sidewalk at a blue awning two blocks away. The flashy lettering on the fabric read *Wok and Roll Restaurant.*

"I can't believe that's the place where John Wilkes Booth and his cohorts plotted the Lincoln and Seward assassinations," Sean said. "A Chinese joint."

"Yeah, I'm not sure how I feel about it," Tommy said. "On the one hand, it's an infamous place from history that should have been preserved."

"Right. And on the other hand, it's a place where an evil plan was hatched. With that thinking, maybe it should have been torn down."

"Exactly."

They stood there in the cold for a moment, gazing down the sidewalk. There were only a few other pedestrians walking around. Most people were indoors, keeping warm.

"You think we'll find anything in there?" Tommy asked.

Sean rolled his shoulders underneath his thick coat. "No idea. But we have to give it a look. I just hope the restaurant owners won't mind us snooping around."

The two trudged down the sidewalk. Little piles of snow lined both sides of the concrete, swept aside by municipal workers. The snow on the roads had melted from salt the city had applied. Soupy gray skies overhead foretold more of the same and already dripped with big snowflakes that fluttered to the ground.

Underneath the awning, Sean opened the door and let his friend pass through first. The smell of onions, garlic, broccoli, and meat filled the air and wafted by the visitors in a steamy cloud, dissipating in the freezing cold outside.

Inside, the kitchen was situated behind a counter. Two cooks stirred various ingredients in giant steel woks. Fire flashed around the pans, rising up toward the ventilation fans overhead before disappearing just as fast as the flames appeared.

A young Asian woman stood at a cash register behind the counter. She wore a polite smile and gave a welcoming nod to the two men as they entered.

"Welcome to Wok and Roll. How can I help you?" she said in a thick accent.

Sean cleared his throat and stepped to the counter. "Hello. My name is Sean, and this is Tommy. We work for a historical agency in Atlanta and were wondering if you could help us with an investigation."

The young woman's face scrunched into a frown. "You're police?"

"No, no. Not police," Tommy corrected. "We're doing some research on the Abraham Lincoln assassination and were wondering if we could have a look around your building."

The moment the words came out of Tommy's mouth, he realized the poor girl probably had dozens of similar requests every single day.

"So, you're not police?"

"No," Sean said.

"Upstairs is a private residence. You're not allowed up there." She was clearly offended by the request. At least it sounded like she was.

"We're really sorry," Sean said in an attempt to smooth things over. "The research we're doing is extremely important. You're sure we can't just have a quick look?"

An older man walked up to the register from a doorway in the back corner. From the potbelly and the sagging face, Sean and Tommy figured him to be in his late fifties or early sixties.

"What's the problem here?" he said in a booming

voice that startled the other two customers in the room.

"They were asking to see the rooms upstairs," the girl explained.

"No." He wagged a finger. "Do you have any idea how many people we get in here every week who want to see the Surratt boarding house?"

"No, but I'm betting it's more than a few," Sean whispered, mostly to himself.

"If you want to know more about the building, read the plaque the government posted outside."

"We've read the plaque," Tommy said. He wasn't lying. They read it online before coming to visit the building in person. "But we think it's possible there is a key piece of evidence for our project somewhere in here. We'd just like to look around and see what we can find."

The older guy—who Sean and Tommy figured was the manager—shook his head. "This building was stripped apart several times over the last hundred years. Anything that may have been hidden here is long gone. I'm sorry, but it appears you've wasted your time."

Sean and Tommy exchanged a forlorn glance.

"Would you like something to eat while you're here?" the girl asked.

Tommy started to say he wasn't hungry when Sean spoke up first. "I'll try the lo mein and General Tso's tofu."

"Your friend want anything?"

Tommy relented. "Fine. I'll get the tofu as well

with a side of white rice."

A few minutes later, the two were sitting in a booth near the back of the building, spinning noodles around chopsticks and shoveling rice into their mouths.

"What should we do?" Tommy asked, looking around at the employees. "Come back later when they're closed?"

Sean surveyed the room. "And what," he whispered, "break in? You heard them. They live upstairs. And besides, the manager said that the place was torn apart multiple times over the last hundred years. It's highly unlikely that something would still be here after all that."

It wasn't like Tommy to offer the brazen option. Tommy's nature wasn't necessarily timid. It's just that he usually chose to do things by the book, follow the rules, rarely step out of line.

In certain circumstances, Sean would have agreed to a little breaking and entering of the old Surratt boarding house. In this instance, he wasn't sure that was the best course of action.

"Then what do you suggest we do?" Tommy asked.

"Excuse me," a new voice interrupted their quiet conversation.

The two turned and saw an older man in the booth behind them. His thick gray hair was combed to one side. Even though the restaurant was warm, he wore a beige trench coat. The skin under his eyes sagged, showing dark circles beneath weary blue eyes. He had the appearance of someone who'd been working in politics for most of his life—the sort of rugged yet refined handsomeness voters loved.

"I couldn't help but hear you two talking to that manager about having a look upstairs," he said.

Tommy and Sean stared at the guy, wondering what else he'd heard.

"There's nothing up there," the man continued. "The manager's right. This place went through several renovations through the years."

The stranger could tell the two friends were curious as to why they should listen to him, maybe even as to who he was.

"Eli Stumper," he said. "I've been coming to this joint ever since I got elected."

I knew it, Sean thought. *A politician.* "I'm Sean, and this is my friend Tommy."

"Nice to meet you, sir," Tommy said, awkwardly twisting his body in the booth to reach over and shake the man's hand.

"Are you a history buff like me?" Eli asked.

Sean let a wry grin ease across his face. "I guess you could say that. We work for the International Archaeological Agency. He's the founder." Sean gave a nod at Tommy.

"You don't say. I thought I recognized you."

Tommy blushed. Sean's face reddened, too, but for a different reason. If this guy—a government official—knew who they were, there could be trouble if he relayed the message to a corrupt coworker. They were already taking a huge chance coming into DC. The last thing they needed was to have some guy start blabbing about them being here.

"We're trying to keep a low profile," Sean said. "The project we're working on at the moment is...sensitive."

Eli's eyes widened. "Oh, I see. Well, I won't trouble you anymore."

The man started to turn around, but Sean stopped him. "That's not what I meant. Care to join us?"

Eli looked at one and then the other as if the question required deliberation. "Sure," he said. "I'd love to."

The older man slipped out of his seat as Tommy moved over. He brought his half-eaten plate of dumplings and set it on the table next to Tommy's.

"So, you know a lot about this place, huh?" Tommy asked.

"Yep," Eli said, shoving a forkful of the sweet and spicy food into his mouth.

"When the renovations happened, did the construction crews find anything unusual?"

Eli chewed and looked up to the ceiling as if the tiles above would somehow help him recall the answer. "Not that I remember. What is it you two are looking for, anyway?"

"A document," Sean said quickly.

Tommy's head swiveled. He surveyed the room, making sure no one else was paying attention. The cooks and the girl working the register were busy running the restaurant.

When Tommy spoke, it was in a hushed tone. "Keep this hush-hush," he said.

Eli nodded that he understood.

"When Booth killed Lincoln, he came back here to get ammunition and food before heading to Doctor Mudd." Tommy shoved a pile of rice into his mouth.

"You think Booth left something here?"

"No, sir," Sean said. "Someone else did."

Eli's forehead wrinkled. "Who?"

"You're a history guy," Sean said. "So, you know Lewis Powell tried to assassinate William Seward that night, too."

"That is correct. Powell also came here that night. He was arrested here the next day." Eli paused to reflect for a moment. "You think it was Powell that brought a document here?"

"Maybe," Sean said. "But I guess we'll never know. We can't very well look upstairs. And this floor wasn't the main floor when Mary Surratt was running a boarding house here."

Eli nodded. Sean was right. It wasn't until years later that the ground floor became the main entrance. By then, Mary Surratt's family was long gone.

"Mary Surratt's family," Eli said.

"Excuse me?" Tommy chirped. "What about her family?"

"This is a long shot. I don't know if it will help or

not. Mary had a son, John Jr. He hung around many of the nights Booth and the others conspired to take down the government. He was involved heavily with the Confederate cause in multiple instances, working from behind enemy lines to get them supplies or let them know about troop movements by the North."

"John was arrested later and then let go. They said he didn't have anything to do with the conspiracy," Sean said.

"That's correct. While his mother and three others were hanged for their crimes, John was not. I'm not sure if it was because he was younger or what. The other men they hanged were pretty young themselves. Anyway, the boarding house was operating at a loss and had to be sold to pay off the family debts. Their family farmhouse, on the other hand, is still standing today. There's a little museum inside it, complete with all the original furnishings, woodwork, everything."

Sean and Tommy sat up a little straighter.

"Let me see if I'm following your thought here. You think if Powell brought the document back here, John Surratt may have hidden it in his family home?" Tommy asked.

Eli confirmed with a nod. "It's possible. I have no idea what you two are looking for or why, and frankly I'm fine with reading about it in the news when you make an announcement. But yes, if Powell did bring something back here, John Surratt may have hidden it at their farm."

Sean listened intensely. He pointed a finger at Eli. "You might be onto something. The conspirators thought through pretty much everything. They'd have to believe that the authorities might connect the dots."

"Right," Tommy said. "And those dots would have led straight back to here."

"So, John Surratt took the document and fled back to the family homestead."

"And if he did that, it's extremely likely he hid it somewhere in the house," Eli said. "Back in those days, people used to hide things in the ground along prominent roads or near local landmarks. If it's paper you're looking for, I doubt he would have done that. The elements would destroy it in no time. If that document still exists, and no one ever found it, it might be worth a look at the family house."

"Where is that property?" Tommy asked.

"Not too far from here. It's in Clinton, Maryland. Nothing but gas stations and strip malls around it, but the historical societies have managed to keep the Surratt farmhouse safe from destruction."

"Thank you for your help," Sean said.

"Happy to lend a hand," Eli said.

He wiped his fingers clean on a couple of napkins and then dabbed one at the corner of his mouth to get a smudge of sauce still lingering on his lips. He stood up and picked up his tray. "It's been nice chatting with you, gentlemen. I have to get going. Perhaps I'll see you around again sometime. Best of luck on your adventure."

"Thanks," the two said in tandem.

Eli disposed of his tray and ventured out onto the cold Washington sidewalk.

"What do you think?" Tommy asked, taking another big bite of his food.

Sean was chewing his own food while searching for something on his phone's web browser. "He's right about the Surratt farmhouse not being far from here. We could shoot over there and have a look. It's definitely worth a shot."

"What if we don't find anything?" A piece of rice dangled from the corner of Tommy's lips.

"From the sound of it, we're not going to find what we're looking for here, either. May as well take a short drive out to the country and take a gander."

"Gander?"

"Yeah, you know, have a look around."

"Sorry, I just didn't realize it was 1954."

Sean shook his head and scooped up the last remains of his noodles. "I like old-school words. So?"

Tommy pouted his lips and rolled his shoulders. "I'm not judging."

"Really? It feels a little like you're judging."

"Like all those times you told me to get in better shape?"

Sean chuckled. "And don't you feel so good now that you are?"

The door opened, ringing the bell over the

frame.

Tommy's eyes flashed to his left, taking note of the big man walking into the restaurant. He had long black hair pulled back into a ponytail and wore a heavy Gore-Tex coat.

"That's not the point," Tommy said.

"Look, I'm sorry if I hurt your feelings when I brought up your health. It wasn't to make fun. Okay? It's because I care. I've known you longer than any of my other friends. You're like family to me. I apologize for wanting you to be around a while."

The big man who'd just come in the door looked over at the two friends. They didn't see him staring, and they didn't notice when he started unzipping his coat, revealing Egyptian tattoos on his neck and upper chest.

"Wow," Tommy said. He sat back against the booth and took in a deep breath. "A tender moment from Sean Wyatt. That doesn't happen often."

Sean shook his head and narrowed his eyes. "Are you done eating? We should get going."

"Aww. Did I hit a soft spot?"

"No. But we need to get out of the city before traffic starts up again."

"It's DC," Tommy said. "There's always traffic."

Sean picked up his and Tommy's trays and spun toward the trashcan next to the door. Then he saw the tattooed man standing ten feet away. He was at least six-six and looked like a body builder. Then

Sean saw the guy pulling two huge handguns out of shoulder holsters.

"Get down!" Sean yelled.

25. Washington

The man whipped the pistols out.

Before he could fire, Sean flung one of the trays like a Frisbee, striking the big man square in the face.

The blow stung and stunned the guy enough that his hands pointed up just enough that when he fired the weapons that the rounds flew through the wall over Tommy's head.

Sean didn't wait for him to recover. He charged the shooter, jumping at the last second to hit him with a flying kick to the chest.

The gunman was faster than he looked for a big, muscular guy. He stepped aside and swung the base of one of the pistols into Sean's back. As he spun around, he swung the other arm in Sean's direction and took aim at the back of his head.

Sean hit the floor and slid into the counter as the cooks dove for cover. The girl yelled and dropped out of sight behind the register.

The shooter's finger tensed, ready to put a .45-caliber bullet through the back of Sean's skull when something struck him on the back of the head. Fresh pain instantly throbbed from the blow, stunning him for a brief moment. A split second after, the ceramic plate that struck him crashed in a hundred pieces at his feet.

He turned and saw Tommy racing for him, lowering his shoulder. The gunman tried to line up Tommy in his sights, but his aim was too slow. He fired the weapon, sending a round a foot to Tommy's right. The next second, Tommy's shoulder dug into the gunman's ribcage.

Tommy pumped his legs as hard and fast as he could until he felt the gunman's bulk shudder when his body hit the counter.

One of the guns fell to the ground a few feet away from Sean. The shooter winced but managed to wriggle free of Tommy's grasp. He spun his remaining weapon around and started to fire again, but Tommy chopped his right arm down on the guy's forearm. The pistol's muzzle erupted. Part of the cheap tile floor exploded as the bullet smashed into it.

Sean grabbed the other weapon and scrambled to his feet. He tried to take aim but couldn't get a clear line of sight while Tommy was grappling with the shooter.

The gunman chopped his elbow down on Tommy's back.

Tommy grunted in pain and dropped to his knees, opening a shooting lane for Sean, whose fingers tightened on the trigger as he lined up the man's muscular chest with his sights.

The shooter's foot kicked up much higher and faster than either Sean or Tommy would have thought possible. The tip of the man's heavy boot hit Sean's hand and knocked the weapon backward toward the rear exit.

Sean's hand flew up. He corrected quickly and put himself into an attacking stance. In the blink of an eye, Sean swung his left arm in an arch, twisted his right foot, opened his hips, and kicked hard with his left.

The gunman attempted a block, but he used the hand with his gun in it. The blow knocked the weapon across the room, just as he'd done to Sean.

Tommy was on his hands and knees with his arms wrapped around the man's legs, still attempting to tackle the shooter.

The gunman yelled and grabbed Tommy by the belt and shirt, hefting him off the floor and then dropping him hard to the tile.

Sean used his friend as a step and lunged forward, vaulting himself into the air. The gunman twisted and clotheslined Sean with a forearm across the face.

The blow sent a surge of pain through Sean's entire head as he crashed to the floor in a heap next to Tommy. He struggled to get up, but before he could, the gunman grabbed him by the neck and picked him up. He did the same to Tommy, wrapping his massive arm around Tommy's throat.

Sean drove his elbow in the man's abs over and over again, desperate to free himself from the gunman's death grip. Tommy wriggled frantically, also trying to get away so he could breathe.

Sean's vision blurred. He was certain his friend was in similar straits. In less than a minute, they would both black out. A few seconds more than that, and they'd be dead.

His arms grew heavy, and the shots his elbows delivered to the gunman's midsection seemed to do nothing but piss him off, like a gnat flying around a bull.

He couldn't get into a position to kick his heel into the man's groin. But there was one idea that popped into his head.

"Tommy," Sean said through clenched teeth. He was barely able to make a sound. "Ears."

Tommy heard his friend and knew what he meant.

With a last-ditch effort, the two twisted their bodies as much as possible and swung their open hands at the gunman's head.

Their palms smacked both ears at the same time. To Sean and Tommy, it sounded like a low clap. To the man choking them, it may as well have been two loaded shotguns going off on either side of his head.

His grip loosened instantly, and the two fell to the floor, gasping for air as the shooter staggered backward into the counter. The big man clutched his ears, wincing in agony and no doubt a sudden dizzy spell brought on by busted eardrums.

Tommy and Sean struggled to their feet, bracing themselves on each other's shoulders.

They gasped for air, relieved to flood their lungs after being deprived for what seemed like an eternity.

Sean looked over his shoulder at the big gunman. His eyes twitched from the lumbering shooter to the sizzling hot woks on the flaming stoves.

"Time to find out who this guy works for," Sean said. "Take out his knees."

He and Tommy stood up straight, their faces still bulging and red from being choked. They rushed forward as the gunman started to regain his balance. Before he could get into a defensive position, Sean and Tommy leaped into the air. They extended their legs, driving their shoes hard into the man's knees.

The gunman suddenly yelped in a tone men his size rarely ever reached. It came approximately two seconds after both knees collapsed inward under Sean and Tommy's weight.

He dropped to the ground, crippled and in agony. He reached for his knees, but what he found was both legs bent at a wretched, unnatural angle. The gunman wailed, realizing the severity of the damage.

Sean ignored the man's screams. "Help me drag him to the kitchen."

Tommy obeyed and copied Sean as he grabbed the guy under the armpit. The two tugged and pulled, their legs and backs straining from the gunman's weight. After a Herculean effort, they dropped him behind the counter in front of the nearest stove. The cooks yelled, and the young woman screamed, all three still crouching behind the counter for safety.

"You might want to hide in the back," Sean suggested in between pants for air.

The workers scrambled to their feet and ran through the back door. The bell over the door jingled as one of the other patrons ran out onto the street, apparently confident enough they could escape now that the fight was over.

The gunman moaned. A tapestry of profanity came in the form of shouts and groans. He cursed nearly everything and everyone, especially Sean and Tommy.

Sean reached down and grabbed the guy by the ponytail. He yanked the man up onto his disfigured knees and lowered his face toward one of the woks. Tommy held one of the man's arms, twisting it behind his back.

"If you think you're in pain now," Sean said in as sinister a tone as he could muster, "wait until you feel your face frying in peanut oil."

"You can go to—"

"Uh uh uh," Sean cut him off. "Remember. The only thing standing between you and the worst possible pain you could ever imagine are my fingers wrapped around your ponytail. One slip"— he loosened his grip for a second and allowed the man's face to drop an inch closer to the pan—"and that becomes a reality."

The gunman wiggled violently.

Tommy punched him in the lower back, probably bruising a kidney. The gunman drooped forward another inch, only pulling back when he felt the wok's searing heat.

"See?" Sean said. "Struggling is only going to make things worse for you. Now, I can shove your face into that wok and not think twice about it. But that's not what I want to do. I don't like the smell of burning flesh."

"What do you want?" the man spat.

"There we go. Now we're getting somewhere. I like that. In spite of having blown out both your knees, you can think logically."

"You can take your logic and—"

"Now, now," Sean said. "Be nice. All I want to know is who sent you to kill us."

The man's head shook violently. "I don't know. I just get money, names, and an address."

Sean looked over at Tommy.

"Feels like he's lying," Tommy said with arms crossed.

"You know, I think you're right." He turned his attention to the gunman. "Is he right? Are you lying to me? I don't like being lied to."

Sean forced the man's head toward the bubbling oil.

"Porter! His name is Drew Porter! I've only worked for him a few times. He sent me." The man's accent was difficult to place through his yelling.

Sean's eyes narrowed. "Who does Porter work for?"

The man spat out an obscenity.

"Oh, that isn't nice," Tommy said. "Sean, go ahead, and stir-fry this knucklehead."

Sean pressed down on the back of the guy's head again. The heat from the wok started burning his eyes. He tried to turn his face sideways, but Sean gripped him tight.

"I don't know who he works for! He didn't tell me. I'm just the errand guy. I swear! He called me up and asked if I wanted to make some quick cash."

"Where is Porter?" Sean asked.

"I swear, I don't know. We used a drop point for the money. He called *me*!"

Sean looked at his friend. "Sounds like he's telling the truth, Schultzie."

"You sure?"

The sounds of police sirens echoed in the distance.

Sean cocked his head to the side and looked down at the man. "No, but I think he's suffered enough for one night. And we should probably leave before the cops get here."

Sean shoved the guy to the ground and hurried around the end of the counter. He scooped up the gunman's weapons on his way to the door.

They burst through the door and out onto the sidewalk. Sirens were rapidly bearing down on their location.

"We should hurry," Sean said.

A short sprint and ninety seconds later they pulled out of their parking spot and zoomed by the restaurant just as police cars whipped around the corner and blocked off the road in front of the historic building.

"That was close," Tommy said, looking out the back window. He turned and faced forward as Sean steered the car to the right and onto the next street.

"Pull up a map with directions to Clinton," Sean said as he accelerated through the next green light. "If you can, find some back roads. Let's try to avoid as much traffic as possible."

Tommy did what Sean said, quickly finding a map. He performed a quick search on his phone to get the exact address for the Surratt farmhouse and entered it into the map's address bar.

"Got it," Tommy said. "We can be there in forty minutes."

Sean tightened his grip on the steering wheel. "We'll be there in thirty."

26 Atlanta

"Did your guy find anything?" Adriana held the phone tight against her ear.

She sat in one of the empty offices of Axis headquarters. When her phone started ringing, she'd excused herself from Emily's office and found a quieter place to talk.

"Yeah," Tara said. "Probably more than either of us expected."

"That didn't take long."

"Clyde has around a dozen computers running at all times. He's constantly downloading information. For what, I don't really know, but I know that when he looks for something and puts all his energy behind it, he doesn't take long."

"That's good for us."

"It sure is."

Adriana stared at the clock over the door, watching the second hand creep along its circular route. "What did he find?"

"As expected, reversing the digital footprint to track where the deposits came from took some work."

"I can't imagine."

"Yeah, but our guy is good. I don't understand all the technical mumbo jumbo he was spewing about it, but he got the job done. He said there were a

couple of sizable deposits that looked fishy, so
those were the ones he went after. They were
connected to other dummy accounts. Clyde said
that whoever laundered that money was working
hard to cover their tracks. They had over thirty
different accounts across the globe."

"How was he able to unravel those knots?"
Adriana asked.

"Every crumb leads somewhere, Adriana," Tara
said. "Leave enough of them lying around,
someone is going to come by and pick them up. At
the epicenter of this particular trail is a company
called Transcorp."

"Transcorp?"

"Yeah. I hadn't heard of it either, so I looked
them up online. They're a humongous
experimental energy company."

"Experimental?"

"Correct. Apparently, their thing is finding new
forms of energy to replace nonrenewable resources
like fossil fuels."

Adriana was puzzled. "So, they're a green energy
company? Usually, those types aren't taking part in
a lot of shady activities."

"You'd think. But this company isn't as granola
as they'd like to appear. They have a significant
infrastructure that spans most of the United States.
I did a little digging around. Turns out they supply
most of California, Arizona, Nevada, and New
Mexico with power, and no one even realizes it.
Some of the bigger energy companies have to buy

their power from Transcorp because if they don't, their supply will run too low."

Adriana knew the problems some of those states had experienced with energy deficits over the years. There weren't enough hydroelectric stations in that region to meet the population's demand for power. There were over thirteen thousand wind turbines in California, but customers there still had to deal with power outages and brownouts.

"How many wind turbines and solar farms does Transcorp own?"

"Great question," Tara said. "None."

"None?"

"Yep. A big fat zero. They have pictures of wind turbines and other green energy generators on their website, but when I did some checking, I couldn't find any properties owned by Transcorp that are power producers. It's like they're getting their energy out of thin air."

"That *is* strange. How long have they been in business?" Adriana asked.

"A little over a decade. But here's the thing. In that short amount of time, they've gone from being a small energy startup to a ten-billion-dollar company."

'Ten billion? With a B?"

"Yep. You heard right. You can thank June for that little tidbit. She's been a big help with the research end of things, by the way. Pass that along to Tommy. Maybe his girlfriend can come to work for us."

Adriana smiled at the thought. "Maybe." She switched back to the subject at hand. "Who's in charge of this company?"

"Ah, now you're opening a different can of worms. Transcorp is a publicly traded company, so there's a board of directors and all that, but one man holds more shares than anyone: the company's founder."

Adriana waited patiently for the name.

"Ever heard of a guy named Kent Foster?" Alex asked.

Adriana jerked the phone away from her ear, surprised to hear his voice all of a sudden.

"Sorry, on speaker phone," Alex said, sensing he'd startled Adriana.

"Hello, Alex. No, should I have heard of him?"

"Probably. He's the president's secretary of state and a trusted adviser."

The information Alex relayed may as well have been strapped to a wrecking ball wrapped in dynamite.

Adriana was floored. "Wait a minute. Are you guys saying that the secretary of state was paying Kendricks?"

"That's not all we're saying," June jumped into the conversation. Now everyone was involved. "Not only did Kendricks receive some rather large deposits from Transcorp, after he died the money vanished."

"What do you mean, it vanished?"

"Someone paid a visit to those two banks and

withdrew every penny. Due to the distance between the two banks, we're assuming two separate people made the withdrawals. They must have known that an online transfer would have left a big trail, so they made the withdrawals on site."

"Sounds risky to carry around that kind of cash. How much are we talking about?"

"Millions."

The wheels spun out of control in Adriana's mind. There was one horrifying theory that kept rearing its head. "If Transcorp paid Kendricks, that means they were trying to eliminate Dawkins. And if that's the case, that means..."

"Foster was behind the assassination attempt," Tara finished her thought.

"I have to tell Emily," Adriana said, her voice nearly drowning in urgency. "We need to warn the president. If Foster really is the one behind all this, the president is still in danger."

She thanked the kids and June for their assistance and ended the call. Adriana couldn't walk fast enough back to Emily's office.

Adriana burst through the door, holding her phone at her side. Emily was on the phone, listening to someone else, and saw the intense look in Adriana's eyes.

"I'm going to have to call you back in a minute. Yes, I know this is important, but I have a national security issue to deal with."

She ended the call and waited for Adriana to speak.

"I just got off the phone with June and the kids."

"Did their hacker find anything?"

"Yes. And it's worse than we thought."

"Worse?" Emily asked.

"Much worse. We think Kent Foster was behind the assassination attempt."

"Foster? But he's the secretary of state. He's been one of the president's biggest allies over the years. What would he stand to gain by getting Dawkins out of the way? Secretary of state is fourth on the list to take over if the president dies."

Adriana's head slowly moved side to side. "I don't think he wants the presidency."

"Then what does he want?"

"They didn't have any theories on that, and—at the moment—neither do I. However, the kids were able to track down the deposits into Kendricks's offshore accounts. They came from several different other accounts. Tara said the people behind it took extreme measures to cover their tracks."

"As they should if they're doing something illegal."

"Correct, but their guy managed to figure it out. He traced the deposits back to a company called Transcorp."

"Transcorp?" Emily asked. It was apparent in her tone that she'd heard of the company.

"Yes. You've heard of them?"

Emily's eyes stared at the wall to the right of her guest. Her face took on a vapid, blank look. "Yes, I know who they are. Big energy company out west. Last I heard, they were trying to get into the East Coast."

"Did you know Foster is the largest shareholder?"

Emily's eyes widened with surprise. "That part I didn't know. I knew Foster was wealthy but never had much reason to investigate where his money was coming from."

"Does Dawkins know?" Adriana asked, the urgency continuing to build in her voice.

"I have no idea. What I do know is Foster has been bugging Dawkins for years about breaking apart Tennessee Valley Authority," Emily said. "He wanted to privatize it. Said that it's not right the government controls an energy company like that."

"Foster wants to break up TVA?"

"Yes. In spite of having some of the lowest energy costs per consumer across the nation, Foster suggested that it was corrupt and that privatizing it could lower consumer costs even more. Now, it seems his real motives might have been of a more personal nature."

Adriana connected the dots. "If TVA was picked apart, it would open up the entire Southeast for Transcorp."

"Absolutely. Once they're in that region, the entire East Coast is ripe for the picking."

"So, what's our next move?" Adriana asked.

"First thing we have to do is warn the president. If Foster is behind all of this, he needs to be taken in for questioning, and Dawkins needs to get somewhere safe."

"Safer than that bunker we were in?"

Emily nodded. "Foster would have access to nearly everywhere, including that bunker. If he gets alone with the president, he may well try to take matters into his own hands."

"That would be a desperate move. He has too much to lose."

"True. But rage and greed make people do crazy things."

The room fell silent for a second as Emily considered what to do next. She picked up her phone and started dialing. After several rings and no answer, she set it down with a frustrated sigh.

"No answer?" Adriana asked.

Emily shook her head. "We were just there," she said, frustrated. "We have to get word to him that Foster might be the man behind the assassination plot."

"How?"

"I know we just got here, but we're going to have to go back to Washington."

"First things first," Adriana said. "We need to check the security cameras and see if we can figure out who redirected the calls. Get your people on that. I can fly back to Washington and warn the president. Give him a call, and tell his people to make sure they let me in."

"He knows you. Most of his team does. That shouldn't be a problem."

"I'd rather be safe than sorry," Adriana said. "With all that's going on right now, I don't want to take any chances."

Emily thought hard about the plan. She didn't like the idea of sending Adriana back up to Washington on her own. There was no reason to take any chances with something as dire as this.

"My people can handle things here and report back to me. I'm coming with you."

27. Washington

Porter let his phone ring four times before he answered. He recognized the number on the screen and wanted to make the man on the other end wait, mostly because of their previous exchange.

He picked up the device and tapped the green button. "Yes, sir?" he answered with a thick layer of snark.

"I sincerely hope you didn't have anything to do with what just happened."

Porter's lips stretched out to one side of his face. Of course, he knew what had happened. He was the one who'd orchestrated it.

He'd heard there was a shootout at the place formerly known as Mary Surratt's boarding house. He also heard one man was severely injured and had been apprehended. Reports said one man was dead. Porter assumed the dead man was the hitter his employer sent to take care of Wyatt and Schultz. Who'd been arrested, though, was still a mystery.

Porter hadn't reached out to his connections yet to get that information. At this point, he didn't care. If Schultz and Wyatt had somehow managed to escape, it was just as well with him. That meant they could still lead him to whatever treasure they were seeking.

"I'm sorry?" Porter said. "I don't know what you're talking about, sir. What happened?"

"The shootout in the Chinese restaurant. The man I sent to take out Wyatt and Schultz is dead. I was told a large man with tattoos came in and started shooting up the place. Before he went in, he cut my asset's throat and stuffed him in the back of his own car."

For some reason, the macabre thought nearly caused Porter to chuckle. He bit back the laughter, though, and defended himself. "Your man was killed? Any leads?"

His former employer remained silent for a moment. The only sound Porter heard coming through his phone's earpiece was an occasional breath.

"The man they arrested will not be a problem again. When the police arrived, they found him with two dislocated knees, which I'm certain would make it difficult to swim."

Porter didn't have to ask what the man meant by that. He knew. The cops on payroll must have taken their new prisoner to the nearest lake or river and dropped him in, probably with cuffs on just to make sure. Anhur would have sunk to the bottom like a lead balloon.

The thought didn't bother Porter. He had no personal affiliation with Anhur other than using him for the occasional assignment. His employer's disposal of the man actually made things easier for Porter, a fact he would keep to himself.

"Can't have loose ends, can you, sir?"

If his boss thought he was going to pry a confession out of Porter, the guy was dead wrong.

"Precisely. I would hate to think you may have had something to do with what happened."

There it was: the bold accusation. Porter expected the man to lead with that and not beat around the bush. Then again, he was a politician. It was in their nature to waste time, dancing around a subject.

Porter had seen it ever since he moved to Washington. It was a different way of doing things. Where he came from in West Virginia, they didn't have time to waste. Life was hard, and if you didn't take on every day like it was your last, you were doing something wrong.

His father's death in the coal mines taught him that at a very young age. His mother's suicide three years later reinforced it. Porter had no intention of ever mincing words, tap dancing around a subject, or worrying about the politically correct thing to say.

He got the job done as quickly and efficiently as possible, which made him a perfect killing machine. It did not, however, make for good conversation.

"If you think I had anything to do with that mess, you need to think again, sir. You told me and my men to sit back and wait for further instructions. You were taking us off the case. Now you have the guts to call me and ask if I had something to do with your little screwup? No. No, I didn't have anything to do with it."

He knew the lie would work. There was nothing linking Porter to Anhur. He'd paid in cash and left nothing in the way of evidence that could connect him to the attack inside the Chinese joint.

The man on the other end of the line exhaled audibly through his nose. What could he do? He didn't have any proof that Porter was affiliated with the tattooed guy who shot up the restaurant, especially since the shooter was probably dead at this point.

"One of my men is following Wyatt. He's heading out of town. I need you to rendezvous with my asset and follow Wyatt to wherever he's going. It is of the utmost importance that we stop these individuals before they can cause more trouble."

There it was, Porter thought: the ask.

His employer waited patiently on the other end of the line for Porter's response.

"I'm sorry, sir, but are you saying you want me and my men back on the case?'

He knew his boss had to swallow his pride to say it. Politicians like him weren't good at doing that. Most of them hated having to admit they were wrong, and while Porter doubted he'd get those words out of his employer, he knew the man was thinking it.

"I need you to meet up with my guy and take out Wyatt and Schultz. Eliminate them at all costs. I don't care what it takes. Just wipe them off the face of the planet. Okay? Understood?"

"Loud and clear, sir. I'd be happy to rendezvous with your guy. My only question is, when and where would you like me to meet your other guy?"

"He said Wyatt and Schultz are heading out of town. Looks like they're going southeast. I'll give you his number so you two can sort it out. He's on the road right now, trailing the marks."

Porter thought it interesting that he had another man on the scene at the Chinese restaurant. That meant his employer either thought he needed a backup plan or maybe he thought Porter might try to get involved. By using Anhur as his trigger man, Porter had avoided direct confrontation, which meant he still had plausible deniability.

"Sounds good, sir. Thank you for the opportunity."

The other man said nothing. No apology. No "glad to have you back on the case." Just an ended call followed shortly by a text message with his other asset's phone number

Of course, Porter would make sure that guy ended up dead as well. Like he'd mentioned to his boss, loose ends needed to be tied up. In the line of fire, all sorts of accidents could happen. Once the tail was eliminated, there'd be no one in Porter's way.

He'd follow Wyatt to the treasure, kill him, and then make his employer pay for his doubt.

28. Clinton, Maryland

Sean and Tommy walked toward the maroon nineteenth-century farmhouse. The wooden siding and fresh paint were a tribute to the constant maintenance done on the historic site to keep it looking as it may have in the mid-1800s.

The area surrounding the Surratt house was less than historic. Gas stations and small shopping centers lined the streets nearby, taking away some of the prestige of such an old building and making it instead look like an out-of-place relic.

The town of Clinton was originally called Surrattsville, named for the family that founded it. After the Lincoln conspiracy came to light, the name was later changed so that any association with that tragic event would be lost to history.

Sean's and Tommy's heads were on a swivel, turning one way and then the other to make sure no one was watching—or following. So far, they'd not seen anything suspicious.

"You don't look comfortable," Tommy said to his friend as they neared the front steps of the Surratt House. "Cold?"

"It's like thirty degrees out. So yeah, I'm cold. That's not it, though."

"What is it, then? We haven't noticed anyone following us."

"That's what worries me," Sean said. "It's been too quiet."

Tommy stopped short of the first step and gave his friend an incredulous look. "Sometimes I wonder if you prefer to have trouble chasing you around."

Sean didn't break his stoic expression. "It's just easier when you see it coming. That's all. The knife you don't see is the one you should fear most."

Tommy sighed. "All right, Sun Tzu. Try not to stress yourself out too much, okay?"

Sean remained silent as they climbed the short set of steps onto the front porch and passed the sign hanging on one of the wooden columns that read *Surratt's Tavern*.

They opened the front door and stepped into a room that time forgot. The old hearth, the tables, the kitchen, the chairs, and every furnishing in the place looked original. It even smelled old, giving off scents of wood and smoke. Fake logs rested in the fireplace, smudging the authentic feel of the room. The only other thing that didn't fit with all the antiques was the yellow paint on the wall. It appeared to have been done some time in the last decade.

A woman with golden curly hair was sitting at a desk near the door when Sean and Tommy walked in. She stood up and smiled pleasantly at them. "Hello. Welcome to the Surratt House. Can I help you?"

Sean's eyes shifted to Tommy, giving him a *you*

wanna take this one glance.

"Yes," Tommy said. "I'm Tommy Schultz, and this is my friend Sean Wyatt. We work for the International Archaeological Agency and were wondering if we could take a look around your museum."

Based on the blank look on the woman's face, she had no clue who they were. "Would you like a guided tour, or do you just want to show yourself around?"

Sean noted the name on her tag. "Janet, is it?"

She nodded.

"If it's okay with you, we'd just like to have a look around. No need in doing a guided tour."

"Okay," she said with a hint of disappointment.

Sean figured she'd been sitting in there all day without a single visitor. Janet probably wanted to show them around just to break up the monotony.

"I'll be here if you have any questions," she said, returning to her seat with a dejected frown.

"Thanks," Tommy said, already wandering away from the information desk.

They made their way around the first room, inspecting every inch of floorboard, every brick, and every stone in the place. Their eyes scanned the walls, searching for a crack or a seam that might have been a hiding place for something secret.

After a short loop around the living room and the adjacent smaller rooms, the two still hadn't found anything that remotely suggested something might be hidden there.

"Is it okay for us to go upstairs and see the other rooms?" Sean asked.

"Certainly," Janet said. "The entire house is open to the public. You'll find the master bedroom and a few other rooms up there, as well as one room with several important artifacts on display."

"Great. Thank you."

Sean led the way up the creaky wooden steps. At the top, the room with the glass displays was straight ahead. Two rooms were on either side of the hall, and then another was back in the other direction. The open doors revealed the interior of every room. One looked like an old sewing room, another a spare bedroom, and the one at the end was the master bedroom.

"Take a look in these two rooms," Sean said. "I'm going to check out the master."

Tommy gave a nod and disappeared into the guest room while Sean meandered down the narrow corridor to the larger bedroom.

Inside the master bedroom, Sean found what appeared to be a queen-size bed. White linens and a comforter were tucked in tight. It looked like the bed had been permanently made. Another fireplace was set into the wall to his immediate left. A polished cherrywood dresser sat under a bright window, opposite the bed's beveled footrail. A matching armoire stood a few feet away, next to an antique rocking chair.

Whoever decorated the room contents had done

an impeccable job. A tall, black top hat rested on
the dresser, next to a bonnet and a few other items
from the era.

On the right side of the room, a little desk with a
mirror stood alone between windows.

Sean took a look back down the hallway and
then hurried over to the desk. He pulled out the
drawer but found nothing of interest inside. He
then moved over to the armoire and the dresser,
investigating the drawers and shelves of both, still
finding empty space.

He put his hands on his hips and considered
looking under the bed, but he decided against it.
Had there been anything there, someone would
have seen it long ago. Probably a custodian or one
of the curators like Janet.

Sean heard footsteps and spun around again.
Tommy was coming his way.

"Find anything?" Sean whispered so the lady
downstairs couldn't hear.

"No," Tommy said. "Just a bunch of antiques
they probably found at some flea market. Some of
the stuff might be original, but not much of it."

Sean ran his fingers through his hair. They'd
only been there for five minutes, and already the
sense of dread had begun creeping into their guts.

"If you were hiding something as important as
the map in question, where would you have put it?"
Sean asked.

Tommy bit the corner of his lower lip and gazed
up at the ceiling. "I'm not sure. In this instance,

John Surratt knew the authorities were probably going to come around collecting evidence."

"Correct. Which means it would have to be even more difficult to find than a mere trinket."

"So, what are you thinking?"

Sean stared down at the floor. He was running out of ideas. They couldn't exactly tear the walls down and rip up the floorboards in hopes of finding a map that may or may not exist. Even if it did, that ridiculous notion wasn't going to happen.

As his eyes ran along the floorboards and came to the spot where stone surrounded a small fireplace, he noticed something unusual. His eyebrows lowered, and he cocked his head to the side. A moment later, he stepped over to the stone tiles and took a knee next to the corner.

"What is it?" Tommy asked.

"I don't know. Might be nothing. Take a look."

Sean scooted to the right so his friend could get a better view.

"Notice anything unusual about these tiles?"

Tommy rolled his shoulders. "No, not really." Then he saw it. "Oh yeah. The grout they used around this one looks a little lighter in color than the rest."

"Exactly."

Sean bent down closer to get a better look. He pressed on the brick surrounded by the different grout, but it wouldn't budge. He tried to dig a fingernail into the gritty bond, but it was too firm to dislodge.

"We need a screwdriver or something," Sean said in a hushed tone.

"Should I run back out to the car? I think I've got something in there that we could use to pry it free."

"If you do, she'll wonder what's going on."

"Not if I tell her I left my phone in the car and want to take some pictures."

Sean raised his eyebrows. "Good idea. Do it."

Tommy scurried out of the room and down the stairs. Sean heard him giving the explanation to Janet. A second later, he heard the door creak open and close again. It only took Tommy a couple minutes to get to the car and back. He rounded the top of the stairs, and when Janet was out of view, pulled a socket iron out of his back pocket. One end was designed to loosen nuts on car wheels. The other end had a flat wedge.

"Good work," Sean said. "You want to start on the grout? I'm going to go downstairs and distract Janet."

Tommy looked puzzled. "Distract her?"

Sean stood up and brushed imaginary dust off his pants. "Yeah. Pretty sure if we start digging up this grout, she's going to hear something grinding through the ceiling over her head."

"Good thinking. I'll see what I can do."

Sean left the room and went downstairs. Tommy waited until he heard his friend begin a conversation with Janet about the history of the building. He chuckled to himself. With the woman eager to talk to anyone about anything, he figured that discussion would easily buy him enough time.

Tommy set to work on the grout, digging the flat end of the little iron into one of the long sides first. Initially, the wedge didn't do much to break down the gritty material. After a minute of applying some elbow grease, though, it started to crumble.

He couldn't hear the two downstairs anymore, and for a second worried he'd been too loud. Then he heard the faint sounds of their voices. They'd moved to a different room. Another smart move by Sean.

Convinced they were out of hearing distance, Tommy began grinding away again, this time with renewed vigor.

It took a few minutes to get the first side of grout stripped from between the brick and the floorboards. He found the short ends much easier, perhaps because he'd learned the trick of breaking it free.

Five minutes of hard scraping and pressure resulted in tired forearms and fingers. As he broke the last piece of grout loose, he felt the brick shift. Tommy froze again, listening for the others. Janet was still droning on about the kitchen and the furniture, so Tommy knew he was in the clear. She hadn't heard a thing.

Tommy worked his fingernails under the bottom of the brick and pried it from the floor. He gingerly set the brick to the side and gazed at the empty spot. The sub-floor had been left in place enough to give support to the brick tile. In its center, though, was a narrow hole cut in the shape of a long rectangle. A yellowish scroll sat inside a black metal container that was held in place around the rim of the cavity.

With a swallow and another cautionary look out into the hallway, Tommy reached into the hole and carefully stuck his fingernail under the edge of the scroll. The vellum bent under the pressure but didn't break as he pulled back, lifting it out of the cavity.

Tommy wished he had handling gloves on, but there was no time and at this point he just wanted to get out of there.

Ever so gently, he opened his jacket and slid the scroll into an inner pocket before zipping up the coat to conceal it. Then he picked up the brick tile and placed it back over the hole.

"Crap," he said, realizing there was grout all around the brickwork and floorboards.

He heard Sean's voice from the bottom of the stairs.

"Yes, that would be nice for you to show us a few of the more interesting pieces upstairs." Sean boomed, loud enough for Tommy to know what his friend meant.

It was a warning. They were about to climb the staircase.

Tommy lifted the brick again and hurriedly began sweeping the dust and debris into the hole where he found the hidden scroll. Sean and Janet's footsteps grew louder; the stairs creaked under their weight as they ascended.

Tommy's heart pounded in his chest. They were almost to the top of the steps where they'd be able to see inside the bedroom.

Sean turned his head as he followed Janet and saw Tommy sweeping the grout remnants furiously with his hands.

"Janet," Sean said in as calm a tone as he could muster, "I was hoping you could tell me about some of the items in the display cases."

"Certainly," she said and led the way into the room at the other end of the hall.

Tommy breathed faster. He finished cleaning up the debris as best as he could and then put the brick back in its place.

Now the problem wasn't the mess. It was the missing grout around the brick. And there was no way to replace it.

He stood up and looked around. Then he realized his heels were pressing into an antique area rug. He raised his eyes and glanced down the hall. Sean was listening to the woman talk about a flag in one of the cases.

Without a moment to lose, Tommy bent down at the knees and grabbed the rug with two hands. He tugged it, putting his weight into it, and found that it moved easier than he expected. He pulled again and let it fall. The fabric covered half of the brick.

One more pull, he thought to himself.

He gripped it again and leaned back. The rug budged again, but this time two of the bed's legs came free and clacked on the floor.

Tommy shuddered. He let the rug fall and looked back down the hall.

"Is everything okay in there?" Janet said. She appeared at the opposing doorway a second later.

"Yes," Tommy said, red-faced. "Everything's fine."

She frowned, dubious about his answer. "Why's your face so red all of a sudden?"

"My face? Oh. Because I just banged my knee on the corner of the bed. I'm terribly sorry."

He reached down and grabbed his kneecap, feigning injury.

"Oh, I'm sorry," Janet said.

"It's okay. I'm such a klutz. I don't think I hurt the bed." He limped out of the bedroom and into the hall. "I'll be fine." He bent the knee and kicked a couple of times like he was testing it.

"Are you sure? You want me to get some ice or something?" Janet asked.

Tommy almost felt bad for lying to the nice woman. "No, really, it'll be good. Just have to walk it off. I think I'll head outside and walk around a bit."

"I'll come with you," Sean said.

"Oh." Janet seemed disappointed her tour had come to a sudden end.

"Thank you so much, Janet. I really appreciate you taking the time to show me some of these wonderful antiques you have. It's always great to experience real history like this." Sean passed her an almost flirty smile.

The grin broke down her defenses completely, and she blushed. "Well, you are so welcome. Come back anytime you like."

Tommy walked tenderly down the stairs, partly to keep up the act with his knee and partly so he didn't jostle the potentially priceless document in his coat.

Once they were outside and the front door closed behind them, Tommy picked up the pace, walking briskly back toward the car. He didn't dare turn around for fear of Janet looking out a window and seeing them.

When they were almost to the car, Sean ticked his head to the side. "Did you find it?" he asked through barely parted lips.

"I found something," Tommy said.

"Is it the map?"

"Don't know. Didn't really have time to open it up and analyze it, you know, with your new girlfriend coming up the stairs and all."

They hopped into the car, and Sean started the engine. Tommy carefully unzipped his coat as Sean backed the car out of the parking space and steered it out toward the road.

Tommy pulled the rolled vellum out of the pocket and held it out for Sean to see.

"Nice," Sean said. "Good work, my friend."

Tommy breathed a sigh of relief. "Yeah. Now let's see what secrets Mr. Surratt was hiding in his bedroom."

29. Clinton

Sean guided the car along the busy county road.
Other vehicles filled the oncoming lane as people
hurried home after a long day of work. Most of
them probably had jobs in Washington, a few on
the outskirts in some of the newer corporations
that took root during years of prosperity and
development.

The yellow-orange sun blazed just over the
horizon, fading rapidly toward the hills and ridges
to the west.

"That looks like a good spot," Sean said, pointing
at a pull-off near the river.

There were picnic tables under huge oak trees, a
loading ramp for boats, and a few charcoal grills
permanently fixed in the ground.

"Yeah, that's fine," Tommy said. He still cradled
the rolled vellum in his lap.

Sean pulled off the road and onto the gravel
parking area. He left the engine running so they'd
still have heat.

Tommy took the letter they found in the cave
and set it on the seat next to his leg. Next, he took
out his laptop and placed it on his lap. The
computer made for a decent makeshift desk given
the circumstances. Then he began peeling back the
vellum scroll. Every move he made was full of

nauseating trepidation for fear of tearing it or ruining the integrity of the map.

Tommy spent a full five minutes unrolling since rushing might have meant disaster. As he pressed down the corners of the vellum sheet, the two friends stared in disbelief.

The document was blank.

"I don't...I don't understand." Sean said. "Why would they go through the trouble of hiding a blank piece of vellum? Did the ink fade?"

Tommy shook his head. He felt the heat coming out of the car's vents. "No, it didn't fade. And I'm pretty sure it's still there."

He held the laptop up close to one of the vents, pinning down the top corners of the map with his fingers.

"Turn the heat up as hot as you can," Tommy said.

Sean reached over and twisted the knob. The temperature of the air pouring out of the vents increased immediately.

The two watched for a moment, waiting for the chemicals in the ink to activate. At first, nothing happened. But as the heat continued to flow and warm the entire document, lines began to appear. Soon, words came to light along with different designs representing mountains, islands, the ocean, and rivers.

Sean and Tommy stared with wide eyes at the map.

"You know, I've seen invisible ink before,"

Tommy said, "but every time I see it appear I am kind of amazed."

"No kidding," Sean agreed.

The map depicted a highly detailed map of Alaska, for the time period. Most modern cities there today weren't listed because the drawing had been created before they'd been founded.

"Now," Tommy said, "let's see if we can find what all the fuss is about."

He picked up the letter next to his leg and opened it, spreading it over top of the map with the greatest of care. He flattened it as much as possible, pressing firmly while making sure the edges and corners lined up.

"You got a pencil or a pen in here?" Tommy asked.

Sean reached into the center console and produced a pen. "You're going to draw on what might be one of the most valuable American artifacts ever found?"

Tommy snorted. "You got a better idea? We need to mark the location."

Sean shook his head. "No, just making sure you understood the gravity of what you're about to do."

"Oh, I understand. Don't think I'm happy about it, either."

Tommy removed the pen's lid and held it over the letter. He continued to press down on the two sheets, keeping them as flush as possible. Then he took the pen and held it over the hole in the letter. He paused for a second, probably to reconsider what he was about to do. After a moment's hesitation, Tommy pressed the pen through the hole and wiggled it around, making a dot.

He swallowed and started breathing again. He handed the pen back to Sean like a doctor passing a scalpel to a surgical technician. After another deep breath, Tommy lifted the letter off the map and stared at the new ink spot.

The dot was located beside two words the two hadn't expected.

Bolshaya Gora.

"Russian?" Tommy asked.

"Looks that way," Sean said, leaning over the center console to get a better look. "It means 'big mountain.'"

"Denali?" Tommy asked.

"I think so," Sean said. "Interesting it's in Russian."

Tommy rolled his shoulders. "Actually, it makes perfect sense. The Russians were the first ones to explore that area, other than the natives, of course."

"Of course."

Both men pored over the map, noting all the other way points written in Russian.

"The guys William Seward sent to Alaska must have brought this map back to him. That means—"

"Seward didn't just send explorers. He sent thieves to steal this thing," Sean finished the thought for his friend.

"Possibly. That's assuming he knew someone

had this. Seeing it right now, though, sure seems that way." Tommy had another thought. "That means someone in the Confederacy must have discovered this two-part map and taken it."

"Right. And Andrews' Raiders were sent to recover the piece with the hole in it. You thought you were worried about damaging something valuable. Think about Private Knight writing his letter on that thing. I imagine he wasn't thrilled about it."

Tommy nodded in agreement. "I wonder what this is," he said, pointing at the dot on the map.

"Let's look at what we know. It's close to Denali. From the looks of it, I'd say it's situated in the hills surrounding the big mountain. What's in those hills?" Sean asked the question already knowing the answer.

"Gold?"

"Yep," Sean said. "At least there used to be."

Then another thought struck him. "One of the men who came after me said that there was something under the mountain that could produce gold."

"You mean like alchemy?" Tommy asked.

Sean snorted a short laugh. "I said those exact words. Yes, just like alchemy."

Tommy dismissed the idea with a scowl. "Alchemy isn't real. There's been nothing in science to prove that you can turn lead into gold."

"Maybe it isn't lead they're using. And maybe it isn't alchemy as we understand it."

"Maybe. There's still a lot we don't know about old, or ancient, technology."

"Right. And remember, a thousand years ago the Vikings thought thunder and lightning was Thor using his hammer. It may very well be that what these Russians were talking about wasn't gold at all. It might have been something else, and the translation down through the last 150 years got screwed up."

"Good point," Tommy said. "Either way, you and I both know the only real possibility we have of knowing what's up there is to go see for ourselves."

Sean sighed. "Yeah, but that's going to be the problem. No way we're getting across the Canadian border. The guys behind all this will have the borders locked down tight. And obviously flying isn't an option. Not even with your private plane."

"What about sneaking across the border?" Tommy offered.

"I considered it. Even so, it would take us way too long to get there. Not to mention that getting up there via the roads will be nearly impossible this time of year. Most of the roads will be closed."

"So, we take a boat. Sail into Anchorage and then make our way out to Denali."

Sean shook his head again. "Coast Guard. And we would still have the problem of getting across the country. The closest port to our destination would be Seattle. Combining the time it takes to sail with the drive out there, we'd be looking at nearly a week of travel."

"What do we do, then?"

Sean didn't have an answer. He tried to think back to a time before he and Tommy had every resource imaginable. Before the private jets, the endless amounts of money, and the connections around the globe, the two friends had managed to get around the country—even the world—with limited resources. Time wasn't a factor back then. If they wanted to drive to Saint Louis for a Braves road game, they could do it without having to worry about anything serious.

Things weren't like that anymore, and their current predicament posed a very real threat to a number of people.

He felt his phone start vibrating in his pocket. Sean looked at the screen and saw it was Adriana's burner phone.

"Hey," he answered. "You okay?"

"I'm fine. Listen, we figured out why you couldn't get through to Emily or anyone at axis."

"Oh yeah?"

"Yes. Someone from the CIA redirected the phone line. We were able to search the camera footage from several video surveillance spots around Axis HQ. One of the cameras got a great shot of the guy who sabotaged the incoming line. It was pretty high tech, too. They rigged it for only certain calls. Since you'd been in Auburn, getting a call from that area code was an easy one to mark. That's why no one else noticed what was going on. They kept getting their normal calls without interruption. Emily sent one of her people up the telephone pole to retrieve it. They're dissecting the device as we speak."

"Wow. I can't believe I didn't think of that." Sean cursed himself in his mind.

"No one did...well, until we did. Don't beat yourself up."

"Thanks. What else did you find?"

"We spoke to June and the kids," she said. Sean glanced over at Tommy, who looked at him with curiosity in his eyes.

"I'll explain later," Sean mouthed.

Adriana went on. "They found some interesting information about who we think might be behind the assassination attempt on Dawkins."

"Really?"

"Yep. They tracked a big chunk of money that was put into a fall guy's account. Two accounts, actually, and in two different countries."

"Fall guy?" Sean knew what the term meant, but he didn't understand the context.

"Some guy named Kendricks. Cops shot him dead outside the hotel where the assassination attempt took place. One day, he had an account in Nicaragua and another in Costa Rica, both loaded with a ton of money. The next day, the accounts were dry. The kids had a friend who tracked where the funds came from. They were filtered through a number of channels, but eventually the money was traced to a company called Transcorp."

"Never heard of it."

"I guess most people haven't unless you're in that sector. It's an energy company. They work under the radar, providing power to a good number of other corporations. They claim to be a green energy sort of deal, but we haven't been able to find anything about their land holdings, solar farms, wind farms, nothing."

"Sounds like Transcorp likes to keep their operations out of the public eye. Easy enough to do when you're a private company and not publicly traded. No SEC breathing down your neck all the time, fewer things to file."

"That's not even the most troubling part." She paused for a second. "The majority shareholder is the secretary of state, Kent Foster."

Sean frowned upon hearing that last piece. He clenched his jaw and stared out at the dark, rippling water. "So, you think Foster is behind all this?"

"Apparently, he's been pushing Dawkins and Congress to take down the Tennessee Valley Authority for a long time. Foster wants it broken up and sold to private entities."

"Break up TVA? We have some of the lowest energy costs in the nation."

"I know. But by breaking it up, Transcorp would have the most to gain. With their green energy initiatives, they'd be lovable to the public and have the money and infrastructure to eventually take over the Eastern Seaboard."

"How much money?"

"Right now, they're valued at around ten billion, but they're locked on the West Coast right now. If they can get across the Mississippi, they'll be the primary energy suppliers to the entire country."

Sean took a moment to let the information sink in. Presidents and vice presidents were under constant financial scrutiny. Most of them put their assets into a blind trust. Dawkins's predecessor kept his money in mutual funds and treasury bonds to keep things on the up-and-up. No one ever really put much thought into the secretary of state's finances. Foster was in the perfect position to make moves that would benefit his company and yet remain largely anonymous through the entire process.

Another piece to the puzzle popped into Sean's mind, and it brought everything into focus.

"Foster found out about what I was doing for the president."

"How?"

"How did they take down Nixon? There must have been a bug somewhere. When Foster found out I was getting close, he sent his CIA goons after me."

"And because the president knew too much already, he had to be eliminated as well," Adriana said.

"Exactly. That either means Foster wants Dawkins out of the way so he can take down TVA, or he doesn't want him to find whatever it is out in Alaska." Sean had another thought. "I can't help but wonder..." His voice trailed off.

"Wonder what?" she asked.

"You mentioned that Transcorp doesn't have any wind or solar farms on record."

"Correct."

"I'm assuming they don't own any hydroelectric stations either."

"Usually, assuming isn't the way to go. We both know why, but that is also correct. They don't own any of those."

"That brings me back to what I was thinking. Is it possible that they're producing their power from something underground, possibly a geothermal station of some kind?"

For a brief moment, Adriana didn't answer. Sean didn't expect her to right away. He knew that sort of thing wasn't her area of expertise.

"I suppose it's possible," she said, finally. "They'd have to run power lines, though. And those lines would have to traverse thousands of miles to get power to the lower forty-eight states."

"They built an oil pipeline that does that. Running some cables would be easier."

"Good point," she said. "You want me to have someone look into that?"

"The power lines? No. I have a feeling they probably kept that under wraps as well. It's also a good bet the lines are underground."

Another concern came to Sean's mind. "Does Dawkins know about Foster?"

"I'm on my way back to Washington to warn

him."

"You didn't call?"

"He's in a secure bunker right now, but he's scheduled to make an appearance tomorrow. All the phone lines going into the White House are jammed. I have to warn him myself."

He continued staring out the windshield at the river. A little single-prop airplane bounced in the air several miles away. It almost didn't look like it was moving.

It sounded like Adriana had thought everything through. With Emily working with her, they'd have all the angles covered. Now he needed them to cover one more.

"I need you to ask Emily for a favor," he said.

"And that is?"

"See if she can get a plane for us. Nothing fancy. In fact, the less fancy, the better. We need something that can make it across the country with minimal stops, and we need it at the smallest airport near Clinton, Maryland you can find."

"Clinton? Is that where you guys are?"

"We're close to there, yes. Can you do that for me?"

"Yep. I'll tell her right now. I have to go. Anything else?"

"No," Sean shook his head. A thin smile stretched across his mouth. "Thank you."

"You're welcome. Thank you, too."

"For what?"

"I'll think of something."

They ended the call, and Sean realized his friend was staring at him. He suddenly became uncomfortable.

"What?" Sean asked.

"You gonna share that intimate moment with me or just the information she gave you about Foster?" Tommy said with a devilish smirk.

"Funny guy. I assume you heard me ask for the plane, right?"

"I did," Tommy said with a nod. "She gonna text or call when they know more about that? Or are you just assuming on that one, too? Seems like you're doing a lot of assuming."

"You're on a roll. You know that?" Sean asked as he shifted the car into reverse and started backing out of the lot.

Tommy shrugged. "Just making an observation."

"She'll let me know soon."

"Great. So, where we going?"

"Right now, we're going to keep moving. The longer we sit still, the easier targets we become. Need to stay on the move."

"I meant, where are we going on the plane?" Tommy corrected.

Sean steered the car back onto the road and glanced into the rearview mirror. Traffic was still heavy coming back from Washington. Soon it would be dark. The sun was already half behind the distant horizon.

"Anchorage," Sean said.

"I thought you'd say that. You know we're going

to need a good bit of cold weather gear if we're going up there, especially if we're heading out to Denali. Not to mention we might need some tools."

"We'll sort out the cold weather gear when we get there. As to the tools...I have a strange feeling we're not venturing into an undiscovered place."

30. Clinton

Porter watched Sean and Tommy through a pair of powerful binoculars. His driver stood outside the car, watching carefully behind some shrubs and small trees that lined the highway.

Porter's two men were in the back, waiting quietly.

They'd met their contact on the outskirts of Clinton and left their car in an empty church lot. The driver, a man by the name of Steve, was apparently running the show for their mutual employer.

Even though he thought it reckless to get out of the car or even to park as close as they were to their marks, Porter kept his thoughts to himself, letting Steve keep thinking he was the one in charge.

The men in the back knew better.

"It's hard to see what they're doing from this far away," Steve said in a hushed tone. The men in the car almost didn't hear him over the sound of vehicles zooming by. "We need to get closer."

"If you get closer, you run the risk of them seeing us," Porter warned. "We don't have to know what they're doing. We just have to keep an eye on them."

Steve shook his head. "I don't like it. Our boss

wants us to intercept them. Why are we sitting back here, watching? They're sitting there in the open. If we're going to take them, we need to do it now."

Porter didn't flinch. If he were a more sensitive person, he'd have felt sorry for Steve. The guy might honestly believe he was doing something like fighting domestic terrorism or something. There was no telling what their employer had told him. Not that it mattered, but Steve was a minor roadblock—a small branch across the road—easily moved out of the way with a little push.

"Give it a minute," Porter said.

He didn't have a reason. Truth was, he didn't need one. Steve was a beta male, and Porter knew it. He realized it the moment they shook hands and their eyes locked. There was a lack of confidence, a timidness that Porter picked up on. It was something he'd seen in other "coworkers." Usually, he had to cut the dead weight. That didn't always mean killing them. But in this case, it definitely did.

Porter reached into his jacket and eased the pistol out of its holster.

"Why would we wait?" Steve persisted. "The longer we sit here, the better chance they have of getting away."

He was right about that, although Porter had no intention of letting his quarry escape so easily. Before he made a move on Wyatt and Schultz, he had to get rid of his employer's errand boy. Then nothing would stand in Porter's way.

He found the sound suppressor in the gear bag at his feet and screwed it into place. Every squeak from the twisting metal sounded like a trumpet blaring, but Porter knew he was just being overly sensitive. Not that he needed to be. He had the feeling he could walk right up to Steve, show him the gun, tell him he was going to kill him with it, and still be able to pull it off.

Steve kept looking through his binoculars. Porter could tell he was getting antsy just from the man's body language.

"See what they're doing yet?" Porter asked, keeping the conversation going.

"No. I'm telling you, we're too far away. Only thing I can see is the car and silhouettes of the men inside."

Porter opened his door and stepped out. He left the door open so as not to startle Steve from his surveillance. With the weapon held loosely behind his back, Porter walked quietly over to the unaware man.

"I think you might be right," Porter said, putting his binoculars to his eyes with his right hand. "We really are too far away to see what they're doing."

Steve turned, now realizing Porter had gotten out of the car. "Yeah, I know," he said in an angry tone. "That's what I've been trying to tell you. If we go over there right now, we can box them in and take them down. I don't know if you realize it, but those two are extremely dangerous. The sooner we can get to them, the better."

Porter shifted closer to Steve, momentarily lowering his binoculars. When he was a few feet away, he craned his neck and narrowed his eyes as if he'd seen something of interest. He put his binoculars back to his face.

"Whoa," he said. "There it is."

"There what is?" Steve asked, hurriedly raising his binoculars to see what was going on.

Porter lowered his binoculars, raised the weapon in his left hand, and squeezed the trigger. A pink mist erupted from the other side of Steve's skull. His body stood still for a second before toppling over to the side and into the bushes.

The two men in the back of the car saw their cue and immediately got out. They calmly walked over to the body, grabbed the dead man by the ankles, and dragged him deeper into the bushes. They worked quickly, kicking leaves and piling branches over the body until it was almost invisible to the curious eye.

Someone would find him eventually, of course. That was a certainty. Porter's only concern was making sure that didn't happen in the next few hours.

Cars continued to hurry by: a road full of witnesses who didn't see a thing.

Porter returned to the front passenger seat while one of his men climbed into the front. Looking through the binoculars again, Porter watched as Wyatt's car backed out of the spot next to the river.

"They're on the move," he said to his driver. "Time to get going. Wait until they're on the main road before you pull out."

"Yes, sir," the driver said.

Porter kept his eyes on his quarry. The car steered out onto the highway and turned to the right.

"Hang back. I think I know where they're going."

"Where, sir?"

"What would you do if you were them and you'd just found the map to a massive treasure in Alaska?"

The driver thought for a second. "Get a flight to Alaska?"

"Bingo."

"But they'll be picked up by our people if they go near an airport."

"Not if they go to a small one. Security is much more lax at those."

"What's the plan then, sir?"

"Let them go to the airport. We take them down before they board. Then...we take their plane. You're a pilot, right?"

"Yes, sir."

"Well then. Looks like we just found our ride."

31. Washington

Emily tapped away at the tiny keyboard on her phone. She'd sent the president six text messages since leaving her Atlanta office. He hadn't responded to a single one.

She wasn't surprised. Only land lines worked down in the bunker. At least that's what she tried to tell herself. The problem with that theory was that phones worked on Wi-Fi as well. So, if there was a wireless internet connection in the president's protected quarters, he'd be able to see the texts.

Adriana drove their rental car down through the dark streets of the nation's capital. It was getting late. The chill of winter had driven most of the pedestrians indoors for the night. There were still cars driving about, but not nearly as many as during business hours.

"Any luck?" Adriana asked as she guided the car through an intersection and merged onto Pennsylvania Avenue.

"No," Emily said. "Nothing. I don't know if he's getting my messages that far underground. They should have the internet down there, but I'm not sure."

"Maybe he set his phone down somewhere to charge it."

"Yeah, it could be for a number of reasons," Emily said with a sigh.

She didn't like the fact that she couldn't get in touch with Dawkins. Over the years, they'd developed a strong relationship, mostly kept out of the public eye for discretionary reasons.

There was no denying Emily's feelings for the president. And she knew he felt the same about her. Those emotional attachments made the attempt on his life that much more difficult for Emily. The thought of losing him had become almost unbearable.

"John is a smart man," Adriana said, using the president's first name. "He may have already figured out who was behind everything."

"Maybe."

"He has every resource in the world at his disposal. I'm sure he has good people on it."

"Yeah. The only problem is that some of those resources may be out to kill him. Like Foster." She shook her head at the name. "I always thought there was something off about him."

"What do you mean?"

"I never really put a finger on it. He just seemed like a shady guy. I'm sure you know what I'm talking about when it comes to politicians. Most of them have a slimy feel to them."

Adriana agreed with a nod. "Yes, I think that is a universal issue, not just an American one."

Emily blew air through her lips, flapping them for a second. "Working for the president has been a real blessing. Most of the other agencies have to answer to committees, boards, other arms of government. We operate with a good amount of autonomy, only answering to the man himself."

"That's definitely got its advantages."

"Yes. It's nice to not have to worry about oversight committees and that sort of thing. They slow down so much of the work that needs to be done."

Adriana turned into the driveway leading up to the White House. After they'd gone through the checkpoints and parked their car, they made their way through another security check in an outbuilding next to the presidential mansion.

Emily led the way through the halls of the White House, showing off her credentials to every Secret Service agent she passed.

"Looks like they brought in a few extra people," Emily said after flashing her badge for the fifth time.

"Can you blame them?"

"No. That's standard protocol. I'm guessing some of these guys are working doubles to make sure they have enough people on hand."

Emily nodded as she turned down another long hall. "Yes. Normally that would be a problem, which is why they work in shifts. During an emergency, however, these agents are able to go longer, probably due to the increased adrenaline going through their veins. Somehow, they find a way to get it done."

They reached the secret elevator, and Emily raised her credentials for the guy standing guard. He gave a curt nod and let them pass.

The two didn't say much on the elevator ride down until they neared the bottom. Then Adriana brought up a good question.

"What are we going to do if Foster is in here with the president?"

"I considered that might happen. If it does, we face him right there, tell Dawkins everything, and let him sort out how to handle it."

The doors opened, and they were greeted by the same sterile hallway from before. It almost felt like they'd never left.

Emily led the way down the first corridor and made a right at an intersection.

"Shouldn't we go that way?" Adriana asked, pointing to the left.

"No. That's where we were before. He'll be in the control room, more than likely."

"Control room?"

Emily didn't need to answer. The two rounded another turn and found themselves staring into a cavernous room with a giant map on the far wall and computer workstations covering three rows of counters.

"Wow," Adriana said.

"Yes, it's impressive, isn't it?"

"You could say that."

"In case of a nuclear attack, this bunker was constructed to oversee response operations."

"Response operations?"

Emily nodded. "Retaliation. Now, though, we don't have as many nuclear threats as we used to, so this room has been altered. The commander in chief can still monitor our nuclear arsenal from here, but modern times call for more clandestine approaches."

"Like when they took out that terrorist a few years ago in Pakistan."

"Correct. There's a similar bunker in Colorado, at NORAD. In fact, NORAD was built for this purpose, but then we got to thinking if the president couldn't get out of Washington in time, it would be good to have a home base of operations, right under his actual home."

"Good thinking," Adriana said, still staring in disbelief at all the lights, screens, and gizmos."

"We think so," a familiar man's voice said.

They turned to the right and saw Dawkins appear from one of the control room's side offices.

His face beamed with delight, especially at Emily.

"Mr. President," Emily said, "we have some disturbing information. Is the secretary of state here?"

Puzzled, Dawkins tilted his head to the side with eyebrows furrowed and forehead wrinkled. "No," he said. "Foster left hours ago. Said he had something pressing come up."

"You're sure he's out of the building?" Adriana asked.

The question only served to add to the president's confusion. "Yes, I'm quite sure. Why? What's this all about?"

Emily grabbed him by the wrist. "Come with me."

The surprised look on his face was mirrored by the Secret Service agent standing by the door. Before the young man could stop Emily, Dawkins waved him off, reassuring him that it was going to be okay.

Emily, Adriana, and the president stepped into a small office set into the back. Emily closed the door and looked around, sweeping the place with her eyes to make sure nothing out of the ordinary was sitting in the open.

"Looking for bugs?" Dawkins asked. "Because this room is clean. Anything said in here is only heard by those present."

"You're sure?" Emily asked.

Dawkins chuckled. "Yes, I'm sure. What's all this about? And why were you asking about Kent Foster?"

Adriana and Emily exchanged a sidelong glance.

"Go ahead," Adriana said with an outstretched palm.

"Okay," Emily said. "Sir, we have reason to believe that Kent Foster is the one behind the assassination attempt."

His eyebrows jerked in surprise. If the accusation hadn't been accompanied by such a serious face, he might have laughed.

"I'm sorry. Is this some kind of joke?" All he needed to see was Emily's stern face before he knew the answer. "Are you serious? Foster? Why? What possible motive could he have?"

"Sir," Adriana broke in, "we will fill you in on all the details later. Right now, we need to know where Foster is. Do you know where he went?"

The president looked baffled. "No. Not exactly. He said he had to attend a security briefing."

"And you don't know where that briefing is taking place?" Emily asked.

"No. I don't usually keep strict tabs on my cabinet members."

"We need to find him. Foster is the primary shareholder in an energy company called Transcorp."

"I'm aware of that, Emily."

"And you're also aware that if the government were to dismantle TVA and force it to go private that would open up a massive market for energy companies?"

Dawkins didn't see where this was going, but he kept pulling the string to the sweater. "I have no plans to dismantle TVA. They have the best power rates in the country for consumers. I'd lose the entire Southeast if I did that. Besides, if it ain't broke, don't fix it."

Normally, his Southern adages brought a smile or a bit of laughter. In this case, he was dead serious.

"Yes, but if you were out of the way, your vice

president is a much more malleable person. With the proper influence, he could be convinced to sway Congress to Foster's side."

Dawkins shook his head, dismissing the notion. "The secretary of state doesn't always get involved with domestic affairs like that. I have another person in charge of those kinds of things. So even if I were gone and the vice president was running the show, Foster would be too busy with foreign affairs and national security."

"Except for the fact that he's been here, with you, for the last few weeks."

She made a good point. Foster had been hanging around more than usual. That didn't necessarily mean he was guilty.

"The man the police killed outside the hotel, the one they're accusing of being the trigger man, he had ties to Transcorp," Adriana said. "We found bank accounts in Nicaragua and Costa Rica with huge sums of money sent from other offshore accounts."

"Go on," the president said with piqued interest.

"So, the deposits all came from Transcorp. Not directly. They were funneled through several dummy accounts before landing in those two places. The real kicker was that after Kendricks was killed, just hours later, someone visited those banks and took the money out. It's gone, and there's no way to trace who took it."

"Wait a minute," Dawkins said, holding up his hand. "You're saying that Kendricks was a fall guy?"

"That's not all, sir," Emily said. "The truth is, we don't know who we can trust. Not even with some of your closest advisers."

Dawkins's face continued to get longer and longer with every additional piece of information. The final comment did him in. Forlorn, he crossed his arms and eased into a desk chair near the window looking out into the control room.

"And you're positive about all this?" he asked.

"Unfortunately," Emily said. "But we're sure your Secret Service men aren't in on it. There may be police and some other advisers, though we have no way of knowing right now. A full investigation will begin in earnest as soon as we make sure you're safe."

"I'm not leaving the White House," Dawkins said. "The last thing I can do right now is project weakness. We shot a press conference earlier. It looks just like our press room above ground. As far as the American people are concerned, I'm still here and doing my job as normal. If I venture out, that might send the wrong message."

"I'm more worried about your safety than a message, Mr. President."

He sighed. "You don't have to call me that, Emily."

"We're at work, Mr. President."

"Is that work Emily or personal Emily that's worried about my safety?"

"It's both, sir. If you're not going to leave, then I

am staying with you."

He smirked at the threat. "If you think that's going to get me to go with you, you may want to rethink your strategy. Besides, we will be going back up top in the morning. All the security sweeps have detected no danger. The White House will resume normal business first thing tomorrow."

"Fine. Just promise me you won't let Foster near the building. He's a snake in the grass. He already struck once. Don't give him another chance."

"Very well," Dawkins said with resignation. "I'll alert security."

"There's more, sir."

"More?" Dawkins said as his eyebrows lifted.

"Yes, sir. Someone redirected the calls coming into Axis from Sean's number as well as areas where he was known to be operating, such as western New York. The phone they were sent to is most likely a burner. I doubt we can connect it to anyone on paper. Our cameras, however, were able to help us ID the person who put the device on the lines outside our building."

"You have a positive ID?"

"Yes, sir. His name is Mark Pinkton."

"Never heard of him."

Adriana and Emily exchanged a knowing glance. Emily pulled a folder out of her bag and passed it to the president.

He opened it and looked at the images at the top of a stack.

"That is Pinkton standing next to a CIA

operative named Drew Porter."

"And look who they're standing behind," Adriana added.

Dawkins lifted the image a little closer so his eyes could focus. It looked like the image had been taken somewhere in Europe. The buildings in the background looked familiar. Moscow, perhaps? The two men were standing in a group of security personnel, slightly in front of the rest. They were clearly protecting the man at the front of the picture as he gave a speech behind a podium.

The speaker was Kent Foster.

The president's face turned pale. "Get me the head of the Secret Service. And call Langley. Someone's going to have some explaining to do."

"We've already made the calls, sir," Emily said. "Porter and Pinkton are missing. They've gone rogue."

32. Washington

"How did this happen?" Foster raged.

"I'm not sure, sir," Porter answered. "I told him to hang back, to keep his distance from Wyatt. He insisted on trying to apprehend the two marks."

"Those were not his orders."

"Yes, sir. I know. I have no idea why he decided to go against what you wanted. Now he's dead, and Wyatt and Schultz are on the run."

Foster wiped his cold nose with a finger. He glanced out the car window and saw the airport fast approaching.

"What happened to the body? The last thing I need is someone finding a dead CIA agent lying around. If anyone at Langley were to find out, there would be an inquisition like the world hasn't seen since the actual inquisition."

Porter knew the ramifications. He didn't care if the CIA investigated the murder. He wouldn't be touched by it. No one would even think to ask if he was involved. Foster—on the other hand—had plenty of reasons to worry. The secretary of state had been cautious with Porter and his men, always meeting in secret, paying in cash for each assignment, and never using the same burner phone from month to month. That didn't mean there was no evidence that could link him to

Steve's murder—or to the president's for that matter.

Porter didn't want to pull that particular string. He knew that if he threw Foster under the bus, the man would retaliate and take down everyone else who worked for him.

Spending the rest of his life in prison—or worse, being executed—didn't sound appealing to Porter. He'd worked too hard, come too far to turn back now.

So, he kept Foster on the line like a striped bass nibbling at a rubber worm.

"No one is going to find the body, sir," Porter said. "And if they do, we'll put it on Wyatt. He's a loose cannon. Every airport and border agency in the country is on the lookout for him. Now we have one more reason to put his face on those wanted posters."

Foster's silence told Porter the man had liked the idea—and the assessment of the situation.

"I'm curious," Foster said, "how did you escape? Were you or your men injured?"

"No, sir. We're okay. I guess Steve was in a hurry to make a name for himself. He rushed Wyatt and Schultz. Tried to ambush them as they sat next to the river a few miles outside of Clinton. He approached the two men, kept his weapon on Schultz, and then Wyatt shot him in the side of the head."

Foster didn't care about Steve on a personal level. He was an asset, an expendable resource.

Types like those were easy enough to find. What he did care about was whether or not Porter was telling the truth. He'd already shown he wasn't dependable. The fact that Wyatt was still alive was a testament to that. There was also no question that Porter was not to be trusted. Any person who was willing to sell out their position for a chance at money and power was a snake. Snakes had to be handled with care.

There was no way to know Porter's true ambitions. The man always kept things close to the vest, which incited a small amount of admiration in Foster. It reminded him of his own way of handling things.

Now, however, Foster was in a tight spot. He didn't have time to call in more help. He was on his way to the airport. A plane waited to take him to Alaska. Interruptions and distractions could wait. This, however, was different. He needed Wyatt and his friend dealt with immediately.

"What did Wyatt find?" Foster asked.

"We're not sure, sir. He went into the old Surratt Museum. When they came out, neither he nor Schultz was carrying anything that we could tell."

"That you could tell?"

"No, sir."

"What is that supposed to mean?" Foster boomed. "You should have taken them down right there."

"Have you ever been to the Surratt Museum?"

Foster didn't answer, so Porter continued. "I

take that as a *no*. That place is surrounded by busy roads, gas stations, shopping plazas, you name it. I've been operating under the assumption you'd prefer us not draw any undue attention. Perhaps I was wrong about that."

Foster fumed, but he couldn't argue the point. He'd never been to Clinton. Based on what Porter was telling him, it sounded like his men made the right decision—well, right up to the point Steve was killed.

"No. You did right," Foster said.

He didn't trust Porter. For the time being, though, he had to—until he could eliminate the asset.

"What's your status now?" Foster asked.

"We're tailing Wyatt and Schultz. Looks like they're heading to an airport."

Foster let a "ha" escape his mouth. "Are they stupid? They'll be taken into custody on sight."

"Not at a smaller airport, sir. There's one not far from here. Best we can figure, they've made arrangements for a plane to fly out of here."

"To where?"

"That part we don't know."

"Then you better find out."

"Actually, sir, the plan is to take them down before they board. If they took something from the Surratt House, we'll find it. The question is, what do you want us to do with it if we find something?"

Foster didn't have to think long. "Destroy it. Everything. Burn it all. I don't care how you do it.

Just make sure there is no evidence of whatever it is those two have."

"Oh. I thought you would want us to bring it to you. I guess that means we don't have to be careful if things get messy."

Foster considered the last statement. Perhaps he could kill two birds with one stone.

"No need to be cautious anymore," Foster said. "Use any means necessary to take out Wyatt and Schultz. Same goes for whatever they might have discovered. I don't care if you have to burn their plane. Get rid of them and the evidence."

"Yes, sir."

He ended the call and slid the phone back into his suit pocket. His driver pulled through a side entrance to the airport and steered the car toward a row of private hangars to the right.

Directly ahead, a shiny white Gulfstream G650 sat on the tarmac. A few men in black peacoats and matching pants stood at the foot of the steps leading onto the plane. To protect their ears from the cold, they wore matching beanies.

Foster's driver brought the car to a stop fifty feet away from the plane. As soon as he shifted it into park he hurried to get out and open the back door for his employer. Foster stepped out onto the runway and looked around the airport, taking in the smell of jet fuel exhaust, the tarmac, and the chilly city air.

The man to the right of the plane's steps approached the car's parking spot before it stopped so that he was there and ready to greet Foster the moment he left the vehicle.

"Sir, the plane is fueled and ready to go." He spoke in a near-shout due to the engines whining as they warmed up.

"Thank you. We are to take off immediately. Notify the pilot."

"Yes, sir," the man said and took off toward the plane.

Foster strode across the asphalt. When he reached the steps, he took a look around, surveying the airfield. Off in the distance, the lights of the Capitol shone bright in the night. The Washington Monument's red warning lights radiated atop the illuminated obelisk.

The nation's capital always stood for power, at least in Foster's mind. It represented strength over everything else. His predecessors knew that, going all the way back to the waning days of the Civil War.

He climbed the steps and turned into the luxurious cabin filled with plush beige leather, black stitching, polished oak armrests and tables, and a fully stocked bar in the back.

There were no attendants on this flight. From time to time, Foster would request a high-end escort to accompany him on the plane. This trip, however, was all business. Things were dangerously close to unraveling, and he had to make certain everything was in order.

He walked to the back of the plane and opened

one of the doors that housed the rocks glasses. He set the glass on the counter and picked out one of his favorite bourbons. The bottle cost over $600 for most people. For him, it was a gift from a Kentucky senator—a small token of gratitude for a favor no one else could perform. The amber liquid splashed into the glass. He stopped his pour when it was half-full and then put the bottle back in its place.

The engines revved higher, and the captain's voice came over the speakers.

"Sir, we are ready to taxi. When you're in your seat, we'll get moving."

Foster took a conservative sip of the whiskey, letting the smoky flavor splash over the tip of his tongue before turning to vanilla, then pepper, as it trickled down his throat.

He took a seat on his right and nodded to one of his men, who immediately went to the front of the plane to let the captain know he was ready.

Foster drew in a long breath through his nostrils and then took another sip.

Staring out the window at the historic landmarks of the capital brought back more reflections of his secret order: the Knights of the Golden Circle.

So many people had dubbed them a hate group, an evil organization bent on chaos. Foster snorted at the thought. There was nothing hateful about them other than when someone tried to interfere with their profits. They were a business, like anything else. Sometimes, Foster considered them more of a union—at least in the group's early days. After all, that's why they'd been behind the killing of Abraham Lincoln. He'd meddled with the profits of the South and ended up paying the ultimate price.

The other guard closed the door to the plane, and a moment later it started lumbering forward.

Foster's mind drifted to the first time he'd seen the incredible structure in Alaska. The previous chairman and leader of the KGC had taken him there and shown him. Foster had done his best to temper his surprise and wonder. If he hadn't seen it himself, he wouldn't have believed it.

It was Foster who figured out how to take the anomaly and use it to produce power. Up until then, his predecessors merely stripped it and the surrounding area of as much gold as they could find, storing it in giant vaults they built underground.

He didn't blame them. The KGC used the massive quantities of gold to fund wars, political candidates, and diplomacy whenever it was to their financial advantage. In that regard, the men who came before Foster were brilliant. What he'd done, however, was far more important.

Gold, after all, was a finite resource. The ability to perpetually create free energy—that was something far more valuable.

In an age where green energy was the new trend, his organization had capitalized in a way no one else could. They had a limitless source of power and could provide it to anywhere in the country so long as the infrastructure was in place.

Delivering to the Pacific Northwest, California, and the Southwestern regions had been an easy enough sell. With the proper amount of funding and enough palms crossed with silver, there wasn't anything Transcorp couldn't accomplish.

No one knew that under it all—the branding, the public relations, the good will—was the secret society that had been responsible for the death of one of the most beloved American leaders in history.

Lincoln, of course, wasn't the only one. Foster snickered at the thought. The public had no idea. They went about their lives, happily chasing their meager dreams, hoping to someday get a scrap from the table. Foster didn't pity them. It was their own fault. They chased the dream of money. Money fades. Power outlives mere mortals.

The plane turned onto the runway and paused for a moment while the pilot got the final go-ahead from the tower. In less than 15 seconds, Foster's head and back pressed against the seat as the plane jolted forward.

He looked out the window again at the lights passing by outside. Soon, he would be controlling the energy that powered those lights—and in every other city on the East Coast and everywhere in between.

33. Clinton

Sean peered through the windshield at the white airplane. It sat alone on the tarmac outside one of the larger hangars at Washington Executive Airport. There were no sounds of big jet engines or planes taking off and landing. Everything was still save for the pilot double checking a few things on the aircraft.

The Cessna had twin turboprop engines and a range of over two thousand five hundred nautical miles. That meant they'd have to make a stop or two along the way since Alaska was almost twice as far away.

While it wasn't as fast as Tommy's private jet, which was still being watched by the feds in Atlanta, the Cessna would get them there a good deal faster than any other means of transportation.

"Looks like Emily came through," Tommy said. "Those are good planes."

"Yeah," Sean said. "I just hope we don't run into any other snags."

"I know that worrying about stuff like that is kind of one of your things, but just this once, can you let it go? We're going to be fine."

Sean nodded as he surveyed the airfield, keeping his eyes open for trouble.

"Come on," Tommy said. "Let's get our stuff and

climb aboard."

"Yeah."

His paranoia was on full alert as he got out of the car and walked to the back to get his bag. His head swiveled one way and then the other, constantly watching the darkness surrounding the airfield.

He hated it when things were this quiet, though he didn't dare say that to Tommy. His friend's reaction would be something along the lines of, "Well what would you prefer? An angry mob of henchmen rushing after us?"

Sean knew better so, he kept his mouth shut and picked up his bag.

He'd already tucked his pistol inside his jacket beforehand in case something happened while they were waiting.

When Tommy finished collecting his things, Sean closed the trunk and started marching across the asphalt toward the plane. They left their car next to one of the hangars a few hundred feet away. It was out of the way and wouldn't draw attention, not that it mattered too much. The plates were fake, and the registration belonged to a false identity, a cover in case of a random traffic stop by the police.

Halfway to the plane, a bright light flashed in the corner of Sean's eye. He spun around as the sound of a car's engine accompanied it.

Two headlights were roaring toward them. The vehicle had come, seemingly, out of nowhere and was closing fast.

"Friends of yours?" Tommy asked.

"I was going to ask you the same question."

"Looks like they're going to run us over. Thoughts?"

Sean wasn't the type to shoot first and ask questions later. Initially, he hoped the car might be Adriana or Emily. That thought changed in an instant as the car picked up speed.

"Wait for it," Sean said. "Dive clear at the last second."

"Or maybe run for it now?"

The two friends stood their ground, staring down the headlights racing toward them. The car was only a hundred feet away now and closing quickly.

"Hold!" Sean said as he pulled out his pistol and took aim at the oncoming vehicle. "One more second..."

Sean lined up the windshield where he thought the driver would be seated. At fifty feet, he fought his nerves to keep the weapon steady. Then his finger twitched, and the muzzle erupted.

The slug smashed through the windshield, sending a web of cracks through its left half. The car jerked hard to the left and careened toward the hangar before coming to a sudden stop.

Sean kept his weapon trained on the vehicle. The engine was still running, and the lights stayed on. He didn't notice any movement inside.

Sean motioned for Tommy to circle around the other side.

Tommy nodded, taking his own weapon out of his gear bag and making sure a round was chambered.

Sean looped around the other way, approaching the plane as he did so. "Stay inside the aircraft," Sean ordered the pilot, who was crouching at the top of the steps, taking cover in the plane's doorway.

The man nodded and ducked back into the interior to stay out of sight.

Emily's pilots were civilians, untrained in most forms of combat. Their primary usefulness was getting agents to and from mission drop points. Other than that, they were pretty useless. Some were armed, but Sean didn't trust a person with a gun if he hadn't seen them use it in the field.

Cautiously, Sean worked his way to the right until he was staring at the broadside of the black sedan. The darkly tinted windows made it impossible to see anything or anyone inside.

He took a step forward, closing the gap between him and the vehicle to about forty feet.

Suddenly, one of the back doors flung open, and the barrel of a gun appeared. Sean reacted fast, firing over and over at the door until he saw the barrel retract inside.

Tommy was approaching from the other side, keeping his angle the same as Sean's to make sure they didn't catch each other in friendly fire.

When Sean started shooting, Tommy's instincts were to shoot, too. He resisted, waiting for a target to appear.

He looked over at Sean. His shoulders raised, a signal that he was wondering if Sean took out the threat.

Then the back left door swung open, and another barrel popped out with the muzzle blazing. Tommy was out in the open with nowhere to take cover. He dove to the ground and shot back, squeezing the trigger repeatedly, peppering the car with round after round until the weapon clicked. He pushed himself off the ground and ran to his left. With no cover in sight, the only thing he could do was make the angle more difficult for the other shooter.

The only problem was that doing so put him in Sean's crossfire.

It was a risk Tommy had to take.

He pumped his legs while reaching into one of his coat pockets for a full magazine. His fingers fumbled with the object and as he tried to eject the empty one, dropped the other onto the ground.

Tommy stopped in his tracks and spun around to pick up the magazine. He crouched to one knee as another round of gunfire erupted from the car.

Sean saw what happened and tried to give his friend some suppressing fire, pounding the car with round after round until his magazine was also empty. He moved fluidly, crossing the tarmac toward the front of the car as he ejected the empty magazine and popped in a new one.

The gunman in the back of the car poked his pistol out again and fired. Sparks flashed around

Sean's feet. One slug whizzed by his head. And then Sean opened fire once more. The window splintered and cracked but didn't shatter due to the heavy tinting.

Tommy grasped the magazine as the shooter on his side stepped out into the open and took aim.

Suddenly, two bright headlights lined up the gunman and the stopped car. An engine whined as a black SUV rumbled across the asphalt.

The gunman turned his attention away from Tommy and started firing at the oncoming vehicle.

He unloaded the contents of his weapon, but the SUV kept coming, faster and faster. Tommy and Sean couldn't see who was driving it.

Sean's gunman also turned away, ducking back into the car to see who the newcomer was and what they were trying to do.

It was a critical mistake.

As Tommy's shooter fired his final round into the SUV's windshield, he tried to dive clear. The SUV smashed into him, crushing him momentarily against the sedan in a thunderous crash. The car flipped over onto its side, grinding on the pavement for thirty feet while the gunman's body flew clear of the wreckage and rolled to a dead stop.

Rubber squealed and steam started billowing out of the SUV's hood until it came to a stop, casting the airport back into an eerie silence. Tommy and Sean stared in disbelief at the wreckage. The smell of coolant, water, fuel, and burned gunpowder filled the air.

Tommy raised his weapon and moved cautiously toward the driver side of the newcomer's vehicle. Sean circled around to the other side, also keeping his gun drawn in case of another threat.

Sean wondered who was behind the wheel. Like the sedan, the windows were tinted too dark to see in. The windshield was cracked, making it difficult to get a good view through the front.

The door clicked and eased open a few inches.

"Don't be stupid!" Tommy yelled. "You've got two expert marksmen at point blank range staring you down. If you're going to get out, do it nice and slow."

Ten seconds went by before the door moved another inch. This time, a pale set of fingers appeared over the top of it. A second later, another hand raised over the door.

"That's right," Sean said. "Keep your hands where we can see them." He hoped it was Emily or Adriana. Upon seeing the hands and forearms, he knew it was a guy.

The door opened all the way, and a young blond man came into view. Tommy's eyebrows lowered. He didn't recognize the driver.

"Anyone else in there?" Tommy asked.

The young man shook his head slowly. "No," he said. His accent was distinctly Russian. "I am alone."

Sean approached the SUV and swung open the front door, then the back, making sure the guy wasn't lying.

"Truck is clear," Sean said.

He hurried around the back and found Tommy pointing his gun at the driver. "I'm going to check the car. Keep an eye on him."

Tommy gave an upward nod as Sean leaned in through one of the broken windows and found the car's driver bent at an awkward angle. A bullet hole oozed thick crimson from his chest. A look into the back revealed two more men. One was lying across the seat with his face bloodied. His chest didn't rise and fall, signaling he was gone. The man who'd been crushed by the oncoming vehicle was still lying perfectly still a few dozen feet away—killed on impact.

"Well, that went exactly according to plan," Sean said to Tommy as he rejoined his friend.

"Plan? We're lucky this guy showed up," Tommy's voice rose.

"Maybe we were a bit lucky."

Tommy ignored his friend for a moment and directed his attention to the new guy. "Who are you?" he asked, keeping a safe distance between himself and the Russian.

"My name is Yuri," he said, twisting his head slightly to the left toward Sean.

"What are you doing here?" Sean asked.

"I think the words you are looking for, Mr. Wyatt, are *thank you*."

"I'll keep my gratitude in check until you tell us what's going on and why you're here."

"Mr. Wyatt, if I had wanted to kill you or your friend, I wouldn't have hit them with my vehicle. Your friend, Mr. Schultz, was—as you Americans say—a sitting goose. I could have run over him easily."

Sean frowned. "Duck. I think you mean sitting...you know, never mind."

Tommy flashed his friend a sidelong glance, wondering what they should do next.

Sean lowered his weapon at an angle, still keeping it at the ready just in case.

Tommy did the same.

"Thank you," Yuri said.

"Start talking," Sean demanded.

"As I told you, my name is Yuri. I work for Russian intelligence."

"Russian intelligence?" Sean asked.

"Spetsnaz, actually. I have been tracking your movements for some time. I was sent here by my president to retrieve something that belongs to us, something that was lost a long time ago."

Tommy and Sean exchanged confused looks.

"What?" they said simultaneously.

"May I put my hands down?"

The two friends nodded, and Yuri dropped his arms.

"Thank you." He took a cautious step away from the steaming SUV and assessed the damage.

"I suppose we should thank you, as you suggested," Sean said. "Why'd you help us just now?"

"Because those men are also after what I seek. You and your friend are looking for something else. Both things, however, are in the same place."

Sean and Tommy were more confused than ever.

"I'd say we could discuss it on the plane," Yuri said, "but I feel like you wouldn't let me on board unless I gave you a good enough reason."

"You'd be right," Sean said.

"Very well. Time is short, so I'll speak fast and frank." He crossed his arms as he addressed the two Americans.

"When the United States purchased Alaska from the czar of Russia, they promised to pay a sum just over $7 million American dollars. The payment was sent in the form of gold bullion, collected in several chests, and sent west to be shipped via boat."

Tommy and Sean nodded. They knew about the history surrounding the Alaska Purchase. What they didn't know was where this guy was going with his tale.

Yuri went on. "That payment never arrived."

"It didn't arrive?" Tommy asked. "I never read anything about that."

"And you never will. It's a part of the history books that was mysteriously omitted. The czar went back and forth with your government over the issue. The United States claimed the payment was sent. The czar claimed it didn't arrive."

Sean and Tommy were dubious. They'd heard about shipments of gold disappearing throughout history. This one was new to them both.

"So, what did the two sides do?" Sean asked.

"What could we do? The czar wasn't interested in going to war with the United States. He had his own problems to deal with. For a long time, no one mentioned the missing gold or the deal with America.

"Now there is a strong sentiment in Russia to try to take back Alaska. Our previous leader already made a move on Ukraine to take back a part of former Soviet land. The current president has no interest in taking such measures, especially with the United States. It would result in all-out war. No one wants that. All he wants is what is due to the Russian government."

"He sent you here to find the gold?" Tommy asked, incredulous.

"Yes. I am to find the bullion and bring it back to the Russian Federation. Then my country will have what it was due, and we will have closure to the issue of Alaska."

Tommy snorted derisively. "He sent you here to find $7 million dollars' worth of gold?"

"No, Mr. Schultz. That bullion is worth over $120 million in today's money. Possibly more. Honestly, it isn't even the financial worth of the treasure that my president is interested in. It's the point. He wants to make a name for himself as the leader who got the Russian people what they deserve. His plan is to use that money for schools and infrastructure. It may seem insignificant to a country with $15 trillion in debt, but to us it's important."

The two Americans couldn't argue that point. Still, it seemed a lot of trouble to go through to get a few treasure chests of gold that may or may not be at the bottom of the ocean.

"How do you know the ships didn't sink on the way to Russia?" Sean asked. "The ones carrying the gold, I mean."

"As far as we can tell, those ships never left. We've learned that they were boarded by what appeared to be pirates. We have reason to believe those pirates were actually KGC operatives. They hijacked the gold transport vessels and took them somewhere secret."

Sean and Tommy were dubious, and they didn't try to hide it.

"You're telling me this assignment from your president is entirely based on the theory that the KGC took Russia's gold and hid it somewhere?" Tommy asked.

"It isn't a theory, Mr. Schultz. I would not be here if that was all we had."

He reached into his coat pocket and withdrew a picture. The image was a black-and-white photo. From the resolution, the two Americans figured it was probably taken around the turn of the twentieth century. Possibly earlier.

In the middle of the image were two steamships sitting in a bay surrounded by enormous mountains in the background.

"Is that Anchorage?" Sean said while looking over his friend's shoulder.

"Yes. The very early days of Anchorage," Yuri said. "This image was taken by one of Russia's sailors who survived the attack on the ships. He and another of his crew tracked down the ships and took this picture."

"With the limited abilities of the cameras back then, that must have taken some doing," Tommy said.

"Not to mention how bulky they were."

"I don't understand. If the KGC took your gold, surely they'd know that could incite a war with Russia."

Yuri nodded in agreement. "Yes, they probably did. Our theory is that was what they were hoping."

"It would make sense," Sean said. "Even though the KGC was more interested in profits than politics, their history of allegiance to the Confederacy was deeply rooted. It's plausible that they may have hoped a war with Russia could further weaken the Union."

"And with a powerful new ally like Russia, the South could have resumed military operations against the North," Tommy added.

"But that didn't happen."

"No," Yuri said. "It didn't. Russia had its own military concerns at the time, and a war with the United States would have been catastrophic, no matter who the allies might have been."

"So, here you are, looking for the lost gold from

the Alaska Purchase."

"Correct. I have been following you, Mr. Wyatt, since you began your search. I knew that you and your friend were the only two people who could figure out the secret in the Seward letter. That's why I had one of my people infiltrate the White House and put it somewhere your president would find it."

Infiltrate the White House? The two Americans wondered how he'd pulled that off considering the intense vetting process required to even visit the historic mansion. Was this person a part of the president's team of advisers, an intern, or something else?

Sean had a feeling he wouldn't get an answer to that question. There was one, however, that was at the top of his list. And he had to press it.

"Were you the one behind the assassination attempt on President Dawkins?"

Yuri raised a finger. "I thought you might ask that. No, we were not behind the attempt on your leader's life. That was the KGC. They must have found out what you were up to and that Dawkins was involved. No doubt the man that was killed by the police outside the hotel was a sacrificial lamb. He may not have even been the one who put the weapon in place, though he certainly assisted in getting it through security."

The three men stood awkwardly on the tarmac for a moment, unsure of what they should do next.

"Based on your sudden appearance and the fact

that you're telling us all this, I'm going to guess you'd like a lift up to Alaska."

Yuri's stoic expression never changed. "I can secure my own means of transportation; however, it would save me a good deal of time if I could come along. All I ask is that if we find the stolen gold, you allow me to take that back to my country. I give you my word, I will take no more than what is owed. If we find anything above what was the agreed payment to Russia, that belongs to the United States."

It was an interesting offer. While allowing Yuri to tag along could be troublesome if the young man was lying, it was also possible that he could be useful. He'd already bailed Sean and Tommy out of a mess a few minutes before.

"You mind if we have a minute, Yuri?" Sean asked.

"Certainly. I will wait."

Sean pulled his friend aside, standing near the airplane as they talked. "You think he's telling the truth?"

Tommy glanced over at the Russian, who was standing with his hands folded behind his back, doing his best not to pay attention to the two friends. He looked off toward the pale glow in the sky that perpetually hovered over the nation's capital at night.

"I was going to ask you the same thing," Tommy said.

"Honestly, my first instinct is always not to trust

someone, especially if they're Russian special forces. But he did save us from those guys." Sean pointed a thumb at the destroyed vehicle with the dead gunmen inside. "His story seems to add up. I don't see the harm in it. Besides, we can always use another gun on our side. There is one thing...."

Sean turned back to the Russian and crossed his arms, eyeing the young man with an analytical glare. "Yuri?"

"Yes."

"You said you work for the Spetsnaz."

"That is correct."

"You must know Ustin Zegrev."

"Yes. He is my commander."

"Good guy, Ustin. Great sense of humor. I spent some time drinking vodka with him a few years ago when I was in Moscow."

Yuri's head titled slightly to the side and his expression changed to one of puzzlement. "No offense, but you must be thinking of someone else. Ustin doesn't drink and he's certainly not a person given to humor. Many of us have wondered if he's ever cracked a smile in his entire life."

Sean grinned and lowered his hands. "Yes, I know. He's kind of a tough pill. Just had to make sure you were telling the truth."

Ustin's lips parted. He could appreciate the American's caution.

Sean turned around and put his hands up. "All aboard," he said. "Grab whatever you need. It's going to be a long flight."

Sean watched as his friend and their new Russian ally climbed the steps onto the plane. He'd have to keep an eye on Yuri. Then he glanced over at the wreckage. No doubt he'd saved their necks. Sean just hoped that wasn't for show.

34. Anchorage, Alaska

"You're sure you can get us there?" Tommy asked.

The gray-haired pilot at the charter desk stared at the map for another second and nodded. "Yeah, I can get you there. It'll cost a little extra since we have to do a snow landing and all, but sure, I've been to that spot a few times." He looked up from the map and eyed the three men standing on the other side of the counter. "You boys looking to do some mountain climbing?"

Sean chuckled and shook his head. "No, sir. Nothing like that. We're looking to do some exploring around the area. Probably be there for a few hours while we walk around."

"That's fine," the pilot said. "I doubt I'll have any other flights for the day, so you fellas can take as long as you like. Just remember that we'll only have a small window of daylight. That's not a problem if you don't mind flying in the dark, but I'd hate for you to get lost out there. Even though this winter hasn't been as cold as most, it's still pretty darn chilly out there. We got reports of temps in the low teens the last few nights. In the day, it warms to a tepid twenty-seven or so." He laughed at his own joke.

"Sounds good," Tommy said.

"Aside from the money, you guys have enough cold weather gear? I know some visitors come out here thinking they have everything they need and then when they get to the wilderness, they experience a cold unlike anything they ever saw back home."

The three had picked up new gear just that morning—heavier coats, snow pants, gloves, boots, and face masks. Sean nodded. "Yes, sir. We've picked up everything we think we'll need."

"Okay," the pilot said. "My name is Rusty. I'll run through my checklist and make sure everything's ready to go. We should be good to take off in the next twenty minutes or so."

"Thanks, Rusty," the three said as the pilot disappeared into an office back and to the left.

After they paid the charter company's manager for the flight, the visitors retired to a side room with chairs and a leather couch. They'd left their bags of cold weather gear in the room so as not to take up space at the counter. They started putting on the equipment even though they figured the plane would have some kind of heat. The reasoning was that they could save time by doing it now instead of later.

Every one of the men was exhausted from their cross-country trip. It had taken them all night to reach the city of Anchorage. That had included one stopover in Seattle to get fuel and something to eat. Sleeping on the plane had been difficult at first—until fatigue took hold.

A little over twenty minutes passed before Rusty reappeared in the doorway wearing a thick overcoat and a cap covering his head and ears. "Ready when you are," he said.

The three stood up, grabbed their things, and followed the pilot out to the red-and-white ski plane.

"You gonna be okay on this thing?" Tommy asked Sean. His eyes gleamed with mischief.

"You know I'll be fine," Sean said.

Yuri looked puzzled. His head went from Sean to Tommy and back. "What does he mean? Are you afraid of flying?"

"No," Sean said as he trudged toward the plane. "I'm afraid of heights, stationary heights like buildings or high cliffs."

"But flying doesn't bother you?"

"No."

"I'm sorry, but that doesn't make much sense."

Tommy's guffaws echoed across the tarmac. "That's what I've been saying for nearly thirty years!"

Sean shook his head and picked up his speed to walk ahead of the other two.

The twin turboprop plane groaned as it climbed into the cold winter sky just outside of Anchorage. The pilot leveled out the aircraft at around three thousand feet, keeping it relatively low over the forests, lakes, streams, and hills as they flew toward the majestic peaks of Denali in the distance.

The sun sat low on the horizon to the west. It hadn't gone much higher during the entire day. Now it was late morning, and in a few hours it would begin its short descent that would once more plunge the frigid land into darkness.

Rusty spoke through the headsets as he flew the plane toward the mountains, talking about the various points of interest along the way and occasionally mentioning historical events that coincided with different landmarks.

"Where'd you boys get that map, anyway?" Rusty asked after a few minutes of radio silence.

Sean and Tommy looked at each other.

Sean answered. "We found it in Maryland," he said, going with straight honesty.

"Looks pretty old."

"We think it is. Probably over a hundred years if we didn't miss our guess."

"Interesting stuff. Is it a miner's map or something?"

Sean wasn't sure why he asked the question in that way. "Miner's map? You mean, did it belong to a miner?"

"Yeah. I've seen a few maps like that from the late 1800s when gold mining really took off up here. Miners always carried maps to make sure they didn't trespass on someone else's claims."

"We actually don't know who it belonged to," Tommy said.

"Well, that area you pointed out is right in the thick of a bunch of abandoned gold mines from the late 1800s. You three best be careful while you're out looking around. And if you get the wise idea to go into one of those old mines, you should think again. They're not safe, especially after being out of use for so long. Most of them are blocked off."

"We'll be careful," Sean said.

He and Tommy were both thinking the same thing: the anomaly they were searching for might be in one of the abandoned mines.

The next forty minutes literally flew by, with Rusty continuing his informative aerial tour of the land.

He banked the plane through treacherous mountain slopes and cut through a narrow passage between two peaks that hiked the blood pressure of the three passengers up significantly.

After flying around the rocky, snow-covered mountains, Rusty found the place he was looking for. There was a long patch of white snow leading up a gradual slope of a hill near the base of the mountains.

"That's where we're going down there," he said, pointing out the window to the right. "The dot on your map will be over there, at the foot of that smaller mountain."

The mountain he referred to was only smaller in comparison to the one formerly known as Mount McKinley. The name had been changed back to the Native title of Denali during the previous president's regime. Some opposed the change, but for the most part, the people appreciated the president's attempt to honor Native heritage.

"Any gold mines along that mountain?" Tommy asked. The second the words came out of his mouth, he regretted them. "You know, so we don't stumble into any."

"Just one that I know of. The entrance usually has a good amount of snow over it this time of year. The winter has been so mild up here, though, you might be able to see it."

The pilot looped the plane around one more time to get a better approach angle to the snowfield and then began his descent. He touched down easily in the powder, and the plane quickly decelerated as it coasted down the hill toward the narrow valley between hills and mountain.

The four men stepped out into the packed snow and looked out on the white landscape through their goggles. A blustery wind rolled across the hills and up to the mountain, sending wispy clouds of snow dust sparkling into the air.

"I'll wait for you guys here," Rusty said. "Got a heater I can run for a while. If you're planning on being more than a few hours, I might have to run back to the airport and return to get you later. With how cold it will be around sunset, I'd recommend having all your exploring done before then."

Sean nodded and handed a piece of paper to Rusty.

"What's this?" the pilot asked.

"If we're not back and you don't hear from us

within the next two hours, call the number on that paper and tell Emily to send the cavalry to this location."

"Emily? Emily who?"

"Don't worry about that," Sean said. "Just do it."

"Oh. All right."

The pilot didn't understand, but he didn't need to as long as he followed Sean's instructions.

"Not a moment before two hours. Got it?"

Rusty nodded. "Yep. I got it." He looked over to the base of the mountain. "That's where the dot on your map is," he said, pointing a finger. "If the mine isn't covered, you'll be able to see it pretty easily just over the other side of that ridge. I know I told you all not to try going into the mines in this area, but it sounds to me like that's exactly what you're going to do. Just remember, if you get lost in one of those, sit tight. The last thing you want to do is start moving around down there.

Sean nodded. No sense in lying about their intentions anymore. Rusty had a good sense of what was going on here.

"We'll be careful. Thanks, Rusty. Remember, two hours."

Sean, Tommy, and Yuri grabbed their gear bags and trudged off toward the ridge. One thing they noticed after only five minutes of marching through the snow was that things in Alaska were much bigger, which threw off their sense of distance much like being out in the American Southwest desert. It felt like they hadn't even moved, and already the three men were out of breath—the two Americans more so than their young Russian counterpart.

He seemed almost cheery to be hiking through the snow across the frozen landscape.

The white powder crunched under their boots. They'd decided against using snowshoes since the snow wasn't more than a foot deep. It was possible they'd encounter some deeper drifts, but they'd deal with that problem if it arose.

"What's put you in such a good mood?" Tommy asked Yuri as they hit the ten-minute mark. He panted for air in spite of his newfound fitness.

"This reminds me of the time I spent in Siberia. We had to go through a month of training there. I always wondered why that was a requirement since most battles are not fought in frozen wastelands. Now I'm glad I was put through that ordeal."

"I'm still waiting for high school algebra to pay off like that," Sean joked.

Everyone was breathing too hard to laugh, but he liked to think everyone thought it was funny.

They reached the bottom of the valley and started the trek around the base of the mountain, just below the ridge Rusty had pointed out. Twenty minutes had already passed, and while moving had kept the men warm, Sean started growing concerned he should have allowed for more time. Their pilot would only wait for so long before he made the call Sean requested.

Sean looked down at his wrist, pulled back the

coat sleeve, and noted the time on his watch.

The wind kept driving against them, more than once nearly knocking the men over as they trudged forward around the bend. Snow flew against their bodies, occasionally finding the cracks in their thermal armor, stinging their skin.

"I feel like we should have tauntauns," Tommy said.

Yuri turned his head and looked at the American with a quizzical expression. Tommy couldn't really see the man's face under the goggles and mask.

"It's from a movie," Tommy explained. After a few seconds, he realized Yuri wasn't going to understand. "Never mind. Let's keep going."

Around the bend, the group stayed close to the slopes to get as much protection from the wind as possible. Up ahead, they saw a point on the hill that was much steeper than the rest of the slopes. Rocks jutted up sharply and then leveled off with the rest of the mountain's grade.

"That the mine Rusty was talking about?" Tommy asked.

"Might be," Sean said over the howling wind. "Only one way to find out."

The three men kept pushing forward until they were less than a hundred feet away from the rocks. From their vantage point, they could see an arched entryway with steel rails coming out. The opening was blocked off by heavy wooden boards and an old sign that read Danger, Keep Out in faded red letters.

"Looks like the mine, all right," Sean said. He noticed the rails and followed them to where they stopped twenty feet outside the mine's entrance. His eyes narrowed, and he scowled under his face coverings.

Sean diverted his path away from the mine and over to the right.

"Where are you going?" Tommy stuck his hands out wide.

Sean didn't answer immediately. He walked past the rails until he could see clearly the oddity he'd noticed. He bent down and pressed a glove into the snow.

"Tire tracks," he said to himself.

The wide troughs had been filled in with fresh snow, but it was clear someone had driven through the area recently. He stood up and followed the shallow tracks until they stopped near the mine's entrance. Sean's instincts suddenly went on full alert. He looked around the area, scanning the hills surrounding them.

"What's wrong?" Tommy asked, joining his friend at the crest near the mine.

"Someone's been here."

"What?" Tommy reached into his coat and pulled out his weapon. "How do you know?" Then he saw the tracks. "Oh."

"Looks like they were here in the last day, maybe twelve hours. Those tracks would be covered if it had been much longer."

"Whoever it was, they appear to be gone now,"

Yuri said.

"Yeah. Seems that way. Still, keep your eyes peeled. It could be a trap."

Sean and Yuri produced their weapons and held them at their sides, ready in case something or someone appeared.

They climbed the remaining thirty feet up to where the rock leveled off. Luckily for Sean, there were no steep precipices or cliffs. A fall from here would just mean rolling back down the snow-covered hill—annoying, but nothing dangerous. The wind was even calmer at the mine's entrance. Sean pulled up his goggles and stepped closer to the boards. He inspected the planks closely, trying to find a crack big enough to see through. The boards had been pressed tightly together and didn't have more than a few millimeters between each. He wedged his fingers into the side and tried to pull, but he couldn't get the barricade to budge.

"Need the tire iron," Sean said to Tommy.

Tommy set his bag down in the snow and tucked his pistol back into his coat. Sean kept looking out away from the mine, constantly watching for any threat that might sneak up on them.

"Got it," Tommy said, pulling the little iron rod from the bag.

Sean took it and moved back over to the barricade.

"You're welcome," Tommy said, zipping his bag.

"Thanks," Sean said. He found a crack big enough for the flat end of the iron to fit and started wiggling it back and forth.

Suddenly, the entire wooden facade started moving. A high-pitched creak from rusty hinges screamed in their ears. The planks weren't a barricade. They were part of a big door. And the door was swinging open. A blast of warm air billowed out of the entrance, washing over the men as they stared into the darkness.

"What's going on?" Yuri asked. He raised his weapon and started looking around frantically.

A motor groaned, pushing the door open from the inside. It swung wide enough to accommodate a mine car on the tracks—even though there were none sitting around at the entrance.

Sean aimed his gun into the tunnel. Dim lights were fixed into the wall, barely lighting the dark shaft. The three moved into the threshold and stared inside. From the row of lights along the wall, they could see the corridor bent gradually to the left about ninety feet in.

Tommy and Yuri lifted their goggles to get a better view into the tunnel.

"Did you hit a button or something?" Tommy asked.

"No."

"Maybe there was a trigger. A laser, perhaps," Yuri offered.

"No. I don't think so. Someone knows we're here."

"That would be correct," a familiar voice said from behind.

Sean, Tommy, and Yuri jerked their heads around, startled.

"Drop your weapons," Porter said with a H&K MP5 hanging from his shoulder. He waved the gun back and forth, making sure the intruders understood they could all be taken out in a matter of seconds. From such a short range, Porter would make quick work of them.

"Drew Porter," Sean said. "I should have known you were behind all this."

Porter raised his goggles, revealing his wicked brown eyes. "Me? Oh, I'm not behind all this. In fact, I'm looking for the same thing you're trying to find. Except I'm not working for the president."

Sean and his comrades were puzzled. "If you're not behind all this, why'd you try to kill me in New York? And what are you doing pointing a gun at us?"

Porter shrugged. "Isn't it obvious? I want this treasure for myself. As to your execution, yes, I was taking orders from someone else."

"But not anymore?" Tommy asked.

Porter's head turned back and forth. "No. Not anymore. They tried to cut me out. Now, though, I have more leverage than I could have hoped for."

35. Washington

"Okay, thank you." Emily ended the call and slid her phone back into the front pocket of her black slacks.

"That was the police down in Clinton," she said. "They found Pinkton and two other men dead."

Dawkins and Adriana looked at her in confusion.

"What?" Dawkins asked. "Dead? What happened?"

"It isn't clear yet. Sounds like there was some kind of shootout on the runway. One of Pinkton's men was shot dead. He and the other guy were killed when an SUV rammed into their car, broadside. Pinkton was crushed under his vehicle. The other guy had a blunt force trauma to the head."

"What about the driver of the SUV?" Adriana asked.

Emily's head turned side to side. "They didn't know. It was a rental. Fake name and ID."

"A ghost."

"Yep. So as of right now, they have no idea who it was."

"Sean texted me this morning to let me know they made it safely to Anchorage. Do you think they killed Pinkton and those men?"

"Not sure, but I'm glad they made it out safely."

The president's face was stern. He was stuck on the missing detail of the SUV driver. "Did they try to run prints on the driver of the SUV?" he asked.

"Yes, but they didn't find a thing."

"The entire time they used the vehicle?"

"Maybe they were being extremely careful. All I know is they came up with nothing. The only lead is the rental car place. Police are making calls now to see what they can learn. My guess is they won't find much."

Adriana paced back and forth for a minute while she listened to the conversation. Something kept poking at her mind like a needle digging into her skin.

"What about Porter?"

The other two turned to her, their faces filled with the same question.

"Drew Porter. You said he went rogue. His body wasn't on the scene at the airport, at least, not that you mentioned."

"No, they didn't say anything about him."

"Which means he's still on the loose. And it brings up the question as to why he'd send his men after Sean and Tommy without being there to lead things himself."

The room descended into silence as the three considered the problem.

Adriana perked up first. "Who was the pilot that flew Sean and Tommy to Alaska?"

"Perkins. Sam Perkins," Emily said. "I've known him a long time. Good pilot. Good man. Why?"

"Call him, and find out what he saw at the airport. If he was there, he'd have seen what happened."

Emily's eyes opened wide. "Of course. Perkins would have seen everything."

"He wouldn't have demanded to stick around until the authorities arrived?" Dawkins asked.

"I'm sure Sean was pretty insistent they get out of Dodge," Emily said. She picked up her phone and started dialing.

"He flew all night. You think he'll answer?"

"It's late in the morning out there. He should."

The phone rang five times before a groggy man's voice came through the earpiece.

"Hello?"

"Perkins, it's Emily."

"Oh, hello Director Starks. I hope you don't mind if I get a little more sleep before you ask me for another favor."

"I'm not calling for a favor. Can you tell me what happened at the airport in Clinton last night?"

The man sniffled and then yawned. "Sure. I got to the airstrip about a half hour before your friends. Then there was a shootout. Some guys in a car tried to take out Sean and Tommy. They returned fire. Then out of the blue some Russian fellow plowed into their car. I assume everyone inside was killed. My copilot and I got the three of them out of there as fast as we could. Figured discretion was best."

The pilot's explanation brought up more

questions than answers.

"You said a Russian guy killed the three in the car?"

"Yeah. I'm assuming he's Russian. Said his name was Yuri when I went into the back of the plane to get some rest while my copilot took over."

"What was a Russian doing at the airfield?" Emily asked, more thinking out loud than expecting an answer.

"That I don't know, Director Starks. Your boy Sean looked like he was giving him a good once-over while I got the plane ready for takeoff. I figured if Sean trusted him enough to let him on board, he was okay."

Sean wasn't the most trusting person in the world, so the fact that he allowed this Russian to fly with them *did* speak volumes.

"By the way," Perkins said, "thanks for sending me that copilot. He did a great job. Not a very talkative guy, but he's a machine. Only took some rest when we stopped for fuel. In fact, I don't think he ever left the cockpit. Guy was a workhorse."

Emily frowned. "I didn't send a copilot. I thought you were arranging for that."

"Nope. The plan was to get halfway to Anchorage, stop for an hour or so to refuel and take a nap, then fly the rest of the way. Thanks to him, we didn't have to stop long at all."

"This guy, did he have a name?"

"Sure. Said his name was Drew. Didn't catch his last name. Said he'd been working for you for a while, though."

Emily's face flushed white like she'd seen the devil himself. "Where is this Drew now?"

"I don't know. He got his own room here at the hotel. Said he had to grab some things in town before he came back to sleep."

"Thanks, Perkins. I've gotta go."

"You're welcome."

She ended the call and turned to face Adriana and the president.

"What's wrong?" Adriana asked before Dawkins could.

"I think I just found out where Porter went. Sean and Tommy could be in grave danger. Mr. President. I'm going to need a plane."

36. Denali National Park and Preserve, Alaska

Two armed guards waited just around the first bend in the mine. They pointed their weapons at the approaching intruders, malice filling their eyes.

"You're trespassing on government property," one of the guards said. He motioned to Porter. "Put down your weapon immediately."

"Tell your boss that Drew Porter caught these three snooping around outside," Porter said.

The guards looked at each other, suddenly thrown off by the order.

"Do it," Porter said in a stern tone. "He knows who I am."

The guard on the left pressed a button on his earpiece and did as told. He listened closely, looking down at the ground as the response came through. A few seconds later, he looked up at the four intruders and waved them on.

"You may proceed," he said. "He'll be waiting for you down below."

The three captives trudged by the guards and into the dimly lit tunnel.

They pressed on, marching ahead for fifteen minutes, seeing nothing more than a bunch of old mining tools, wooden beams supporting the ceiling, and some side tunnels the branched off in

perpendicular directions. Those were blocked off
by flimsy wooden boards.

"What's all this about?" Tommy asked as they
marched through another bend in the tunnel. "You
abandon your country to work for some madman?
And for what, money?"

"Everything is about money," Porter sneered.
"Countries, even this one, have murdered millions
of people for nothing more than profit. I see no
reason why I shouldn't get a piece of the pie."

"You have no idea what's down here, do you?"
Sean said. His statement was half button-pushing,
half feeling out their captor.

"Honestly, Sean, I don't. I have no clue what
we're about to see. My former employer is down
here. You'll probably recognize him when you see
him."

"We already know about Secretary Foster. He'll
be tried for high treason, not to mention
attempting to murder the president of the United
States."

"Along with like forty other charges," Tommy
added.

"I don't care if he is or not," Porter said.

"Because you've gone rogue?" Sean asked. "You
think that's going to keep you safe?"

"Oh, I am safe. And Foster will do as I say, or
he'll burn. But there's no reason why he and I can't
be civil. After all, the right amount of money can
mend the most jagged of rifts."

The sounds of machines began to echo through

the corridor. They whirred and hummed with an occasional clanking sound. The noise grew louder as the group progressed farther into the mine.

"Sounds like generators?" Tommy said.

Sean thought the same thing but kept quiet. His mind was already working on how to get away. If they rushed Porter, he'd mow them down like tall summer fescue. They'd have to wait for the right moment, when Porter lowered his guard. Since the man was CIA, that was going to be tricky.

They rounded another bend to the left and were greeted by a giant opening in the tunnel. Bright light poured into the corridor from beyond. Ahead was the most astonishing thing the four men had ever seen in their lives.

"That's...impossible," Tommy said as he stared at the giant structure.

The mine tunnel opened into the largest underground room they'd ever seen. The ceiling was easily two hundred feet high, and the circumference took up acres of space.

In the center of it all was something that didn't belong anywhere near that part of the world.

The four smooth sides of the structure rose dramatically to a single point at the top. From the looks of it, the top piece was made of pure, glimmering gold.

"It looks just like one of the pyramids in Giza," Sean said.

Yuri said nothing. He merely stared in disbelief.

Giant floodlights were positioned all around the

cavernous room, pouring bright white light onto the ancient structure. Cables and wires ran along the walls and disappeared into other tunnels. Where they went, the four visitors didn't know.

Their tunnel veered to the right and wound its way down to the ground floor about fifty feet below. Down at the base of the pyramid, dozens of men in hard hats were working at computers, checking cables and running control panels with hundreds of buttons and knobs. One was running through a checklist on a clipboard, making an occasional note as he did so.

A gray trailer was parked off to the side. It looked like ones Sean had seen at construction sites. On the opposite side of the room, far away across the massive interior, was an electrical power station. Power lines ran from somewhere inside the pyramid out to the station, which then ran lines into some of the other tunnels.

"This is unbelievable. What is that pyramid doing here?" Tommy asked.

"It's a generator," Yuri said.

Porter looked at him like he was crazy. "A generator?" He hadn't engaged with his prisoners much since entering the mine.

"He could be right," Sean said. "I've read several studies about how the ancient Egyptians were able to harness electricity from various natural sources. The hieroglyphs at the Hathor temple in Dendera show an image that looks like a lightbulb attached to a simple battery."

Tommy nodded. "There's speculation that they were somehow able to harness geostatic electricity. I read a book that theorized that was how the Ark of the Covenant worked."

"That doesn't explain what this thing is doing here," Sean said.

"I don't care how it got here," Porter said. "Where's the gold?"

It was a good question. If there was a large cache of gold in the mine, they couldn't see it except for the pyramid's golden top.

"Get moving," he grunted a moment later. Sean and the others could tell Porter was irritated. Finding an ancient pyramid in an abandoned mine wasn't what he'd planned.

He motioned with his weapon toward the narrow path leading down below.

His prisoners obeyed and reluctantly started down the trail. As they rounded the first turn, some of the workers below saw them approaching. One ran hurriedly over to the office trailer and disappeared inside.

A minute later, he reappeared with a similar weapon to Porter's and stood at the trailer's front door.

A man in a gray sweater and black pants appeared in the doorway. As Sean and the others walked slowly across the main floor, the man in the sweater moved closer.

He stopped a dozen feet away, surrounded by men in hard hats with submachine guns. They all wore stern faces and kept their weapons pointed at the trespassers.

"Mr. Secretary," Sean said. "Interesting little operation you have here."

Kent Foster crossed his arms and tilted his head to the side. "Yes, Sean. It's impressive, isn't it?" He turned and looked up at the pyramid towering over them. "I have to say, I only get out here a few times a year, but when I do it's still quite the imposing figure. I never really get used to it."

"I caught them trying to get in, sir," Porter interrupted.

So that was his angle. Sean figured he'd play it that way. Porter wasn't the inventive type.

"I see that, Porter. My question is, what are you doing here? Who is this guy? And how did you find this place? You realize I'm going to have to kill all of you, don't you?" Three of the men with submachine guns stepped closer, leveling their weapons at their waists.

"He's a Russian spy, sir," Porter said as calmly as he could. "He's working with Wyatt and Schultz. As to your other question, I followed them, told their pilot I was the copilot, and flew out here with them. They never knew I was on board. You should know, however, that if you kill me, this entire story goes public. You'll lose everything: your position, your company, whatever all this is. You'll be tried and executed."

Foster tilted his head back, sizing up Porter's eyes, searching for a sign of bluffing.

Sean and Tommy frowned. They were puzzled as to when Porter could have gotten aboard the plane in Clinton. Then they remembered the shootout. The whole thing had been a distraction to get them away from the aircraft so Porter could climb on board. The plan nearly fell apart when Yuri showed up and killed his three men.

Foster appeared uncomfortable for a moment. He saw no sign of dishonesty in Porter's story. Then he stiffened and motioned to some of his guards. "Take these three, and put them down below. Porter, you may come with me."

Four of the guards surrounded the three captives. One of them waved his hand for them to follow.

Sean, Tommy, and Yuri resisted at first, then one of the guards elbowed Sean in the lower back and he stumbled forward.

The guards ushered them toward an opening on the side of the pyramid. A path was carved into the rock, leading down at an angle into an open doorway. Tommy followed the lead guard as they moved single file down into the belly of the pyramid.

Inside the megalithic structure, they found themselves in a remarkably preserved corridor. Hieroglyphs colored both walls of the hallway, featuring people, animals, and scenes of agriculture. Presiding over all of the artwork were some of the more famous Egyptian deities, all of which Sean and Tommy recognized instantly.

The path turned sharply and then went down at an even steeper angle than the one leading into the pyramid. It did a 180-degree turn at a landing and then continued downward, deeper and deeper into the base of the mountain.

"How far down does this thing go?" Sean asked, not expecting an answer from any of the guards.

"These pyramids are like icebergs," Tommy said. "Beneath the tip is a labyrinth of tunnels, rooms, and secret chambers."

"Thanks, Nat Geo," Sean said. "I was looking for a more specific answer from the guys who work here. Not that they'll answer."

The procession went down another two levels before they arrived at the bottom. It was a square room with doorways leading in all four directions. Floodlights lined the floor, casting their radiant glow on more ancient artwork.

In the center of the room, a long cable hung from a hole in the ceiling. It stretched down to a tall stack of gold bars sitting a few feet off the ground, held up by a wooden platform. Wires and cables spread across the precious metal like spiderwebs.

"That your gold?" Sean asked Yuri.

The Russian stared with wide eyes at the incredible treasure. A sign was posted on every side of the platform that read *High Voltage*. "Dah," he said—the Russian word for *yes*.

Tommy followed the main cable up into the ceiling where it disappeared into the upper parts of the ancient structure. "So, this is how he does it," he said. "He's harnessing the power of geostatic electricity—just like Yuri was saying."

To the men standing in the center of the room, it felt like the entire structure was vibrating.

"In there," one of the guards said to Tommy.

Before he could resist, the guy shoved Tommy in the back and sent him sprawling forward into the empty room.

Sean and Yuri were directed to separate but similar rooms, each with a guard watching over the doorway.

"I'm going back up top," the lead guard said. "Keep an eye on them until we have further instructions."

The other three nodded and turned to face their prisoners, fingers wrapped tightly around their weapons.

Sean looked across the center room at his friend who stood in the doorway. "Not going according to plan, huh, Schultzie?"

"When does it go according to plan?"

"Maybe next time we need a better plan or at least a backup."

"That would be good."

"Quiet, you two," one of the guards said. "I suggest you try and relax. Mr. Foster will be down to deal with you shortly."

37. Denali

"What is it you want, Porter?" Foster said as he slid into the leather chair behind his desk.

The room was decorated with wood panels and bookshelves that stretched to the ceiling. For an office trailer, the interior appeared more like something one would find on Capitol Hill.

"What does anyone want, Mr. Secretary?" He asked the question with a snide glare on his face. "I want to retire on a beach, maybe have a cabin in the mountains. Women, cars, all of it. That's what I want."

Foster bit his lower lip and nodded, taking in a long breath through his nose. He turned his chair at an angle and looked up at the ceiling. "Or I can kill you right now and no one will be the wiser."

Porter snorted. "I guess you forgot what I said. If I don't get back aboveground in the next hour, my partner is going to tell everyone what you've done. You'll be finished. There won't be a safe haven for you anywhere in the world. You can't run to where they won't find you."

"I think you underestimate the power I wield, Porter. We are everywhere. We control everything."

"Yeah, well, that doesn't change the fact that in one hour my man goes live with everything we know about you. You may be able to lie low for a bit—a year, maybe two—but eventually someone will find you and take you down. President Dawkins is a beloved leader. The agencies might not find you, but one of his fanatics might."

Foster seemed unimpressed. "Very well, Porter. What do you want?" He folded his hands in his lap and returned his gaze to the man across the desk.

"A hundred million," Porter said in a flat voice.

Foster's eyebrows shot skyward. "A hundred? Really? That's a considerable sum of money, Agent Porter. What makes you think I have that kind of coin lying around?"

"Don't play dumb with me, Kent," Porter said. He kept his eyes level with Foster's. "I know how much Transcorp is worth. You netted billions last year. From what I've read, the next fiscal year will be even better. The environmentalist nut jobs love the company because of its green energy. A hundred million is a drop in the bucket. Now that I think of it, maybe I should ask for two hundred."

He waited for a reaction from Foster, but got none.

"I'm not greedy, though, Kent. There's only so many things you can buy before it gets boring. I know that. I just want to live comfortably for the rest of my life. A hundred million should take care of that."

Foster tapped his fingers together. He drew in another long breath and once more looked up at the ceiling as if searching the tiles for an answer.

"Very well, Drew," he spat Porter's first name with bitter derision. "A hundred million it is."

Porter did his best to hide his surprise. He didn't think it would be that easy. In fact, he expected Foster to see through his bluff. There was no partner topside. And he had no connections to break the story about the secretary of state's betrayal. Yet here he was, about to be wealthier than he ever dreamed.

"I'll make the necessary arrangements," Foster said, standing up. "It will take a couple of days to get the money moved around. That large of a sum doesn't get shifted quickly. I'll need your account numbers, that sort of thing."

"Of course," Porter said. He stood as well. Foster stuck out his hand, and the two shook for a moment. "Pleasure doing business with you, sir."

Foster nodded and pointed a finger at Porter. "I have to say, I'm a bit surprised. I knew you were a good agent, but I didn't know you had this in you. Well played."

"Necessity is the mother of invention."

"Indeed it is."

Foster picked up a radio from his desk and pressed the button on the side. "Bring the prisoners up to level eight. I have something I want them to see."

He set the radio back on the desk and looked over at his guest.

"Something you want them to see?" Porter asked, curious.

Foster flashed a toothy grin. "You need to see it, too. After all, it's what's provided you with a lifetime of drinks, golf, fast cars, and fancy homes. Come, let me show you."

The two made their way out of the office and into the giant cavern. They crossed the ground floor and walked down into the pyramid's entrance. Inside, a ramp proceeded down and then another ascended into the upper reaches of the structure. Foster led the way to the one going up, holding onto a wooden rail as he did.

A long cable hung in the center of the spiraling ramp way, disappearing into a hole below and a similar one above.

"This is quite the little setup you have here," Porter said as they climbed higher into the pyramid.

"Yes," Foster said, panting slightly. "It certainly is."

He didn't say anything else for the rest of their climb. Porter wondered if it was because he was keeping something back or if it was due to the exertion of the hike.

They reached a room with high angled ceilings that rose toward a single point at the top. A golden square loomed over them. Porter figured it was the underside of the pyramid's gold top.

The ceiling, however, wasn't the most interesting thing in the room. The same cable that stretched down below also ran down to one of the most spectacular sights Porter had ever seen.

In the middle of the room—on a wooden platform held up by four legs—was a box made of pure gold. On top of it were two jackals bowing toward the center with long ears pointed at each other, nearly touching over the top of the box.

"Is that..." Porter struggled to find the words.

"The Ark of the Covenant?" Foster asked. "No. It isn't the ark Moses carried through the Sinai."

"But it's one heck of a replica," a new voice said from the other side of the room.

The two looked over and saw Sean, Tommy, and Yuri along with their guards.

Sean stared at the shiny yellow object. "I have to say, I'm impressed, Kent. How'd you figure out how to make one of those?"

Foster took on a smug expression. "Sadly, Sean, we didn't make it. This ark was here when we discovered this pyramid over a hundred years ago. Although my predecessors had no idea how to harness its power. That was my doing."

"So, you're using static electricity to build your energy empire," Tommy said.

"Geostatic power, yes. The ancients knew about this sort of thing, as it turns out. They knew there were pools of energy all over the globe. The Egyptians were some of the first to utilize it. Their places of worship were built almost exclusively in such locations so they could use the electrical display as a sort of show for their feebleminded believers. Ordinary citizens didn't understand what was happening, so seeing lightning come out of one of these things looked like the acts of a deity, not some boring scientific experiment."

"This was what Seward's explorers found," Sean said, still staring at the ark.

"Correct," Foster said as he sidled up next to Porter. "William Seward and his men understood the gravity of this incredible place. He had the vision to see that this thing could be harnessed for electrical power. That vision was nothing short of remarkable considering electricity was still in its infancy during his lifetime. Of course, the Confederacy wanted the gold to fund the rebellion. Our organization attempted to get them what they wanted, but when the tide of the war turned, we protected our interests and withdrew support. The Confederacy died, and we flourished."

"Bet on the winning horse, I always say," Sean said.

Foster almost appeared pleased at the comment. "That's right, Sean. For the last 150 years, the KGC has done just that. And in return we have become one of the most powerful organizations on the planet."

"All the while manipulating the American public," Tommy sneered.

Foster chuckled. "Tommy, of course we have. Someone is going to manipulate them. If it wasn't us, it would be the government. Oh, sure, they do their best to control things to suit the needs of those in power, but behind the scenes we are pulling all the strings."

"How many?" Sean asked. "How many of you are there? These secret societies usually have a high council or something." He pried for the information, not really expecting an answer. He was surprised when Foster responded.

"Our hierarchy has many members, though I'm not at liberty to tell you how many or who they are. That, my friend, will remain a secret for all time. Only members of the circle can know those things. I'm afraid I'm sworn to secrecy in that regard."

Foster shifted his feet, inching a little closer to Porter.

"And what does he get out of this?" Tommy asked, pointing at Porter. "A seat at the table?"

Foster was a little surprised by the question, as evidenced by the wrinkles on his forehead. "Agent Porter? Oh goodness, no. He'll be getting a reward, nothing more."

"Thirty pieces of silver," Sean said through clenched teeth.

"That's right," Porter said. "If you were smart, you would have gotten yours a long time ago as well."

Sean noticed Foster's movement. The secretary was trying to be subtle. Porter didn't notice; at least he didn't seem to. Sean, however, anticipated the politician was about to do something. What it was, he didn't know yet, but he focused his senses on the guard behind him.

"So, the KGC killed Abraham Lincoln and attempted to kill Seward—all so they could claim power for themselves?" Tommy asked, pressing the conversation. He was doing his best to stall what he believed would be their inevitable execution.

Meanwhile, Yuri just listened, staring fiercely at the two men opposite them. Like Sean, he was waiting for a chance to make his move.

"Don't be so judgmental, Tommy. Look at history. This is how things have always been done. Ancient Rome, Greece, even Egypt all embraced assassination to bring about change for those seeking power. Besides, it isn't like we're running some evil empire here. Look around you." He put his arms out wide. "We are providing clean, renewable energy to the country and perhaps someday, the entire world. Transcorp will lead everyone into a new golden age of power without relying on fossil fuels. This! This is good for the people of America. This is good for the world!"

"Of course, the bottom line is good for you, isn't it?" Sean asked.

"Obviously, Sean. And why is that so bad? After all, we're providing something of incredible value. We will reduce the average energy costs and carbon footprint per household fourfold, maybe even more."

Foster turned his gaze to Yuri. "As for you," he said, "I suppose you've been sent here by your president to claim what is rightfully yours."

Yuri was a little surprised at the sudden comment, but he kept his icy stare in place. "That's right. Your government promised us the gold you have down in the basement of this place. It's rightfully ours."

"Well, that may be, comrade. And I apologize for the actions we had to take in order to make all this happen. If it makes you feel better, you're about to die, so there's that."

"So, you kill us and continue to spread Transcorp's tentacles across the globe?" Sean said, still trying to squeeze every drop of information out of their captor.

"Funny you should say that, Sean. I tried for years to get Dawkins to break apart the Tennessee Valley Authority. Their stranglehold on the power supply to the Southeastern United States is corrupt and un-American. He wouldn't listen. So we had to take matters into our own hands. You may have temporarily interfered with my plan, but we have other ways of getting what we want."

"He knows about you. He knows you're behind the assassination attempt. Right now there's a nationwide manhunt going on, and they're looking for you, Mr. Secretary. If you turn yourself in, maybe they'll show you mercy."

Foster snorted. "Mercy? I doubt the president knows anything. I closed off all your connections to the government. In fact, right now there are police in over two dozen cities across the country looking for you two in connection with the assassination attempt. So, don't kid yourselves. I don't lose."

He put his hand on Porter's shoulder and gripped it tight. Foster's knuckles whitened, and his jaw clenched.

"What should we do with these people who dare threaten me, Agent Porter?"

Porter's lips creased. "I'd kill anyone who threatened me, sir."

Foster nodded. "I completely agree."

He shoved Porter hard and took a step back. The sudden force against his shoulder threw Porter off balance. He stumbled sideways toward the ark only a few feet away.

Instinctively, Porter put out his hands to catch himself. His palms pressed against the side of the ark, and suddenly his body stiffened and started gyrating. He screamed as electricity coursed through him. Everyone else took a horrified step back, including the guards.

Smoke started seeping from Porter's clothes and hair. The screaming stopped, and suddenly his body hurled through the air and smacked into the wall fifteen feet away. He dropped to the floor in a heap.

The second Porter's body was thrown clear of the ark, Sean knew it was his only chance.

In a flash, he bent at the hips and put his hands on the floor, kicking out his right foot behind him and snapping it up with his hamstring. His heel struck the guard's gun just as the man squeezed the trigger.

The muzzle popped loudly as the weapon rode up from the force of Sean's kick. Sean pushed himself back up and jumped, hurling himself through the air and striking the guard in the chest with his boot, driving the man backward until the back of his head struck the angled wall.

Yuri saw Sean's move. He twisted his head around in time to see the guard behind him spinning around to point his weapon at the American.

Yuri snapped his heel back and kicked the guard in the groin, pivoting as the man doubled over and then driving his knee into the guard's nose.

Sean's guard fell to the floor while Sean took an exaggerated step and kicked him in the side of the head as he would an American football.

Yuri whirled around with a roundhouse to his guard's face.

Meanwhile, Tommy tracked the chaos taking place around him. The guard behind him turned his head one way and the other as if trying to decide who to help first. The man's confusion cost him.

Tommy rushed him before he could aim his gun. The guard tried to swing the weapon around, but Tommy grabbed the guy by the shirt and punched him square in the teeth. Over and over Tommy pulled with one hand and punched with the other until the guard collapsed to the floor, unconscious.

Tommy bent down and picked up the weapon lying next to the man. Sean and Yuri did the same, stealing the guns from their guards.

They all turned to face Foster, intent on dispensing justice.

But Foster was nowhere to be seen.

Sean's eyes flashed across the room. He stepped around to the other side of the ark and saw a coat flap and then disappear as his quarry hurried down the ramps toward the ground floor.

"There he is!" Sean said, pointing down below.

The three of them took off, hurtling down the ramps, using the railing to balance their descent.

Yuri stuck his weapon over the edge and fired a shot at the secretary of state as he wrapped around the final leg of the ramp. Rounds pinged off the ancient stone, sending sparks and debris flying.

Foster sprinted out the pyramid's entrance, yelling for his other guards.

"They'll have this place surrounded in a minute," Sean said. "Then there won't be any other way out."

"There might be," Yuri said.

"What are you talking about?" Tommy asked, turning to face their Russian friend.

"Down below, where they're keeping the gold, there was an opening underneath the platform. I think we can fit between the wood and the hole. It might be a way out."

"A way out or a deathtrap," Tommy said.

"If we stick around here, we're going to be dead or trapped anyway," Sean said. "And we can't win a shootout with these guys. We've only got one magazine each. They'll have dozens. Not to mention when Foster calls in reinforcements."

Tommy sighed. "Show us the way, Yuri."

38. Denali

The three men raced to the bottom of the pyramid. They skidded to a stop when they reached the mound of gold resting atop the wooden platform.

"See?" Yuri said, pointing at a narrow space under the wood.

"That's going to be a tight squeeze," Tommy said.

"Good thing you lost so much weight, eh, buddy?" Sean slapped him on the back.

"What is it? Looks like some kind of ventilation."

"Doesn't matter what it is right now," Sean said. "At the moment, it's our only way out."

"It matters if there's a hundred-foot drop down there."

Yuri was already on his belly, crawling under to look down into the darkness. He'd grabbed one of the floodlights from the floor and positioned it over the edge of the cavity so he could see what waited for them in the abyss.

To everyone's surprise, including Yuri's, he sounded positive.

"It's not that bad. The drop is about three meters. We can hang from the edge and lower ourselves down."

"Shh," Sean said, holding up a hand. "I hear

something."

A second later, the sound of footsteps pounding the stone of the ramp echoed down into the chamber.

"Are they going up or coming down?" Tommy whispered.

"Doesn't matter. We're going down the shaft."

Sean got on his belly and started inching his way toward the hole.

Tommy looked up at the ramp. The footsteps were getting louder. Even though he'd lost a ton of weight over the last few months, he was still thicker than his friend, and far larger than the skinny Russian.

He got down on his hands and knees and put his face close to the ground. If he could get through, it would be by less than two inches.

Yuri had already dropped down into the hole and switched on the light attached to his weapon.

Sean swung his legs over and let himself hang for a moment to make sure Yuri was out of the way.

Tommy struggled to worm his way to the edge. He shimmied and wiggled, grinding his cheek on the hard stone more than a few times. He finally reached the edge and scooted his legs over the lip of the shaft. Then he pushed himself backward until he was hanging on by his fingernails and let himself fall to the ground.

Sean and Yuri were waiting with their gun lights on. Yuri was staring ahead into another passageway.

"See?" Yuri said. "This corridor goes somewhere."

"Could be a dead end," Tommy hissed.

"Be positive," Sean said and took off into the tunnel.

Yuri followed close behind while Tommy reluctantly brought up the rear.

They rushed ahead, barreling their way forward up the slow incline. The narrow corridor was different than the mine shaft they'd walked through on the way in. It was cut smooth from the rock with laser precision, unlike the rough-hewn walls of the mine.

The tunnel turned left after they'd been running for a minute. The grade increased to a steeper angle before it leveled off and turned right.

"I hope this doesn't lead to a dead end," Yuri said as he rounded another corner.

"It was going to be a dead end back there," Sean said between breaths. "This way, at least it might be faster."

A few minutes in, the tunnel made a sharp left and then flattened out again. The men slowed to a walk as they made their way forward, their flashlight beams dancing along the ground several feet ahead.

"The air's cooler up here," Tommy said. His breath was coming quickly but not like it would have a year prior.

"Yeah, I was wondering if I felt that right," Sean

said. "We must be closer to the surface."

"Or the main tunnel coming into the mine," Yuri said. "Listen."

The sound of men shouting orders echoed into their secret passage.

"Keep going," Sean said. "Put your palms over the top of the lights so the beams stay on the ground. Last thing we want to do is give up the element of surprise."

The others did as instructed and pushed ahead. The sounds of footsteps grew louder for a moment and then faded away. Probably reinforcements heading either to the gate or down below. If it was the latter, that would mean Foster had more men aboveground. Sean hoped it was the former.

He and the other two slowed down as their lights cast a faint glow on something obstructing the path ahead.

"This passage must be one of the ones that was blocked off," Sean said in a hushed tone.

No sooner had he gotten the words through his lips than the three heard a new sound. It was an engine—like a motorcycle.

Suddenly, lights danced on the wall beyond the barricade.

"It's a four-wheeler," Sean said.

"How do you know that?" Yuri asked.

"He's got a thing with motorbikes," Tommy explained.

Sean waited for a moment until the ATV was close. The engine roared and the lights grew brighter. From the sound, Sean could hear it pass by, and the second it did he charged forward, breaking through the old boards like a dump truck through a stack of matchsticks.

He turned to his left first to make sure no one else was coming and then spun to the right, aiming his weapon up the gradual ascent.

The four-wheeler was speeding toward the mine's entrance.

Sean took aim and squeezed the trigger.

The submachine gun fired round after round, forcing the muzzle upward. Sean's muscles tensed, fighting to keep the weapon steady.

Rounds sparked off the walls and floor. One struck the back right tire of the ATV. He didn't see one of his bullets tear through the driver's left shoulder. He did, however, see the man fall out of the saddle and roll to the ground as the ATV smashed into the wall.

The driver stood up and started running toward the door that began slowly creaking open.

Sean took aim at the driver's back and squared his sights. He squeezed the trigger, but the weapon clicked.

"Shoot him!" Sean yelled to Tommy and Yuri as they clambered out of the side shaft and into the main tunnel.

They raised their weapons and opened fire, but the wounded man had already slipped out the door.

"Hold on," Sean said. "He's out."

He tossed his gun aside and took off at a dead sprint.

His legs burned after the climb through the secret corridor. Now he was running uphill. The cool air burned in his chest, but he kept going.

Up ahead, the door to the mine hung wide open. Snow blew into the tunnel from the pale gray beyond.

Sean burst through the door, and his face smashed into something. He fell over sideways, his jaw throbbing with a sudden sharp pain. He rolled around in the powder for a second before he felt something dig into his ribs.

He swung both arms forward and wrapped around a leg. He looked up and saw Kent Foster standing over him with a bloody shoulder and a pistol in one hand.

"Goodbye, Sean."

Sean didn't let the words fully escape the man's mouth. He reached up and grabbed the barrel Foster fired. The muzzle popped loudly, ringing both men's ears, but the round dove harmlessly into the snow.

Sean wrenched the weapon away and smashed the secretary across the side of the face with his forearm. Then Sean tossed the weapon aside, far out of Foster's reach.

"It's over, Mr. Secretary. You've lost."

"Lost?" Foster huffed. "I don't lose, you imbecile. You do!"

Foster pulled a long hunting knife out of his coat

and lunged forward.

His attack was reckless, but dangerous nonetheless. Sean sidestepped the charging madman like a matador in an arena.

Foster slid to a stop and spun around. He rushed at Sean again, shrieking a war cry as he charged.

Sean faked one way and then dipped to the other. Foster took the fake and swung his knife that direction. Sean grabbed the secretary's good arm and then swung his left foot at Foster's heels.

The kick flipped Foster's feet out from under him, and he hung in the air for a second. Sean yanked down, helping gravity to slam him to the ground.

Foster's head hit the snow hard, jarring him for a moment and loosening his grip on the knife. Sean pried it from his fingers and pressed the sharp edge to Foster's neck.

Foster breathed heavily. He swallowed hard, raising the blade slightly as Sean kept it firmly against his skin.

"Go ahead, Sean. Do it."

"I could," Sean said. "Not my style."

"Then do it. This is your last chance. I won't go to prison. It won't matter if the president himself tries to make it happen. I'll go free. We are everywhere."

"What was that you just said?" A new voice startled Foster from just over the ridge. "Something about how the president himself couldn't make it happen?"

John Dawkins crested the snowy hillside along with Adriana and Emily. Secret Service men and special ops surrounded him, clad in white winter gear. They swarmed the area and started pouring into the mine.

"Tommy and Yuri are down there," Sean said as he tossed the knife into the snow.

"My men know to look for them," Dawkins said.

He pulled up his goggles as he neared Sean and the wounded Foster.

"With all due respect, sir, maybe you should hang back until we get this cleared up. There are armed men down there."

"With all due respect, Sean, I've been in combat. And even though my men told me not to do this, I'm here. Deal with it." He winked as he said the last line.

"Yes, sir." Sean bowed his head and stepped aside.

Dawkins stood over Foster, looking down at him with disdain. Emily and Adriana gathered around, Adriana wrapping her arms around Sean and squeezing him tight.

"Secretary of State Kent Foster, you're under arrest," Dawkins said in a thunderous voice.

A sinister, sickly laugh escaped Foster's mouth. The volume of his voice continued to rise, and he put his hands up, waiting for someone to put cuffs on them.

"Go ahead. Arrest me."

39. Juneau, Alaska

President Dawkins stood on the other end of the room in front of a mirror. He straightened his blue tie and pressed out his suit jacket to make sure there were no wrinkles. He must have done the same thing a thousand times and never found a problem. Old habits and all that.

Sean sat in the corner, staring at his phone.

Adriana had taken off the previous day. She said her father found a lead on a piece of artwork she'd been trying to find for some time.

Sean and Tommy had stayed with the president. Emily, too, had lingered behind to spend some time with the commander in chief.

"Mr. President?" His press secretary poked his head in the door of the green room. "It's time, sir."

"Okay," Dawkins said.

Sean scrolled to a newsfeed that caught his eye. He read the headline and studied the image that accompanied it.

Former Secretary of State Kent Foster Dead.

Sean read a little farther. The article said Foster committed suicide while in protective custody.

"That's gruesome," Sean said.

"What is?" Tommy asked.

Sean showed his friend the screen. "Foster committed suicide in protective custody." Sean thought for a moment in silence. "I guess he was right about never going to prison."

"You think that's true?"

"No," Sean said, "but the public will believe it. Who knows? It might be true. He was being kept at a military base. Easy enough for a double agent to sneak him a razor blade or a special pill and give him the option to go out on his own terms."

Dawkins caught the last bits of what Sean and Tommy were saying. "You talking about the Foster suicide?"

"Yes. Bizarre turn of events."

"It's a shame." Dawkins's eyes lowered to the floor as he drifted away in thought for a second. "You think you know someone, and then you find out they're trying to undermine everything you're doing. And then they try to kill you on top of that. I guess that's a lesson to us all. Keep your eyes open."

"Indeed," Tommy said. He didn't mention the fact that the president had completely ignored the conspiracy theory.

"Well, I'd better get out there. Lots of questions to answer."

"We've included all the notes you need for almost every conceivable question you could get in regards to the history of the pyramid. Information is still coming in, but we wanted to get you what we have in case anyone brought it up."

Sean and Tommy stood, beaming with pride.

The president eyed both of them as he would his

own sons. "I can't thank you both enough for this. For everything."

The two friends blushed.

"Well, you did get us our money back in the banks," Sean said.

"Yeah, and I think we're okay to fly on normal airlines again," Tommy added.

"Not that you would with your private jet and all."

"Oh, because you hate using it so much? What about that trip to Thailand you took last year?"

"That was for an assignment."

"Gentlemen," the president interrupted the spat. "I'll see you after the press conference. Try not to kill each other while I'm on the air."

The president turned and walked out of the room.

"Yes, sir," the two said at the same time.

They eased back into a couple of seats and looked over to the corner of the room where a flatscreen television displayed a podium with the presidential seal. A moment later, Dawkins appeared from behind the curtain and stepped in front of the podium.

"Hello and thank you for taking the time to attend this historic announcement." He paused and allowed more cameras to flash before beginning again.

"As many of you already know, some of my friends at the International Archaeological Agency have made an incredible discovery, one that will change the future of humanity.

"A few days ago, they uncovered an ancient Egyptian pyramid under the mountains of Denali."

Some of the reporters in the room gasped at hearing the information for the first time.

The president reached over to his right where an easel was covered by a dark blue drape. He pulled the cover back and revealed an image of the underground pyramid.

"This pyramid is believed to date back to around 3200 BC. Information is still coming in on that as we speak. One thing we do know, however, is that this ancient structure is capable of producing massive amounts of energy. We have scientists and engineers on site at this moment trying to understand how this generator works and how we can make it better."

Sean turned to his friend as the president continued talking in the background. "Yuri get out okay last night?"

"I think so," Tommy said. "It was no easy task trying to get him and $160 million in gold bullion past the reporters."

"How'd you do it?"

Tommy shrugged. "Stuffed it in some old maintenance vans and drove right by them."

"Huh."

"Yeah. We figured they wouldn't think much of a maintenance vehicle going by. He should be home soon, if not already. It's not that far to Russia from here."

Sean stared at the screen. The president was talking about the clean energy implications of the new discovery.

"I suppose Yuri's president will be happy," Tommy said, staring at the television the same as his friend.

"Oh sure. He'll probably get a medal or some piroshkis."

"Piroshkis?"

"It's a small pie dish." Sean stared at his friend in surprise. "You've been to Russia."

"I didn't realize you were such a connoisseur."

Sean sighed. "Anyway, it was awfully cool of Dawkins to let him take it. I'm sure there were some members of Congress who wouldn't have approved that move."

Sean smirked. "That's probably why he didn't tell them."

"Good point."

"What are you doing this weekend?" Sean asked.

"Flying back to Atlanta. Going to spend some time with June before she heads back to work. You?"

"May head down to Seattle, catch some music and fresh salmon while I'm there."

"Oh. That sounds really good. You think June will wait an extra day?"

Sean chuckled, and his friend laughed, too.

"No, I think she'll dump you before you get back."

They shared another laugh, and then the room

fell silent—except for the sound of the president talking about an economic boost of historic proportions.

"What do you think about what Foster said?" Tommy said after a moment of reflection.

"What part?"

"The part about having people everywhere. Dawkins just mentioned the different levels this thing could impact. Made me think about all the various positions that must be occupied by Foster's people."

Sean drew in a slow breath. "Yeah, it can drive you crazy if you think about it too much. The president told me he's going to use an infiltrator to start weeding out some institutions and agencies, but he'll need several if he wants to have an impact."

"Infiltrator?"

"Yep. Someone who gets behind the lines, gets embedded with the threat, and then neutralizes it."

"Who's he got in mind for that job?" Tommy asked.

"I don't know," Sean said. "But it won't be me. I guess we'll learn more about that eventually. For now, think about the fact that we just discovered a pyramid underneath the base of Denali. So, I say we celebrate our success."

Tommy's face scrunched in a frown. "Actually, we didn't really discover it. That thing was found 150 years ago."

Sean groaned. "Fine. We brought it to the public

after more than a century of being hidden. Not to mention the fact that we shed new light on the Lincoln assassination."

Tommy thought for a second. "You're right. We should celebrate. Let's—" Whatever he was about to say was interrupted by his phone ringing. He looked at the caller ID. It read *The Kids*.

He hit the green button and put it to his ear while Sean looked on with a curious look.

"Hello? Oh hey, Alex. Yeah, it's okay. I'm free. What's going on?"

Tommy listened intensely for a minute before saying anything else. "Wow. Okay. You're sure about this?" He waited for confirmation. "Yeah, absolutely we'll tackle that. Tell them I'm on my way."

He ended the call and slid the phone back into his pocket. He stood up from his seat and put his hands out with palms up.

"The celebration will have to wait, my friend. Duty calls."

"Another big project?" Sean asked with an eyebrow raised.

"Always."

Thank You

Writing a book is a heck of a thing.

It takes an incredible amount of time, research, energy, and mental focus. That last one is extremely difficult for me.

When I say thank you for reading my work, I truly mean it and I cannot express how much I appreciate you choosing to spend your time with my words.

Perhaps you're a loyal reader who has read every single book in the series. Maybe this is your first one. Either way, at some point you took a chance on purchasing a story from a guy you'd probably never heard of. I can't thank you enough for that.

I've always been a storyteller, no matter the career in which I worked. To be able to write books for a living is an honor and a privilege. I owe that to good people like you.

Again, thank you for trusting me with your time. It is the most valuable resource a person has. And you chose to spend some with me.

Sincerely,
Ernest

Other Books by Ernest Dempsey

The Secret of the Stones
The Cleric's Vault
The Last Chamber
The Grecian Manifesto
The Norse Directive
Game of Shadows
The Jerusalem Creed
The Samurai Cipher
The Cairo Vendetta
The Uluru Code
The Excalibur Key

War of Thieves Box Set
(An Adriana Villa Adventure)

Sci-Fi/Fantasy
The Dream Rider
The Dream Rider 2: Retribution

From the Author

Author's Notes

One of the things that makes history so interesting is the stuff that we don't know. I'm talking about those connections—real, possible, or imagined—between the people and events that drive the story of who we are—the how and why that the history books often leave out.

It's probably my favorite part of writing stories like these.

Through the eyes of Sean, Tommy, Adriana, Emily, and now June, you and I can explore behind the curtain of "official history" as we entertain what might have been (or what is but still isn't known).

Although this tale is my own invention, I always try to connect the dots to the historical record in a way that makes things plausible for you. There are certainly a few moments that may stretch the possibilities, but I wanted to make this tale as realistic as possible.

Speaking of which: I love it when other authors talk about the fact versus fiction of their books, so I've included some notes here (hopefully for your enjoyment) that shed light on which aspects were true—and which I played around with.

Seward's Assassination Attempt

In case you didn't realize it, the attempt on William Seward's life was very real. The event happened the same night Lincoln was shot at Ford's Theater. Sadly, his wife was so distraught about the incident that she took ill and died not long after.

Seward House

The Seward mansion is a historical landmark in the beautiful city of Auburn, New York. Many people don't realize how pretty the New York countryside is, and I always recommend people give it a visit. The rolling hills and mountains make for a picturesque setting in every season of the year. The towns, too, are perfectly situated in the natural surroundings and make for a lovely stay.

The home is now a museum, and visitors are welcome to come by and check out the property to see it as it was in the 1800s. The home is in amazing condition and is certainly worth visiting to take a journey back in time. As far as I know, most of the furnishings are originals and have been kept in good condition. It's an incredible thing to stand in a place where such a remarkable and tragic historical event took place. Kind of sobering.

The Surratt Boarding House

The Surratt Boarding House was the real meeting place for John Wilkes Booth and his associates. While the conversation at the beginning of the story was fabricated, the people involved were all real, as were their roles in history.

For her actions in harboring and assisting the conspirators, Mary Surratt became the first woman to be executed in United States history. Her son, John Jr., however, was released. After his work as a spy in the Confederate Secret Service, John remained in Baltimore where he lived out the rest of his life. He lived until he was 72, working as a United States postmaster, school teacher, lecturer, and farmer.

This place still stands today and really is the home of the Wok and Roll Chinese restaurant. While I have not eaten there, I almost always recommend General Tso's tofu (or chicken) if you're in the mood for something sweet and spicy. Of course, there's nothing spicier than a little conspiracy.

The building has gone through many renovations since the time of Lincoln. If anything was hidden there, it would have been removed long ago.

The Surratt Farmhouse

This place, also known as Surratt's Tavern, is still a historical landmark in Clinton, Maryland, and is an interesting place to visit if you're passing through the area, though maybe not worth going out of your way to investigate.

Many of the rooms and furnishings are as I described in the story. The only device I used with this particular scene was the oddly colored grout between the stone tiles. That was a figment of my imagination.

The bed that Tommy claimed to have bumped his knee on, however, is very real. Watch out that it doesn't get you, too.

The Note and Map

To my knowledge, the Seward letter to Lincoln about the anomaly in Alaska and the map with its location do not exist. It would be pretty cool if they did. There is, however, speculation that a pyramid does remain hidden somewhere underground in Alaska. It might be fanciful dreaming or just rabid conspiracy theorists letting their minds run amok. Either way, I thought it was a fascinating idea.

The General

The story about Andrews and his Raiders is absolutely true. My parents' home rests on the mountain that overlooks the railroad where the final leg of the Raiders' journey took place.

I imagine about the time those guys crossed the trestle in the valley below that they knew they were in trouble.

The cave is also a very real thing. The opening is only a few hundred feet away from my parents' house, on our neighbor's property. The trenches I mentioned are also still there and quite visible.

The neighbor has been kind enough to allow us to do some exploring through the years, though now the cave entrance has collapsed and no one will be able to go in there again.

I had the good fortune of going back pretty far in several years ago. At one point we thought we could hear cars going by, which meant we'd descended a few hundred feet to get that close to Highway 41 below.

The Russian Gold

There is a sentiment among some Russians that Alaska should be taken back from the United States. So wide-ranging is this feeling in some quarters that, in fact, there's a plaque near Crimea that suggests this should happen.

As for the gold in dispute in the novel? Most people claim the United States paid its gold debt to Russia. Others say "nyet!"

Based on my research, I do not have a definitive conclusion. I can say that if I were asked, I'd lean more toward the side that claims the gold was never paid. Maybe that's because I just enjoy a good conspiracy. I like to think it's more than that. The thing that bothers me the most about the USA's side of the story is the historical unwillingness to offer an explanation or defense. The U.S. Government has few records of the gold shipment being sent and no eyewitness testimony. There's almost nothing about the actual payment other than the ceremonial check used to make the deal.

It is sort of fun to imagine Russia and America at odds over gold and ancient pyramids instead of elections and other wild accusations. It's is a lot more interesting than almost anything the day's headlines could bring.

For Carol Griggs. If not for you, the second book would have never been written, much less all the others. I and all my readers thank you.

Acknowledgments

None of my stories would be possible without the great input I get from incredible readers all over the globe. My advance reader group is such an incredibly unselfish and supportive team. I couldn't do any of this without them.

My editors, Anne Storer and Jason Whited, must also be thanked for their amazing work and guidance in crafting these stories. They make everything so much better for the reader.

Last but not least, I need to give a big thank you to Elena at L1 Graphics for the incredible cover art she always delivers, along with beautiful social media artwork.